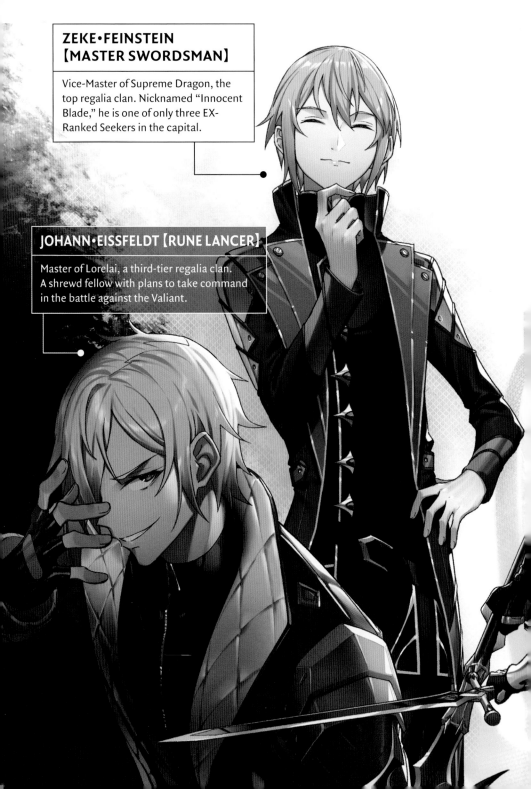

ZEKE·FEINSTEIN [MASTER SWORDSMAN]

Vice-Master of Supreme Dragon, the top regalia clan. Nicknamed "Innocent Blade," he is one of only three EX-Ranked Seekers in the capital.

JOHANN·EISSFELDT [RUNE LANCER]

Master of Lorelai, a third-tier regalia clan. A shrewd fellow with plans to take command in the battle against the Valiant.

VACLAV (SUMMONER)

Member of the Winged Knights. A large wolf-man with a calm demeanor that belies his appearance.

OPHELIA·MERCEDES (HAWK EYE)

Member of the Winged Knights. A long-lived elf and friend of Lycia.

KEIM·LAZAR (WARSPEAR)

Member of the Winged Knights. Unpretentious big-brother type from the same town as Leon.

LEON·FREDRIC (KNIGHT)

Leader of the Winged Knights. Has achieved a great deal but is wary of rushing into registering as a clan. From the same hometown as Keim.

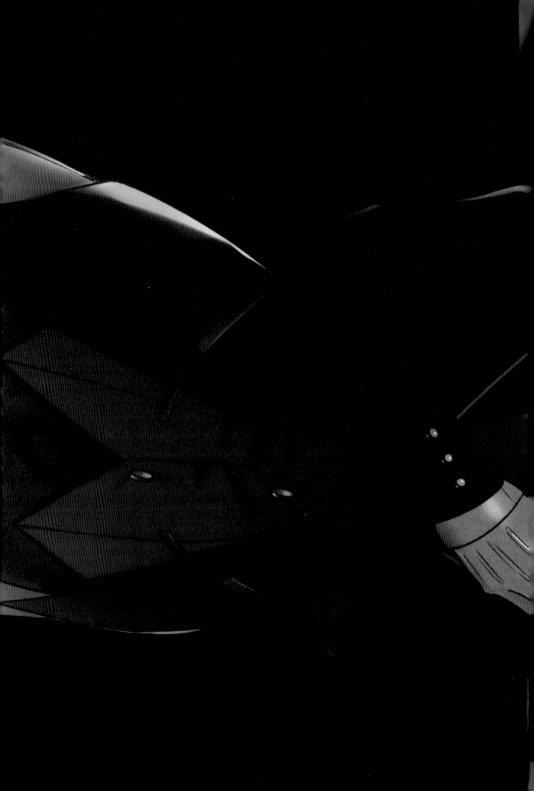

"Everyone, do you remember the name
Hugo Coppélia?"

CONTENTS

KEYWORDS

CLASS

The class of abilities that appear in an individual after an appraisal by an official appraiser. Determines one's skills and physical limitations. Classes are ranked from A to C. In rare circumstances, individuals can achieve the rank of EX.

BEAST

Enemies of humanity that manifest from the Void. The space known as the Abyss causes reality to degenerate, so the beast at the core of an Abyss must be defeated. Beast strength is measured by depth—beasts with a depth of 12 are known as beast lords. Lords with depths of 13 are called Valiants.

REGALIA

An organization of seven clans recognized by the emperor for their high-ranking achievements. Not all regalia clans are equal. There are four spots for third-tier clans, two spots for second-tier clans, and one spot for the top tier.

THE MOST NOTORIOUS ⟨TALKER⟩ RUNS THE WORLD'S GREATEST CLAN

NOVEL 2

WRITTEN BY

jaki

ILLUSTRATED BY

fame

Airship

Seven Seas Entertainment

The Most Notorious "Talker" Runs the World's Greatest Clan Vol. 2
© 2020 jaki
Illustrated by fame
First published in Japan in 2020 by OVERLAP Inc., Ltd., Tokyo.
English translation rights arranged with OVERLAP Inc., Ltd., Tokyo.

Seven Seas press and purchase enquiries can be sent to
Marketing Manager Lianne Sentar at press@gomanga.com.
Information regarding the distribution and purchase of
digital editions is available from Digital Manager CK Russell
at digital@gomanga.com.

Follow Seven Seas Entertainment online at
sevenseasentertainment.com.

TRANSLATION: Jenn Yamazaki
ADAPTATION: Nick Mamatas
COVER DESIGN: Erika Terriquez
LOGO DESIGN: George Panella
INTERIOR LAYOUT & DESIGN: Clay Gardner
COPY EDITOR: Meg van Huygen
LIGHT NOVEL EDITOR: T. Anne
PREPRESS TECHNICIAN: Melanie Ujimori
PRINT MANAGER: Rhiannon Rasmussen-Silverstein
PRODUCTION MANAGER: Lissa Pattillo
MANAGING EDITOR: Julie Davis
ASSOCIATE PUBLISHER: Adam Arnold
PUBLISHER: Jason DeAngelis

ISBN: 978-1-64827-639-2
Printed in Canada
First Printing: January 2022
10 9 8 7 6 5 4 3 2 1

Prologue

"I'LL BECOME the strongest Seeker ever... No matter what it takes."

I repeated my vow before the smoldering ruins of the town. My grandpa, whose body I held in my arms, was already gone. No words or laughter would ever leave his lips again. My mind was flooded with memories of Grandpa, only for them to turn to bubbles and float away. I wondered how long it had been. The sun, high in the sky, burned my eyes. A strong wind kicked up ash and dust that stung my cheeks. I gingerly laid Grandpa down on the ground and stood up.

"They're all gone..." Grandpa had been my only living relative, and now he was dead. The town in which we had lived was nothing but ash. Looking out at the charred ruins made my heart ache, but I felt oddly calm. It was clear to me that I was thinking rationally.

"Maybe this is one of the perks of being a Talker." Each Seeker class provided not only super abilities—skills that we could use—but also augmentations to preexisting capabilities, unique characteristics, and tolerances. Talker tolerance was an abnormal mental function. It helped me resist psychological attacks from enemies and made it easy for me to keep my cool.

"I never thought the day would come when I'd be grateful to be a Talker." I laughed at myself. This class, which had manifested in me at a young age, was a buffer role. Although I possessed strong support capabilities, my fighting abilities were underwhelming compared to those of combat classes. I could easily die in battle; Talkers were considered the weakest class. After dreaming for so long of becoming a Seeker like my grandpa—my hero—I was tormented by a sense of inferiority due to my class.

However, I never gave up. By studying under Grandpa, I gained the power to fight, even as a Talker. I mastered hand-to-hand combat and strategies to tackle beasts from the Void, which were both feared enemies and coveted prey for Seekers.

My current capabilities were comparable to a mid-level Seeker of a combat class.

"But still..." I wasn't even close to what my grandpa had been. I was an encumbrance. That was why Grandpa had entered the fight alone against the beast lord that had transformed this town into an Abyss—a space where beasts could run amok. Were I a combat-class Seeker instead of a Talker, could I have come to Grandpa's aid? No...probably not. I was a C-Rank. Nothing more than a pesky fly to the lord who had squared off against my EX-Ranked hero.

"I still have such a long way to go."

I was dead serious when I vowed to become the strongest Seeker. However, the road to my goal would be long and hard.

Furthermore, my class was Talker. How in the world could a lousy Talker become the strongest Seeker? As my thoughts unwound, I realized something.

"Where are they?"

Two important things were missing. One was Grandpa's beloved battle-axe. The other was...the corpse of the lord.

"No way! Where did they go?!" I ran around the nearby area, suddenly flustered. I didn't find the battle-axe, and among the many beast corpses, there were none that could have been that of the lord.

"But..." I stood there, dumbfounded. As far as I knew, the only way to purify an Abyss was to defeat the beast at its core. The town was gone, but the Abyss had been purified. Ergo, Grandpa must have defeated the lord.

"Could he have missed?"

A hateful thought flashed through my mind, and a chill ran down my spine. But that was the only possible explanation. The lord must have suffered grave wounds while fighting Grandpa and fled to the Void before dying.

"Dammit!" Just as humans grew stronger through battle, beasts also gained strength through experience. Just imagining how the experience of fighting Grandpa—a major hero nicknamed Overdeath—would strengthen a lord was too much.

One month after the tragedy, I'd gathered the other surviving staff, and we were living in another town. Using my inheritance from Grandpa, I decided to rent a large manor and start a company.

It wasn't that I'd forgotten my dream to become the strongest Seeker. I knew that if I could just get the business on track, I would be able to leave it in the capable hands of the staff. Then my plan was to leave for Etrai, the imperial capital of the Velnant Empire. Still, I had to be an adult before I could become a Seeker. I was only fourteen, meaning I would have to wait another year. My idea was to continue my training as a Seeker while also building a business for the staff to maintain. My family had once run a reputable winery, but now that the vineyard had been destroyed, it would take time to rebuild. I decided to start with a wine-consulting business, offering our expertise on making and selling wine.

My sales pitches paid off, and the heart of the business began to thrum once more. At the same time, we worked to restore the winery and even started developing new products. By the time I was ready to leave, the company was stable enough that the staff could handle it. I was actually quite pleased with how much I had achieved with my knowledge, despite being a novice in running a business. Apparently, I had some sort of talent in managing people and business operations. Once that finally dawned on me, I knew what I had to do.

That also happened to be the day that the inspector from the Seekers Association came from the imperial capital.

The old man in his tailcoat suit stood at the entrance to my manor and flashed his ID, introducing himself. "I am very pleased to meet you. My name is Harold Jenkins, and I am the third inspector of the Seekers Association. I hope to be of some assistance." Seekers Association inspectors provided management and instruction to regulated Seeker groups, known as clans.

This man, Harold, was seventy years old. His crinkled eyes and mustached mouth were gentle, and his demeanor that of a kind old chap. However, despite his age, he was tall and broad-chested. I could tell that even his coat was exquisitely tailored. He was also packing a pair of guns.

Common folk admired Seekers, but they *were* basically hooligans in the business of violence. Even this old inspector wouldn't go down without a serious fight.

According to Grandpa, only A-Ranked Seekers could become inspectors. The job of inspector included controlling—and sometimes terminating—clans that broke the rules. It was clear that Harold was tough, and a veteran to boot.

I invited Harold and a man who seemed to be his assistant into the parlor.

Taking a seat on the sofa, I tilted my head to one side and asked, "So what brings an Association inspector here?" As a representative of the survivors of a terrible tragedy, I had already told the imperial military police everything I knew.

In response, Harold set a single photograph on the table. It was a picture of a humanoid beast covered in white shell-shaped armor, with two horns sprouting from its forehead. It held a familiar-looking battle-axe. I had never seen this beast before, but I knew what it was immediately.

"This is an image of a lord taken with the latest surveillance

technology. Judging by the battle-axe it's holding, it is undoubtedly the same lord that destroyed the town you were living in."

"When...was this taken?"

"Just the other day. A surveyor in the Association managed to capture the image. A major clan, Night Rage, tried to subdue it, but they were obliterated. Not a single member returned."

"Night Rage, you say?" Night Rage was a distinguished clan, even by the capital's standards, and was considered to be equal to the regalia clans—the seven star-ranked clans who were granted various exclusive rights by the emperor.

"You don't seem surprised."

"Oh, I'm surprised," I said. "But as I said in my interview, I knew the beast was still alive. It's not *terribly* shocking news. Have you defeated this lord?"

"No. As soon as Night Rage was annihilated, Supreme Dragon, the top clan in the regalia, moved in. But by the time they arrived on the scene, the lord had already left for the Void."

"It left again?"

Powerful beasts needed an ultra-high concentration of mana to manifest in our world. It wasn't possible for them to travel as they pleased between this realm and the Void. I couldn't comprehend why this beast would simply choose to go back.

"They say that beasts are driven to invade this world by an irresistible instinct," Harold said with a mysterious look on his face. "That's why both lower-level and higher-level beasts manifest. This beast, on the other hand, seems to be acting freely according to its own will. That's what brings me here today."

That was when it clicked: They thought I had given a false report.

"I'm sorry, I've told you everything I know. I haven't left anything out intentionally."

"I don't think you've acted in bad faith, but this is a grave situation," the inspector told me. "This lord has battled against humans twice, and not just any humans. It grappled with Overdeath and Night Rage. Using that experience as fuel, this lord may reach a depth of 13 and become a new Valiant. I don't think I need to tell you how terrifying a Valiant is. At any rate, the only clan that was able to take down a Valiant in the past was your grandfather's— Bloodsword Federation."

A Valiant was a powerful lord with an abyssal depth of 13. Since the dawn of time, only ten Valiants had been confirmed. Each of these Ten Dark Lords wielded a power great enough to destroy the entire world.

FIRST WORLD: Limbo of the Underworld

SECOND WORLD: Francesca the Lustful Eclipse

THIRD WORLD: Pluton the Star Scavenger

FOURTH WORLD: Styx the Sorcerer

FIFTH WORLD: Dis the Black Death

SIXTH WORLD: Fotinos the False God

SEVENTH WORLD: Phlegethon of Starvation

EIGHTH WORLD: Malebolge the Chaotic

NINTH WORLD: Cocytus the Silverfish

TENTH WORLD: Purgatrio of Inferno

Valiants embodied entire mythical worlds and were named accordingly. They were so powerful that they required hundreds of times more mana than normal lords to manifest in our world, but once they did, they brought about unmeasurable chaos and calamity. Desperate battles against them ended only once they were sent back to the Void.

It had been decades since the last time a Valiant had manifested in this world. Cocytus the Silverfish—massive enough to fill the sky from horizon to horizon—had obliterated three countries the moment he emerged.

Back then, everyone had been sure the end was nigh. However, the Bloodsword Federation, of which Grandpa was a member, achieved a miracle. It was the first time anyone in history had succeeded in defeating a Valiant. I'd heard the battle was so perilous, it was like dancing the waltz with the god of death. Grandpa told me many times that the only reason they were victorious was thanks to a stroke of luck. I could still remember the fear on his face as clear as day.

"Can you remember anything else? Even the smallest detail would be helpful."

I shook my head. "If I knew anything else, I would have told you already."

"See, I don't buy that," the man sitting next to Harold suddenly cut in harshly. "You're the grandson of Overdeath. We know you would do anything to achieve your goal."

"My goal?"

"Revenge," the man replied, as if trying to provoke me.

"You're withholding information about the lord so you can get revenge yourself, right? Of course you are. But you're just a Talker, so you don't stand a chance. Then again, you could hire excellent Seekers to do it for you. Your new endeavor seems to be doing pretty well. How do you plan to spend your profits?"

All I could do was chuckle at the man's attempt at inquisition. It was a wild misunderstanding. However, he wasn't completely off the mark. "Pay them back a thousand times over" was my motto. I *did* want to avenge Grandpa, but I didn't yet have the means, and I certainly wouldn't have given them a false report.

"Hmm. How pitiful," I tutted. "How dare you assume that I'm as pathetic as you—it's ridiculous. Insulting, in fact. You would do well to know your place, you half-wit Seeker wannabe."

"What did you say?!" The man leapt to his feet in fury, but Harold held out his hand, motioning for him to stop.

"Settle down. We didn't come here to squabble."

"But Harold! If this brat hadn't been hiding something, Night Rage might still be alive!"

"Shut up. I won't say it again."

"Ergh!" At Harold's glare, man bit his lip and kept quiet, looking frustrated.

"I apologize. He oversaw Night Rage, so this issue is a bit emotional for him," Harold said.

"That's your business. It has nothing to do with me."

"Ha ha, you're right about that." Harold then narrowed his eyes, which smoldered with a subtle anger. "I find it interesting that you said 'half-wit Seeker-wannabe.' You're welcome to test him yourself, just to confirm whether he really is a half-wit."

I shrugged. "Sorry about that; it was a little excessive. But you're the ones who came here and hurled groundless accusations at me. Makes me a bit testy," I said, my voice laced with sarcasm. I had no intention of backing down. Grandpa always said that once you're no longer respected, that was the end of it.

Harold chuckled. "You really remind me of your grandfather."

"What do you mean by that?"

"I was in charge of Bloodsword Federation, your grandfather's clan."

"You were?"

"Yes. Your grandfather and I were close. The clan no longer exists, but it really was phenomenal." He pulled a pack of cigarettes from the breast pocket of his fine jacket. "Do you mind if I smoke?"

"This is a nonsmoking house...but I'll allow it, out of consideration for my grandfather."

With my permission, Harold lit his cigarette. "Let's go back. Why did you start this business? You're still only fourteen. Luckily, you've been successful, but it was a risky move, considering the consequences of failure. You could have lived an easy life with what your grandfather left you, no?"

"If I were alone, maybe. But I needed to start a company for the sake of Grandpa's staff, instead of just relying on the inheritance for it."

"For the staff? I'm sorry, but you just don't look like the type."

"Type has nothing to do with it. *Noblesse oblige*. I just did what I had to do."

Harold nodded and smiled as if deeply interested. "That's a lovely story, but it *is* hard to believe."

"I'm sure it is. Well, I'm going to step away from the business. Then you'll believe me, right? It's really unpleasant to have the horrid Association breathing down our necks." It was spiteful, but nothing good would come of unnecessary scrutiny from the Association. I needed to pull out. Although I was worried about entrusting the business to the staff at this stage, my presence would only have a negative effect on their futures. As long as I gave them a large chunk of Grandpa's estate, they would surely be fine without me.

"You won't regret it?" Harold snorted as he pierced me with his gaze, testing me.

"Regret what?" I asked. "We're done talking. If there's nothing else, you may go."

"Understood. We'll trust what you say," Harold said, standing up. This only further incensed the man beside him.

"You're going to trust what this brat says?!" his companion cried.

"Yes, I am. We shall return to the capital. Don't embarrass me." Harold shot him a sharp look, and the man fell silent. His gaze then flitted back to me. "Thank you for having us. I am very sorry about Brandon—your grandfather."

With that, they turned toward the door of the parlor.

"I'm sure we'll meet again," I called after them. "Make sure you remember my face."

The two men looked at me one last time.

"I'm going to become the strongest Seeker ever."

1 Beyond Good and Evil

I N THE SWAYING horse-drawn carriage, I nodded off and entered the realm of dreams. Here, I relived my memories since becoming a Seeker, the images gradually growing clearer.

I formed Blue Beyond. We worked so hard that my friends and I were called "Rookie Giant-Killers." Then those friends betrayed me, and our group broke up. I met the prodigy, Alma. I took on the Gambino family. I beat that gang. I gained a new ally, Koga, from an island nation in the far east.

As I was going over these events in my mind, half-asleep, I was abruptly woken up by a peculiar sound.

"Mwah."

"Eep?!"

Directly in front of me was a girl's face, her lips puckered. Just when our lips were about to touch, I swung my head down and slammed into her with a headbutt.

"Huh?!" The silver-haired girl, Alma, gripped her nose tightly. "Why would you do that?!"

"Because you're trying to attack me while I'm sleeping! I'll kill you!" I shouted, shaking my finger at her.

She shook her head, pitying me. "You're such a baby, getting so worked up over a little kiss."

"That's right; I'm a baby. So stop harassing me. If you do it again, I'll turn you in to the military police, no questions asked. You pipsqueak nympho."

"Pipsqueak nympho?!" Alma acted insulted, but the facts were these: She was short, and she wore very revealing clothing. Considering her height and lack of common sense, it was hard to believe that Alma was twenty-one years old. Killer rack, though.

"Ha ha ha, pipsqueak nympho!" Belly-shaking laughter came from Koga, who sat next to me, wearing his deep-red armor.

"Koga, why didn't you stop her?" I asked, a threat in my voice.

He immediately turned pale. "I-I tried, but she threatened me with a knife! It ain't my fault!"

"I see. In that case, stop her next time, even if you have to take a knife for me. That's the role of the avant-garde."

"Huh?! B-but that's—"

"What's the problem?"

"N-nothing... Fine." Koga nodded, hanging his head pitifully.

"Ha! You're in trouble. Serves ya right," Alma said.

"It's your fault!" Koga wheeled on her, spit flying. Even though we were the only passengers in the carriage, I couldn't help but feel ashamed of these two immature kids.

"Well, I guess it's better than being so nervous that you're petrified..." I murmured, shifting my gaze out the window. We were traveling down this peaceful highway to fight beasts. Alma and Koga were well aware of the task before us.

"Koga, time to review," I said. "Tell me about the beasts we're going to fight."

"Huh? Well, they're goblins, right? If I remember correctly..." Although flustered by the sudden test, Koga started to explain goblins.

Of the thirteen levels of abyssal depth, goblins were level one, the weakest of beasts and merely residents of the Void. They were short and had green skin. While their abyssal depth was low, they had a unique societal structure and the ability to wield weapons and use tactics similar to humans'.

There were four types of goblin fighters. The most abundant were the armor-clad goblin soldiers, which used clubs, wooden shields, and bows. Goblin mages could perform magical spells, such as summoning fire or lightning, according to their attributes. Some goblins found themselves transformed into powerful, two-meter-tall beasts called hobgoblins, and from the tanks of hobgoblins came the heavily armored goblin champions. The most intelligent hobgoblins, goblin generals, commanded the troops. Musters of these four goblin types formed combat forces of anywhere from a few dozen to a hundred members.

"How'd I do?" Koga looked at me, lacking confidence.

"Pretty good." I nodded, smiling. Blue Beyond, our party of three, had accepted a mission from another clan to wipe out some goblins. I'd taken on the job of fighting simple goblins in order to test the proficiency of my current group.

Alma, the Scout, and Koga, the Swordsman, were new members of Blue Beyond. They were both excellent fighters. Through training, they had further refined their remarkable talents. Even though they were both C-Rank Seekers, they were as powerful as many B-Rankers. There was just one problem: Neither of them had experience fighting beasts.

"There is a saying among Seekers: 'Those who laugh at goblins are eaten by goblins,'" I told them as I sat upright in my seat. "While it's true that goblins are weak compared to other beasts, they have weapons and armor, and they can use complex military tactics. If you don't take them seriously, it is you who will become the hunted. More than a few skilled Seekers have fallen to goblins due to unfamiliarity with group combat. The death rate is especially high for Seekers who don't attend training school because they miss out on this crucial information."

They were both listening and looking at me somberly. They wore the expressions of Seekers ready for battle.

"I know how strong you both are, but you're still rough around the edges. I'm going to see if you're worthy of becoming shining jewels, or if you're just gravel to be tossed away."

"Leave it to me," Alma replied.

"Piece of cake," Koga said.

I let my drawn lips go slack. They were ready, and I need say no more. It was then that the carriage came to a stop. Outside the window, we could see a dome-shaped red space. It was an Abyss, an erosive space from the Void generated by an excessive accumulation of mana. At the core of each Abyss sat a beast, and unless the beast was eliminated, the Abyss would continue to grow. A goblin general awaited us at the core of this Abyss, which had manifested on an outpost atop a low hill. The crumbling fort, long since abandoned, was now an Abyss and the home base of the goblin force that had been generated.

I turned to my companions as I stepped out of the carriage. "It's time to fight."

†

The number of goblins we faced had already increased to 200, twice the maximum our intel had told us to expect. However, it was the perfect number for the new party's first battle.

"Order! Alma, kill the goblin mages and archers stationed on the fortress wall!"

"Roger!"

Following the order of my *Tactician* Talker skill, Alma threw two great handfuls of steel darts, using her *Perfect Throw* Scout skill. Her darts flew along impossible trajectories, each one seeking—and quickly finding—its mark. The goblins went down immediately.

Now we'd be safe from overhead fire.

"Koga, break the enemy line! Alma and I will make an opening!"

"Ready!" Koga raced forward at lightning speed. A pair of goblin champions with thick shields moved to intercept him.

"Alma, use *Armor Piercing*!"

Alma hurled another round of darts. Scout skill: *Armor Piercing* decreased the target's defensive power by half. Her perfectly thrown darts, augmented by my skill, easily punched right through the shields, and the champions fell where they stood. The other goblin champions panicked and rushed to close the gap in the line, but my Talker skill: *Stun Howl* was faster.

"Stop!"

The champions jerked to a halt, as if slamming into an invisible wall.

I aimed the barrel of my silver flame at them.

"Koga, duck!"

The thunder bullet I shot flew over Koga's head and hit the enemy's formation, then exploded in a peal of lightning and thunder, blasting the flash-fried goblins away. The line had been broken. Beyond that was the core of the Abyss, and then the goblin general.

"Koga, take out the general!"

"Roger!" Koga rushed through the hole in the line, reaching the goblin general. The massive goblin, almost three meters tall, swung its huge longsword down at Koga.

"Too slow, Joe!" Koga said as he dodged. He drew his own sword, used his Longswordsman skill *Iai Flash*, and sliced off both of the general's arms.

"You're mine!" he yelled. On the backswing, he targeted the general's neck, and—

"Wh-what do you think you're doin'?!"

Alma was there already, but the general's head wasn't. Her knife had beat Koga's sword to the kill.

She giggled. "Tee hee. You're super slow, so I gave you a hand."

"What did you say?!"

Great. The two idiots were now arguing on the broken front line.

"What the hell? Seriously?" I was disgusted. Having lost its core, the Abyss started to purify. The goblins had stopped moving, and the sulfuric odor of the Abyss gradually dissipated.

I let out a sigh and gave my final order: "Battle, complete."

Afterward, we all took a breather.

"The Abyss ain't as scary as I thought," Koga said with a laugh.

We were surrounded by goblin corpses. Their horrible stench wafted into the air. However, we had to wait for the material collection team dispatched by the clan who'd hired us. According to our contract, they would arrive within thirty minutes of purification. The transaction was a simple one: goblin corpses in exchange for one million fil. Goblin livers were often used in alchemy, so they were in high demand.

"Hey, dumbass, I can't believe you're so excited over taking out the weakest beasts," Alma said.

Koga grimaced. "Y-yeah, but..."

"You couldn't even cut off the boss's head."

"That's 'cause you got in the way!"

"Your excuses sure are quicker than your sword."

"Noel, this lady's nuts! Everything she says is insane!" he complained, looking to me for support.

I almost told him to leave me out of it, but stopped myself. As a leader, one of my jobs was to resolve any feuds between members.

"That's enough bickering. Alma, don't engage anyone in battle except on my orders. Koga, stop getting so hyped up. You both got it?"

"'Kay."

"Fine..."

They meekly nodded, making me chuckle. I appreciated their obedience, but clearly, neither of them was suited to be my second-in-command. No matter their skill, this was a personality issue. The biggest obstacle was that they both had blind trust in me. If my second was just a yes-man, we would lack for diversity, and the organization would grow stagnant. While respect for the leader was important, the number-two spot needed the aptitude to prepare backup plans in an emergency. Considering my goals, I needed to find a second right away.

"Anyway, you both did well. It was excellent for our first battle. I'm really proud to be in a party with you."

"Heh heh..." They both laughed and bashfully scratched at their heads. The gesture completely changed my mind. They weren't just compliant—they were simpletons.

"After this battle, I'm certain that we're strong enough to form a clan. Once we're back at the capital, I plan to apply to the government to make this official. Thereafter, we'll be a clan, not a mere party."

"So a clan is like an official Seeker organization, right?" Koga asked me, and I nodded.

"Exactly. Only officially certified clans can accept anti-Abyss missions from the government. Seekers who are unaffiliated with clans cannot be involved with Abyss cleanup, unless subcontracted by a clan. The mission we just completed was a request from the national government to a local clan."

Alma cocked her head to one side, idly spinning a knife in her hand. "What about a clan house? Don't we need a base for the application to be approved?"

"I already bought it," I said.

"You bought one?! Seriously?!"

"Yeah, the other day." It was a property I'd had my eye on for a while. I used most of my savings for the deposit. I still had to pay it off, but I was listed as the owner of both the land and building on the registration. I also had the deed.

"Why is this the first I'm hearing about this?!" Alma said, indignant.

"I'm the one paying for it, so why would I need to check in with you first?"

"Grrr!" Alma puffed out her cheeks, looking grumpy.

I'd snapped at her, but I hadn't withheld the information for any reason other than that I knew she'd object to the idea.

"What kind of house is it? I wanna go see it once we get back," Koga said. In contrast to sourpuss Alma, he was brimming with enthusiasm.

"It's still being remodeled. I'll show you when it's done."

"All right. I can't wait."

I stood up straight and looked at them both.

"We're strong enough, we have a base, and we have the mandatory insurance. We're ready to establish a clan. Once we become a clan, I have no intention of taking weak guppy jobs just to earn a buck. We're only going for whales. Starting with our next battle, we'll be fighting for our lives. Make sure you're prepared."

"Roger!"

"You got it!"

They were ready. I could sense them not only perking up at my words but actually getting excited. They were warriors through and through. I was actually very grateful. If only their personalities were up to the level of their prowess. Well, as they say, "God doesn't grant people more than one talent."

"Hey, Noel, what's that?" Koga asked abruptly, pointing to my right hand.

I tilted my head to see. There was a book-shaped pattern on the back of my hand. "Ah, this is the proof that I can move up to the next rank," I explained.

All classes had a certain set of conditions they needed to meet before they could move up in the ranks. When it was time, a mark of proof would appear somewhere on their body. The one I'd acquired was clear as day. To be honest, just moving up to B-Rank wasn't exciting to me.

"Wow, congratulations!"

"Congratulations, Noel. Now that you can move up too, Koga is the only one left out," Alma said.

Koga's eyes grew wide. "Huh? You can move up already, Alma?"

"That's right. Easily."

"Th-that so?" Koga asked, flustered. I nodded. "I-I see..." He was so disappointed, I couldn't help but laugh at his silly expression.

"Don't look so pathetic. You'll be able to move up soon."

"Is moving up ranks really that easy?" he asked.

"It's not, but once you've met all the conditions, it's pretty likely that you'll get to move up from C to B. Or so they say, anyway." That was why I wasn't excited about this promotion. Even with a high possibility of moving up, nothing was guaranteed. There were plenty of Seekers who were unable to achieve a new rank, even after fulfilling all conditions. However, Koga was truly talented.

"For example, the condition for a Talker to move up is to accumulate a total of 10,000 experience points through providing support in battles."

"How do you know if you've got the 10,000 points or not?" Koga asked me.

"Statistically, you get one point for each battle against an equivalent opponent. This point value goes up exponentially according to the enemy's strength. So if we were only fighting safe battles against equals, it would take an incredible amount of time to move up in rank, but against stronger enemies, we can improve far more rapidly."

"I see. Guess I'll be able to move up soon, then. You said we're going to be dancin' with death from now on, right?"

"Exactly. Plus, you earned lots of experience from your underground fighting career, so I can't imagine it will be long before you're ready."

Known as the Rookie Giant-Killer, I spent a year working almost nonstop to finally establish this routine of gaining experience quickly. Despite that, the path to promotion was still a thorny one. Moving from C to B was simply quantitative; anyone unafraid of battle could achieve it. Getting to Rank A was another story.

Before long, we could hear a carriage approaching. "It looks like the collection team is here. Time to say goodbye to this stinkpot. Once we're back in the capital, I'm going to move up to Rank B. What about you, Alma?"

"Sorry...I need more time."

"Okay. Let me know when you're ready."

Changing ranks was a one-way street. Once you moved up a rank, there was no turning back, and therefore, many Seekers— Alma included—had trouble deciding. It didn't bother me at all. I was sure I would be able to use Alma no matter which rank she decided on.

"I want a class that lets me light up Koga's crotch in rainbow colors."

"You what?!"

The only problem now was their personalities.

†

Just as an appraiser was necessary to determine a class, they were also vital to help Seekers climb up in ranks. An appraiser was unique in that their ability was innate and did not require assessment, like standard classes. They also didn't have ranks.

People born as appraisers were gathered up from the provinces and brought to the imperial capital to be given a specialized education at the Appraiser Association.

The main role of an independent appraiser was to generate the classes of people in the imperial capital and various towns. When there were no classes to assess, they did research on classes they had assessed in the past. The numerical values of the various skills were also calculated based on data that was collected and analyzed by appraisers. Appraisers were vital to the workings of the society, but to be honest, I really hated them.

The Appraiser Association building was a dignified, shrine-like construction made of limestone. After waiting there for what felt like eons, I was ushered into a meeting room. When I entered, I found myself face-to-face with a young gnome.

"Thank you for coming today, Noel Stollen," she said. "So you want to move up a rank? That is wonderful. I am delighted to have the privilege of witnessing the next step in your journey." Her customer-service smile didn't reach her eyes.

Perhaps because of the education she'd been subjected to since childhood, this girl had absolutely no interest in people, and her thirst for knowledge was limited to Seeker class research. She was looking at me as if I were a lab rat, so obviously we weren't going to get along.

"Now, Mr. Noel. You are a Talker, so you have three options for class specialty: Minstrel, Strategist, and finally, Beast Tamer."

I had already researched all three of these options before coming. The Minstrel class allowed for even stronger support skills through song. Strategist was useful for myriad support skills specific to group battle. Then there was Beast Tamer, which would allow me to subdue other species via mutual comprehension.

The stronger support aspect of Minstrel was appealing, but it would be difficult to fulfill my role as commander while also singing, so that was out. What about Beast Tamer? If I could make other beings work for me, I would be able to resolve the biggest weakness of a buffer—lack of combat prowess. That was a huge advantage. There was also a certain romance to riding a massive mutant into battle. However, it was very difficult to get mutant species to follow directions. While they would obey orders, there was often a several-second gap between hearing an order and comprehending it, which would make the beast useless in battles that required split-second coordination. It was pointless to trade one weakness for another.

Thus, there was only one class suitable for a commander like me.

"Which class would you like to choose? My own personal recommendation is Beast—"

"Strategist," I interjected. "Strategist, please."

"Strategist? I see. It is true that as a Seeker, the universal Strategist class may be preferable. However, Beast—"

"Strategist. I have no intention to become anything except a Strategist."

"Hmm... I simply must stress that—"

"I don't care about your recommendation. I said Strategist!" I was getting annoyed.

The appraiser frowned, looking sad. "There's no changing your mind?"

"None."

"Tch." This freaking gnome clicked her tongue at me! The only reason she wanted me to become a Beast Tamer was because she didn't have a lot of data on them. The rare and less-than-desirable classes had real research potential.

"I understand," she relented. "Strategist, then?"

"How many times do I have to say it? Hurry up. I don't have all day."

"Fine. I will now explain rank procession."

The appraiser explained it thusly: Moving up a rank involved augmenting the body, which would improve skills that I'd already learned and grant me some new skills. However, it did not change the core of the class. Even after becoming a Strategist, I would still be a Talker—just as water is water even when it's a solid or a gas.

"Even after moving up a rank, the general practice is to refer to you by your original class name. Don't grow overconfident just because you have this new power. There is no such thing as omnipotence in this world," the gnome told me.

"Obviously. I know my limitations so well, it's sickening."

"Good. This concludes my explanation. Now I shall begin the ceremony."

The appraiser spread out both arms and began singing in a language other than the common tongue. I was no expert, but it sounded like an ancient gnomish song. Gnomes were the first appraisers, after all. Even now, nearly 80 percent of appraisers were gnomes. Any non-gnome appraisers could trace their ancestry back to a gnome at some point in time. This was what the song meant:

"I open thy new door. I open thy new door. Thou, who desires great power. Turn thine eyes to the sea within. It is the wisdom of light that will illuminate the dark water's surface. The light becomes a door that leads to this world. I open thy new door. I open thy new door..."

Finally, a blue glow enveloped me, and a mysterious force started to well up from deep inside my body.

†

Talker Rank B, Class: Strategist. This class's main attribute was ultra-augmentation of cognitive speed. The basic intelligence augmentation for Talker was the highest among all classes. Thanks to my newly acquired abilities, I was even more powerful. I could already compartmentalize my thoughts, create pseudo-personalities, and even entertain parallel ideas while maintaining the processing speed of those personalities. Thus, I could analyze battle situations in real time from multiple perspectives, which meant that I could essentially predict what would happen in a battle with near-perfect accuracy. While the temporal parameters of what I could predict were extremely short, the attribute was truly suited to a Strategist.

In the end, whether I could make this attribute useful in battle was up to me. Even if you know the future, it's not easy to react in a split second. Also, the gap between making a prediction and conveying those results to the other team members could be an issue. My coordination with Koga and Alma—who served as my fists and feet—would be even more important than before. If just anyone could do it, the class of Talker wouldn't be considered the weakest.

Once my rank-up ceremony was finished, I left the Appraiser Association and headed to the Seekers Association. My next goal was to officially establish our clan. Along the way, I noticed that a crowd of shrieking women had gathered on the street ahead of us.

"Squee! You're so cool! Look over here!"

"Let's go eat! It's on me!"

"Excuse me, could you sign my sword sheath?!"

Whoever was in the center of the crowd seemed to be very popular with the ladies. There were women of all ages, from young to quite old, and not only common folk—some Seekers were also among the rabble. While Seekers were like celebrities, very few Seekers had other Seekers as fans. Curious, I craned my neck to try to see who it was in the middle of the crowd. Since the crowd was all women, I was easily able to see over their heads at the subject of all the commotion.

There stood a pretty boy, his flaxen hair topped with a cowlick. He looked to be in his mid-twenties, and he was about a head taller than me. He had gentle features and looked to be squinting. The navy coat draped over his shoulders really made his hair color pop. On his hip, he wore a sheathed longsword.

I knew this man, and it made sense that he'd attracted so many women. The vice-master of Supreme Dragon, top regalia clan and best clan in the capital, was famous in the capital as a young prodigious Swordsman.

"Zeke Feinstein, the Innocent Blade!" I called out, prompting Zeke to turn his head toward me.

"Aha! Noel Stollen, is it?" he responded, loud enough for me to hear even over the squealing. Zeke shouldered the women aside and headed toward me.

"It is you, Noel. What a coincidence." His gentle yet brazen manner of speaking was proof that he had been waiting for me the entire time. And there was a reason for that.

†

"Who is that girl? It looks like Zeke knows her, doesn't it?"

"Uh, I think that's a boy, not a girl..."

"Really?! With such a pretty face?!"

"I know him! He's the leader of Blue Beyond!"

"I-I don't know what that is, but it sounds like a beautiful ocean!"

"Totally! Look, there are roses blooming behind them!"

The women were excitedly going on and on, delighted to see us together. My temples started to throb a little, but I looked straight at Zeke and forced a smile. "Well, well. If it isn't Zeke Feinstein, vice-master of Supreme Dragon, the strongest clan in the capital. How lucky I am to meet you. Seriously."

"Oh, no, *I'm* the lucky one. To think that you even know my name, Noel," Zeke said, flashing a buttery smooth grin.

He was a sarcastic fellow. As if there were any Seekers who didn't know his name. There were only three people of EX-Rank in the capital. One was the master of the third-tier regalia clan Pandemonium, Leo Edin, also known as the King Slayer. The second was master of Supreme Dragon, the top clan of the regalia, Victor Krauser, also known as the Beginning One. The third, naturally, was the vice-master of Supreme Dragon, the man standing before me.

According to what Alma once told me after a few too many drinks, the head of the Society of Assassins was also EX-Rank, but since I'd never met him, I didn't know if it was true. What I did know, and what was important there, was that there were only three Seekers of that rank. However, Victor was already approaching sixty, well past his prime. Even though he was EX-Rank, his battle prowess was hardly better than an A-Ranker. However, he'd also been cultivating knowledge, experience, and skills over many years, so he was still pretty much the cream of the crop.

At this point, the only two EX-Rank Seekers who could unleash their full potential in battle were Leo and Zeke. They were the two strongest Seekers in the capital. When a guy like that tried to act humble, it just came off as sarcasm. Maybe it was genuine, but his strong confidence was obvious from every aspect of his behavior, proof that he clearly understood his position. It seemed to me like the rumors that he was always scheming behind his wholesome front were true.

"So?" I asked him. "What might a prolific hero such as yourself want to discuss with a worthless Seeker like me?"

"Who ever said you were worthless?!" He balked. "Your name has been on the whole clan's lips. Not only are you the grandson of the legendary Overdeath, but you also expelled the Gambino family with only one person's help."

"It's public knowledge that I'm the grandson of Overdeath, but I don't know anything about the Gambino family. Maybe you're mistaking me for someone else?" I shrugged.

"There is no mistake. Plenty of Seekers saw the trouble brewing between you and the Gambino family. While it's not public knowledge, the Gambino family got a new leader one week later. Sure, no one actually saw you lay a hand on Albert directly, but there's enough information to figure out what went down," Zeke said, his smile growing ever wider.

"If that were true, it would make me an extremely dangerous person. The head family—the Lucianos—wouldn't just let something like that go."

"That's right! That's what got me!" Zeke opened his usually narrowed eyes wide. Looking at his silver pupils, I could sense a silent but dark heat, like a banked fire.

"I'm just *very* curious as to what sort of trick a normal Seeker like you could pull to achieve something like that," he continued.

"Now, now, I'm starting to suspect that this isn't just a coincidental meeting. What are you hoping to achieve here? While this is all very interesting, this worthless Seeker is busy. If you don't mind, I'd like to be on my way," I said, turning on my heel. Then I felt Zeke's hand on my shoulder.

"Hey, get your hand off of me."

"So sorry. But I'm not finished yet," he said.

"What does that have to do with me? It seems like you're confused about what you can and can't do just because you're the vice-master of the strongest clan in the capital," I shot back at him.

"Such bitter words." Zeke stepped back, pulling his hand away. "As you've determined, this meeting was not a coincidence. I came here to speak with you. I apologize if that's not to your liking."

"I don't need an apology. You're nothing but a complete stranger to me."

"Come on now, just a minute. I promise it's good news for you. If we could just get a cup of coffee and talk—"

"Were you listening? I said I'm busy. I don't have time to get coffee with you. Not now, not ever."

"So stubborn."

"Hmph. There's nothing stubborn about it. I know why you're here. You came to scout me."

It was common for a successful clan to take in parties with potential. Not only did it help strengthen their clan, but it also helped to eliminate future rivals, so it was disadvantageous not to headhunt. The recruited members also got the chance to earn high pay, so he was right when he said it was good news. But I already knew my answer.

"You disgust me," I spat.

"What did you say?!"

"Why be so forceful? It's like you really do believe you're greater than you are. Do you think that everyone will just do what you say because of who you are? If so, you're gravely mistaken."

Zeke was always brimming with arrogance, picking and choosing the deeds he would perform as favors for people. I would rather die than follow the orders of a guy such as him.

"I didn't mean any harm, but it sounds like I may have offended you." His tone had changed.

"Not 'may have.' You did offend me."

"What you say is correct. My objective was for Supreme Dragon to absorb Blue Beyond. But you've got something wrong here."

"Huh?"

"I'm not mistaken; I really *am* great and important," Zeke said, emanating with a fighting spirit so potent, it seemed sky-high. He was prepared for battle. I would be lying if I said that an EX-Rank's bloodlust wasn't frightening in person.

Faced with this overwhelming opponent, I...let out a snort. "Once you know you can't convince me, you decide it's time for brute force? How small-minded."

"It's true," he replied. "I'm a small man. That's exactly why my principle is to never hold back in getting what I want, no matter what it takes."

So Zeke was aware of his own mental weakness. Regardless of how powerful a Seeker was, most were preoccupied with appearances and unable to recognize their own flaws. Zeke was different; he accepted them. He didn't even try to hide his shortcomings from a rookie like me. Even with the pride and dignity he must've possessed as *crème de la crème* of the imperial capital, he had an unbelievably open mind. It would be hard to corner someone like this in an argument. No matter what I said, he would shrug it off, and in the end, he would use force to get his way.

"Look, I don't want to resort to violence either. I know a place with great cake, so let's just go talk," Zeke proposed with his bright smile. He was a tough opponent, but I knew that there was one topic that no one, not even tough warriors, could brush off.

"I must be pretty lucky for the vice-master of the strongest clan in the capital to be so interested in me. Okay, I get what you want. But there are some conditions I just can't budge on."

"Yes, of course there are. You're welcome to fill me in. No matter how difficult, I'll pass them on to the clan and do what I can."

"You don't need to do that."

"Hmm? What is it you want?" he looked puzzled.

"I can't work under anyone. But if I were to work under someone, they would have to be strong by my standards. Right, Zeke? So who is stronger, you or Leo?"

The effects were immediate.

"So...your condition is that I prove myself against Leo?" Zeke's formerly relaxed face started to twist into a rictus.

"That's right. Makes sense, doesn't it?" I said. "I couldn't possibly operate under the person in the number *two* spot. Your clan might be number one, but that's because of the achievements of your clan master, Victor. If you want to subjugate me, then prove to me that you're the strongest."

Who was the strongest in the capital? It was a frequent conversation topic not just among common folk, but among Seekers as well. There were a few people arguably deserving of the title of the strongest of all time. One of those was Overdeath. More interesting, however, was naming the *current* strongest Seeker. Surely, the candidates themselves thought about it too.

Zeke was flexible, but he was also prideful. Otherwise, he wouldn't have been so fixated on me. That was why he couldn't just let it go. Still, it wouldn't be easy to prove who the strongest was. Even if Zeke wanted to fight such a decisive battle, it would be pointless unless Leo agreed.

Most of all, if two rivals at their level decided to go all out, one of them would undoubtedly be seriously injured or even die. A full-on duel wasn't something that lowly Seekers could just casually partake in, let alone important clan leaders. It would be easy for Zeke to just declare himself the strongest, but that wasn't proof, and even Zeke wasn't completely shameless. In other words, it was almost certainly impossible for Zeke to fulfill my condition.

"I see... So that's the kind of person you are. No wonder you were able to take on the Gambino family," he said slowly.

"I'll take that as a compliment. Now, I've given you my condition. Please let me know if you're prepared to meet it. In the meantime, I'll be waiting. Bye, then." I smiled and waved as I took my leave. Zeke didn't try to stop me this time.

Just then, I heard a stupid voice from somewhere that I *really* didn't need butting in.

"Hey, look. It's Zeke, the second-strongest Seeker in the capital."

There was an oft-spoken adage: "Tickling the dragon's scale." It meant to incur a powerful person's wrath, and it came from the idea that of the many scales on a dragon's body, there was always one that grew in the opposite direction from the others. If anyone were to touch that one scale, the dragon would fly into a rage.

"Was that you?" Zeke asked, jerking his finger in the direction of the speaker. There stood a male Seeker, an ordinary fellow with no distinguishing features to speak of. He was probably a rookie fresh out of training school.

"Huh? Yeah, is that a problem?" Slow on the uptake, the boy fired back a question instead of apologizing.

"No, it's no problem at all," Zeke replied, his voice calm. "But you clearly said I was second strongest, right? I wonder why? Leo and I have never fought, you know."

"Ah, w-well, Leo is clan master so..."

"Mm-hmm, so you believe that since I am vice-master, I'm inferior to Leo, and there isn't even a reason to fight?"

"N-no, that's not what I..." The boy finally realized what he had done, but it was too late. Even if he were to beg and grovel for forgiveness, there was no taking back what he'd said. He was already in Zeke's sights.

"Then what did you mean by it?"

"U-uh, well... Can you just give me a second, Mr. Ze—"

"No can do."

I had no idea what happened in that second, but the next thing I knew, that boy who'd taken a crack at Zeke was suspended in midair. His body then slammed into the side of a building with

incredible force. Zeke had used the flat of his sword to hurl the boy like a stone and was now holding it aloft, but he'd unsheathed the blade faster than the eye could see.

Evidently, he'd held back so as not to kill the boy—despite the terrible impact, he was still breathing. However, all his limbs were facing the wrong direction. He was severely injured; even a skilled healer would have a hard time treating him. I'd had a view from the rooftop of the building, which I'd climbed using the wire gimmick in my watch.

"No matter how much of a position he is in to keep the military police quiet, committing violence so confidently in such a public place... That's something," I muttered.

Had I stayed on the street, the same thing might have happened to me. When I thought about how I could have ended up had I made one wrong move, the very marrow in my spine froze. Despite the danger, I would still need to face Zeke again with strong resolve. If I kept timidly refusing Supreme Dragon's headhunting offers, misunderstandings would come about, and silly rumors would start to spread. I'd already had enough of that.

There were probably others thinking the same thing as Zeke. If I didn't nip this in the bud, I would just be caught up in this crap for a long time.

"I gotta get the clan registered before something gets in the way."

I leapt from rooftop to rooftop in the direction of the Seekers Association.

✝

Three days had passed since I submitted the clan application. A letter had arrived at the Stardrop Inn, where we were staying, inviting all members of the party to come to the Seekers Association for the final certification. As the letter instructed, we'd made our way there and were now standing out front.

"I-I dunno, I'm kinda nervous..." Koga said, which made Alma snort.

"If you can't take it, just go home."

"I-I can take it!"

"Stop it," I snapped. "You're embarrassing me."

The Seekers Association was the largest public building in the capital. It was so ornate, it looked like a palace. There was a large clock tower above the front gate. Everything about the building was huge. I had been there a number of times, so I wasn't nervous like Koga, but I remembered how overwhelming the Association building was the first time I saw it.

"Let's get on with it, then," I said. "You two behave yourselves."

With that, we went through the front gate. Once we'd made it inside, I told the receptionist our business, and we were shown to a luxurious waiting room. The three of us sat on a blue velvet sofa and received complimentary tea. Koga propped his elbow on it as he awkwardly sipped his cup.

"H-hey, Noel."

"What is it? You gotta piss?" I asked him.

"Nah. Did that before we came."

"Then what?"

"We're about to meet the...inspector guy, yeah? So he's gonna interview us, and when that's over, we'll be an official clan?"

"Right."

"Ya think they'll ask me things too, not just you?"

"Maybe."

"I-I've never done nothin' like that before. Ya think I can do it?"

"I don't think they'll ask anything complicated, so you'll be fine," I reassured him. Even if they did ask him something, it would be why he became a Seeker or what his goals were. It was just a simple aptitude diagnosis. The point of it was to confirm that we didn't have any members who could cause an issue.

Even if we *did* have a misbehaving member, our application would still go through, so long as that member wasn't a major handful for the master of the clan. Seekers were generally hooligans, after all. If only the honor-roll types were allowed to join clans, there wouldn't be any clans. I explained all of this to Koga, but he still looked uneasy.

"R-really? Ya sure it's all right?"

"I told you, it'll be fine," I said.

"If one of my answers pisses off the inspector, they really won't deny our application? You swear?"

"Trust me, we have nothing to worry about."

Outside of battle, Koga was a complete scaredy-cat. I understood, considering his history, but I wished he had a bit more confidence.

"That's nice of you, Noel. I heard that if you offended the inspector, they would refuse the application right away. If we're denied, it will definitely be all Koga's fault," Alma cut in.

I didn't get a chance to intervene before Koga started to freak out. "I-I thought so! If I fail, I'll ruin Noel's dream right here 'n' now! What should I do?! What do I do?!"

Alma didn't miss a beat. "All you can do to make amends is commit suicide. We didn't know each other for long, but thanks for the memories, Koga. You rest in peace and leave everything to me."

"If killing myself means he forgives me, I'll do it! Will you forgive me, Noel?! I dunno what else to do!" Koga was properly worked up by now.

"You guys..." Just listening to those idiots go back and forth made my head pound. Alma just lied about everything constantly, and Koga took everything she said at face value. There wasn't a shred of intelligence between them.

"If you don't stop, I'm going to lose my patience—"

Just then, I felt intense bloodlust coming from the other side of the door. By the time I stood up to brace myself, Alma and Koga had already drawn their weapons and were prepared to defend me, eyes on the door. Then the door opened slowly. Standing on the other side of it was a white-mustached old man wearing a black tailcoat.

"My, *what* is going on here? Why are your weapons drawn? You look scared. Did you see something frightful?" the old man—Harold—asked with a bewildered look on his face, but it was clearly an act. He was undoubtedly the source.

"How frightful. Would you mind putting your weapons away? I'm not your enemy; I came to interview your future clan. Let's all get along."

"You're the one to talk, Harold. You started this fight." I had met this man before. Harold Jenkins was an inspector for the Association and had once managed my grandfather's former clan, Bloodsword Federation.

"It's been a while, Noel. Completely preposterous to accuse me of picking a fight. All I did was show a bit of enthusiasm so you would know that I can still hold my own against the bright-eyed, bushy-tailed youth of today. One-two, one-two, you know?" Harold did some quick stretches, and I clicked my tongue in frustration.

"You haven't changed a bit. Still a hoity-toity old man," I said with a frown. "Hey, you two, put your weapons down. We have to be nice to the elderly. If he goes incontinent, you won't be able to take him to the bathroom with your blades out, will you?"

Harold's face twitched. With the change in atmosphere, Koga and Alma relaxed out of their fighting stances. They must have been pretty nervous, since they let out deep sighs as they sheathed their weapons.

"You've not changed either. Absolutely no respect for your elders..." Harold said.

"It's precisely out of respect that I'm treating you with such familiarity, without concern for the generational difference. Would you prefer if I treated you as an expensive object instead, oh, elderly nobleman?" I asked.

"Apparently, Talkers are as skilled at impudent talk as they are at providing support. I must say, I'm jealous of all your talents," Harold grumped, but then he gave a cordial bow. "Allow me to introduce myself properly. My name is Harold Jenkins and I am the third inspector of the Seekers Association. I hope to be of some assistance."

"I am Noel Stollen, leader of Blue Beyond."

"Hmm? The clan name on your application is different. Is this correct?" he asked.

"That's right. I plan to change the name when we become a clan. Blue Beyond is a bit of a bad omen," I explained.

"I see. Now, then, let's tuck into the details."

We sat down and listened to Harold's explanation of clans, though all of it was old news to me. Becoming a clan meant that we could accept contracts from the government. When forming the clan, and every six months thereafter, we were required to pay the compulsory insurance fee. There were also periodical assessments, and our available jobs would change depending on the assessment results. Harold himself would be handling our assessments.

Once Harold had finished, he tossed us some casual questions. They were exactly what I expected. Koga stuttered multiple times thanks to his nerves, but he was able to describe his own history and state his ambitions clearly. Alma looked sleepy, but her answers were fine too. Although I was happy that they both said their goal was to lift me up to the top, it must've looked rehearsed to a third party, so I was a bit embarrassed.

"This concludes the interview portion. Mmm, you have a good party here. While you are all young and you've only just started working together, I sense a strong bond of trust between you.

You're still lacking in results, but judging by your history, I see no issues with your abilities. I've also checked into your base, and the 20-million-fil compulsory insurance payment seems to be in order."

Harold smiled and pulled out his stamp. "Good. I'll be approving this for you here and now. As soon as I stamp this form, you will officially be a clan. I have high expectations of all of you."

"Thank you, Harold. We look forward to working with you."

"The pleasure is all mine. However, before I stamp this, there's something I want you to know."

"What is it?"

"This is off the record." Harold had a docile look on his face and continued with a firm tone. "According to reports by the Association's search team, one year ago, a massive amount of mana erupted from an underground vent west of the empire."

That was a surprise. "What...?"

"An underground vent—a river of mana flowing deep underground—gradually gains speed and erupts aboveground once it achieves the adequate velocity. This happens once every hundred years or so. When a mana explosion occurs, the ground is saturated with an extremely high concentration of mana, which will generate an extra-large Abyss. In other words..." Harold paused for a moment, staring me directly in the eye. "A beast lord with an abyssal depth of 13, the very embodiment of disaster—a Valiant—will manifest."

"Is that true?" Upon hearing this, I felt an icy bead of sweat run down my cheek.

"I wouldn't lie to you. The beast that destroyed three countries decades ago will appear in the capital once more. Believe me when I say that the entirety of the human race is at risk," Harold said with a wry smile, pulling out his cigarettes from his breast pocket.

"I see. I..." Unable to continue, I trailed off. This certainly wasn't what I'd been expecting when I came to set up our clan. My clan members on either side of me seemed confused, and even I was in a state of disbelief.

"C-can't you stop it?" Koga piped up.

Harold shook his head as he exhaled a cloud of violet smoke. "It's impossible. Naturally, there are ways to disperse the mana, but the volume of mana we're predicting is just massive. It's beyond human control. It will also be hard to take measures before the mana manifests. The underground vents are just like blood vessels. If a problem occurs in the flow, you'll see earthquakes, eruptions, soil pollution, and so on." He shrugged. "Once that happens, even if we *could* prevent an Abyss from manifesting, the land would no longer be able to support human life."

"Can you win...?" Alma asked. Her voice was unusually heavy.

"Humans have expelled Valiants numerous times in the past. That's why we have been able to survive and prosper. Last time, we were even able to completely defeat one. However...all of those successes involved a fair amount of good luck." He exhaled a lazy stream of purple smoke, staring at the ceiling. Then he looked back at us.

"It would have to involve a major coalition. The military, prominent Seekers in the capital, and the regalia, of course. The first-tier

Supreme Dragon, second-tier Kahn and Cave of the Universe, and the third-tier Blade Flash, Goat Dinner, Pandemonium, and Lorelai. All of these clans are worthy of the regalia title, but as someone who has seen a Valiant in the flesh, I'll tell you that even the power of these clans is no guarantee we can win. There's no way to know."

Unlike us, who hadn't yet been born during the last manifestation, Harold had seen the true threat of a Valiant with his own eyes. His words rang true. He didn't know if all the regalia and all the military in the capital could win—in reality, the odds were tilted heavily against us. That battle would be waiting for us a year from now. I felt goosebumps spread over my body, and I couldn't stop trembling. But it wasn't fear. It felt like this was fate.

"That's all I wanted to tell you. Now, continuing with the clan procedure—"

"Wait!" I swiftly stopped Harold's hand just as he was about to stamp the application form.

"Oh, what's wrong?" Harold lifted his head with a profound smile on his face. He really was hoity-toity.

"Put our clan application on hold for a bit," I told him.

"Sure. But why?" he asked.

I stood up and looked down at Harold. "I'll tell you when it's done."

"Why did you stop the application?!" Koga shouted as we left the Seekers Association building. "Wasn't it your dream, Noel?!"

I turned back and smiled at him. "You mean you don't know? We're gonna take a giant leap."

"Wh-what do you mean?" he asked, puzzled.

Alma came up beside him and teased, "Koga, you really are a dummy. Think about it for yourself."

"Er, uh, I-I'm just too dumb. You don't have to remind me."

"Idiot. Baldy. Useless. Tiny wiener. Just kill yourself, donkey balls." Alma was ruthless.

"Why you gotta insult me like that?!" Koga started to tear up. "That's enough outta you! If you're so smart, then just tell me!"

"You really don't have to be smart. Anyone could figure it out."

"Okay, then say it."

"Hey, don't blow your load yet. You don't even know what it's about!" Alma glared at Koga with contempt and folded her arms, growing silent. She stayed that way for thirty seconds, then turned to me and smiled. "C'mon Noel. Explain yourself."

"You don't know either?!" Koga and I cried out in unison. I'd had a feeling she was bluffing, but it was infuriating once she showed her empty hand.

"Hey, Koga, feel free to punch this dumb cow in the face. I'll allow it."

"It's so dumb, I can't even bring myself to do it..."

I let out a sigh and started to explain why I'd put the clan registration on hold. "Now, there's no arguing that if a Valiant manifests, humanity as we know it is in peril. But it's also a great opportunity for us. When there's a flood, or when a volcano erupts, the land is fertilized. In the same way, if we can defeat a Valiant, the capital will be prosperous again."

After Cocytus the Silverfish was successfully defeated, it ended up providing the capital with a constant water source. The beast's heart was synthesized into a device that generated endless drinking water from thin air, which facilitated the empire's development. Not only could the government ensure clean, potable water for all, but crops could be grown and harvested year-round. As long as there were no floods, locust plagues, or widespread infections, the food supply was stable.

Cocytus's eyes were also utilized to clean polluted water. Thanks to a purifying facility using these eyes, the water table was no longer tainted. This greatly improved hygienic conditions and decreased the mortality rate, further improving civilization.

"This land has been prone to Abysses since long ago," I explained. "That's why this country has been able to hunt so many beasts and use those materials to cultivate magic-engineered civilization far in advance of any other countries."

It was precisely because Abysses formed here so easily that we had fallen *behind* other countries in some industries. But this wasn't the time for that discussion.

"The Valiant that will manifest a year from now will be the same. The scale is different, but if we defeat it, we'll accrue massive benefits. That's why I want to make sure we can participate in the battle, by any means necessary. No—we need to make sure we're on the battle's front lines."

History would remember the clans that fought against the Valiant very differently than those that refused the call to battle. No matter how powerful we were, if we didn't put that power to use, it was pointless. Facing down a Valiant was the perfect opportunity to strut our stuff.

"Normal clans will only be allowed to provide support. In other words, if we want to get on the front lines, we need to become part of the regalia as soon as possible. Then we'll strive to be assigned to supreme command—the ultimate position. If we can achieve that, then we'll definitely go down in history as the strongest Seekers."

Alma and Koga nodded.

"You did say that we'd be part of the regalia within a year," Alma said.

"So a Valiant is both a blessing and a curse, huh? If we lose, we'll all be wiped out, but just thinkin' about losing won't do us any good. But why does that mean we gotta wait to set up the clan?" Koga asked.

"If we set up a clan right now, we'll have to start without any record of achievement or claims to fame. That won't help us push out the higher ranks. We need to be valued enough from the beginning so that they give us good jobs." I chuckled. "The Association inspectors are very good at their jobs, but they're not known for their precision. If they predict a massive mana eruption a year from now, we should expect it in eight months."

"S-so we're going to be in the regalia in just eight months?" Koga asked.

"No, there's far too much to do *after* joining the regalia. We'll need at least two months to prepare, so we have to do it in six."

"H-half a year?!" Alma and Koga cried out in unison, their eyes wide.

"There's no way we can do that in just six months!" Alma shook her head, her expression somber. "I've done a lot of research since becoming a Seeker, and every regalia clan is a group of super-humans. There's no way we can reach that level in just six months."

"There is a way. I have a plan."

"A plan?!" Alma said.

"We're gonna take down strong beasts, right? That's the fastest way to get results," Koga offered.

Alma held her head in her hands. "Duh, I know that's the fastest way. But we can't just suddenly start slaying beasts way above our level. As we are now, there's no way we'll rack up results so incredible, they make us invaluable."

"So then first we gotta get new members, and get stronger," Koga suggested.

"Are you stupid? We can't just pick up capable members off the street," Alma said.

"I-I know that, but..."

Alma was correct. Most capable folks were already in other organizations or leading their own. They wouldn't want to join a bunch of rookies like us. It was practically a miracle that I'd even gotten Alma and Koga to join me. There was potential in the Puppeteer, Hugo Coppélia, the Seeker I wanted most of all, but he had been falsely convicted of murder and was on death row. I still hadn't finished the preparations to prove his innocence and get him released.

That meant it was impossible to get an ideal start using ordinary means.

"We don't have time to dilly-dally. If we want to become part of the regalia as quickly as we can, starting out with a reputation and a record are the bare minimum. There's no side-stepping that."

I wouldn't have been in such a rush had there been no talk of a Valiant. But now things were different.

I went on, "We can expect that the Association will focus on developing the superior clans to prepare them to face the Valiant. They'll get all the good missions, while new and unproven clans will get crappy ones. There's no point in registering if we're just going to get awful assignments."

In order to have a chance of success, we needed the Association to recognize our value very quickly.

"We need drama. Right now, we're just the heir of Overdeath, the heir of a legendary Assassin, and an undefeated Long-swordsman from the far eastern islands. It's not enough. We need to instigate an event where we can grab the attention of the masses. With their voices, we'll persuade the Association." I motioned for the other two to come closer and lowered my voice. "Listen carefully. This is my plan..."

Once I'd finished, Alma and Koga stepped back, looking dumbfounded.

"That's dirty!"

"It's dirty!"

They both yelled out the same thing at the same time.

"Well, it looks like you two finally agree on something."

Outside the window, the three young people waved goodbye to each other. Harold's eyes narrowed as he watched them.

"Noel Stollen, you really are an interesting and exceptional young man."

He vividly recalled the boy's brazen assertion from before.

"I will become the strongest Seeker in the world."

His colleague had just burst into laughter; he couldn't take such nonsense from a child seriously. Harold, on the other hand, hadn't let out so much as a snicker. Not only was Noel the grandson of a great hero, but at only fourteen, he already demonstrated the qualities of a superior leader. Just as Harold had predicted, as soon as Noel had become a Seeker, he'd started to make a name for himself, despite the immense shortcomings of the Talker class.

Of course, not everything was smooth sailing. Harold knew that Blue Beyond had broken up once due to the treachery of Noel's teammates—though Noel was partially to blame. However, even while experiencing the collapse of his party, Noel had come out on top. Harold was also aware that Noel had triumphed over the Gambino family, a side branch of the Luciano family, the largest organized crime syndicate in the capital.

Today, he'd cemented his belief in the boy's potential.

Noel had been completely unruffled at the A-Ranked Harold's immense bloodlust. In addition to his impressive courage, Noel had seen through Harold the moment he'd heard about the Valiant. He'd even read how the Association would proceed. Harold hadn't just wanted to notify Noel of the looming threat; he'd also wanted to see how Noel would use that information.

Harold closed his eyes and thought back to the late hero.

"Be happy, Brandon. There is no doubt this child is your grandson. Even if he didn't inherit your gifts, he will definitely become an even greater hero than you."

"Of course he will, idiot. That's my boy."

Harold's memory was so vivid, he could practically hear Overdeath's voice. Although Bloodsword Federation had been boisterous, his happy memories of the clan had never faded through the years.

At that moment, the door opened with a bang, interrupting Harold's reminiscing.

"I'm home, Grandpa! I'm here to see you!" came a voice from the threshold. "Man, I'm tired. Why are Seekers so incredibly stupid? They're just impossible."

Harold's grandchild and fellow inspector, Marion Jenkins, came in and plopped down on the sofa. Apparently, there had been a fight with the clan under Marion's charge. Specks of blood dotted the uniform's undershirt.

"Hi, Marion. It looks like you've had a rough day."

"They wouldn't stop complaining about the assessment, so I beat them all up. The useless ones are the most annoying. If they want to complain, maybe they should try accomplishing something first," Marion said.

"Sounds beastly, but that's the job, Inspector 26."

"I know that. Don't lecture me, Grandpa. By the way..." Marion's expression suddenly turned serious. "Are you really going to manage a new clan? I mean, you haven't managed a clan for almost ten years now. Are they really that great?"

Harold chuckled softly and nodded.

There were a total of thirty-six inspectors at the Seekers Association. Each one managed at least one clan. For the last decade, however, Harold hadn't managed any clans on account of his old age. It was just an excuse, of course. While it was true that he was well past his prime, Harold was still capable of fulfilling his duties as an inspector. The reason he had avoided managing a clan was simply due to the lack of Seekers who caught his interest.

"No way! Who is it?!"

"It's a team led by a young man named Noel Stollen."

"I know him—the small fry who was born a Talker, despite being the grandson of Overdeath! Seriously?! You're gonna manage that pipsqueak's clan, Grandpa?!"

"That's right. Is there a problem?" Harold tilted his head with a smile, and Marion's expression stiffened. Though Harold was smiling, Marion sensed his silent anger.

"W-well, if you're getting back in the game, then I'm glad. Yeah..."

"What about you, Marion? How is it going with Pandemonium?"

"They're impossible. There's nothing I can do!" Marion huffed with crossed arms, openly grimacing. "Pandemonium was only admitted to the regalia in the first place thanks to Master Leo's extraordinary strength. The rest of the clan is just average. But Leo is so stuck-up and lazy, he only shows up for missions he likes. The vice-master is working hard to manage the clan, but they're all so pathetic that it's exhausting to watch."

"That is a problem..."

"Dammit! If Leo would just try a little, they could be the top-tier!"

"Marion, I know how you feel, but don't overstep your bounds as an inspector. Nothing good will come of it."

"I know that! Shut up!"

How little Marion really knew. Harold sighed at his grand-child's attitude. "Anyway, what brings you here today?"

"Oh, I wanted to ask you something."

Harold cocked his head to one side, ready to listen.

Marion continued, "The inspectors can't agree who to appoint as supreme commander of the battle against the Valiant. Since I'm the newest inspector, they told me to come ask for your opinion."

Harold smiled. Since he wasn't in charge of any clans, he didn't attend important meetings. In terms of seniority, he was the number-three inspector, but his actual position was basically emeritus. But here, they needed his savvy.

"Normally, the master of the strongest clan in the capital—in this case, Supreme Dragon—would be assigned the role, but..."

"Master Victor's age is a concern, right?" Harold cut in.

"Yeah." Marion nodded gently, tentative about discussing issues of age with the elderly Harold.

"You don't need to tiptoe around the subject. Everyone de-clines as they age, both physically and mentally. Victor under-stands that. It would be better to assign someone else."

"So if the top-tier master can't, then I should pick the next one down?"

"No, neither Kahn nor Cave of the Universe could manage it."

"Huh, why not?"

"Kahn is a special sort of clan composed only of blood relatives. That means they have better teamwork than other clans, but they aren't capable of leading people outside of their family," Harold explained.

"That's true..."

"The master of Cave of the Universe is a foreigner. That doesn't mean he's untrustworthy, but when it comes to defending the country, a countryman would be more dedicated to the cause. That will affect those under his command."

"I see. So we should choose someone from the third tier."

"What do the majority of inspectors think?" Harold asked.

"A slim majority think it should be Supreme Dragon, despite any issues. Everyone else thinks the second tier is the right choice, so it's pretty much split down the middle."

Basically, they were trying to choose someone uncontroversial so they wouldn't have to answer for their selection later. There was absolutely no sense of crisis, even though the very existence of the human race was at stake. As a senior inspector, Harold found it shameful.

"What about you? Who do you think is right for the job?"

"Me? I..." Marion thought for a long time before making a declaration. "I think Leo from Pandemonium is the best."

"And why is that?"

"Leo is definitely a crappy person, but he's one of the best Seekers in history—maybe even *the* best. I mean, you should know. He was already EX-Rank when he became a Seeker at age fifteen."

Harold was well aware of Leo's strength. He was also familiar with the man's many heroic exploits. Leo was always hiding his true identity behind his lion's mask, but he was undeniably one of the strongest.

"But can Leo take command?" Harold pressed.

"He doesn't need to. So long as he charges the enemy, everyone's morale will undoubtedly improve. The regalia is too strong for anyone to control anyway. In that case, Leo's style of taking the reins without any detailed directives makes him the best option for supreme commander. He's just that powerful. The idea of facing a Valiant would definitely motivate him too."

"Right, there is some truth to that." It wasn't a bad idea. Marion had given more thought to this than the other inspectors, who were just looking for someone who wouldn't cause them headaches later on. Before today, Harold would have agreed with Marion's idea.

But now Harold had met someone truly extraordinary.

"Who would you pick, Grandpa?"

"My recommendation would be Noel Stollen," he said matter-of-factly.

"What? Ha ha ha, the Seeker who only registered his clan today?!"

"Actually, he deferred the registration."

"So he doesn't even have a clan?! You can't assign someone like that as supreme commander! Grandpa, are you feeling all right?!"

Seeing Marion in such a tizzy made Harold laugh.

"What are you laughing at?!"

"Oh, ha ha. Sorry. I just thought it was only natural that you were so surprised."

"Of course it is!"

"Marion, how about a wager? My recommendation is Noel, and yours is Leo. Let's bet on which one will reach a position suitable for supreme commander by the day of the battle. If you win, I'll relinquish my position as head of the Jenkins household to you."

Marion's expression suddenly changed. "Grandpa...are you serious?"

"Absolutely."

"Well, I don't think there's a chance in hell, but...what if I lose?"

"If that happens, you will go to finishing school. You will learn proper etiquette and housework, and you'll be reborn into the perfect lady."

"Eeeek! Seriously?!"

Indeed, Marion Jenkins was Harold's granddaughter. She was eighteen and had inherited a gorgeous face and a curvaceous figure from her mother. Her bright, golden hair, currently pulled back in a ponytail, had an orange tint to it. The strands' lovely sheen made the already healthy girl even more attractive. Even disregarding her grandfather's personal bias, Marion was exceptionally beautiful.

Unfortunately, she was also unrefined and excessively violent. The way things were going, she would never find a husband, despite her beauty. Harold wasn't such a dotard that he would tell her that she had to live as a proper lady, but he wanted her to at least learn basic manners.

"How about it? If you're afraid to lose then you can back out."

"A-afraid?! Who's backing out?! I'll take that bet!" she shouted.

At that, Harold's face broke out in a wide grin.

†

After leaving the Seekers Association, I headed to The Orc's Club on my own. Every month, Seeker leaders held informational meetings at a pub, aiming to make everyone's professional activities run more smoothly by swapping the details of our work. Tavern owners also shared whatever intel they had gleaned over the past month.

Anyone who wanted to stay up to date on the latest intel would attend. According to Lloyd, the previous leader of Blue Beyond, no one was ever absent. Staying on top of the most recent intel could spell the difference between life and death. Since cutting ties with Lloyd after his betrayal, it fell to me to participate in the meetings. This would be my first and last time attending.

When I opened the door to The Orc's Club, everyone else was already there. The tavern was normally closed at this time of day, but the team leaders were granted entry.

"Noel, over here!" Wolf, a friendly brown-haired guy and the leader of Lightning Bite, was smiling and motioning for me to come over. He was sitting at a round table in the center of the pub. Next to him was the massive, bald-headed Logan, leader of King of Dukes.

The fact that two enemies were sitting next to each other didn't mean they were getting along. Seating arrangements were determined according to party results. This round table was reserved for Wolf, Logan, Red Lotus leader Veronica Redbone, and me.

Veronica was a Magician. She was a smart-looking beauty with long, chestnut-colored hair. She was wearing a lightweight scarlet robe, befitting a rearguard fighter. When I sat down between Wolf and Logan, Veronica raised her eyebrows unpleasantly.

"How thoughtful to be the last one to arrive to your first-ever meeting, Noel."

"I believe I arrived before the scheduled start time," I told her, puzzled.

"That's not the point," she replied coolly. "It's a matter of manners."

"I see, it's contemporary etiquette to nag others regarding trivial matters, then? I'll be sure to etch that clearly on my chest. Thank you for the totally useful, free advice, Veronica."

Her eyebrows rose even higher. "Noel, you've really been cultivating a bad reputation lately. Forget about being late—you invited the mob into this bar, correct? Don't you have even a mite of respect?"

"Oh, Miss Veronica, are you afraid of the big bad mafia? In that case, I'm very sorry. I apologize from the bottom of my heart."

"Are you done making fun of me? This is important."

Bringing up the Gambinos put me at a disadvantage. I put both arms up in surrender. "Okay, I really am sorry—to all of you. That was my bad," I admitted, but I didn't stop there. "Don't worry; I won't be coming to this bar anymore. This is my last day. I've moved up in rank, and I plan to set up a clan. I'll be moving on without you."

"Wh-what?!" Veronica cried out, and the surrounding tables also erupted in commotion.

"Hey, Noel, are you serious?!" Wolf leaned in close, and I nodded. "Wow! Congratulations, man! I can't believe you didn't tell me! Let's call Lycia and celebrate!" Wolf was a good guy, straightforward, and he treated me like one of his own. While I was grateful, I wasn't exactly comfortable with a rival being so buddy-buddy.

"I appreciate it, but I know you're always broke, so you're not gonna throw a party. Your words are enough. Thanks, Wolf."

"Uh, whoops. Sorry, pal."

Most of the other Seekers looked envious. I could hear them talking trash under their breath. Only Wolf and Logan abstained. Logan didn't congratulate me the way Wolf did, but had his arms crossed and eyes closed without a hint of agitation.

Veronica, who looked more frustrated than anyone, took a number of deep breaths to calm herself, then looked at me with a smile so fake, it looked like she was trying to fill a mold.

"Congratulations, Noel. I am *genuinely* happy for you. Really."

"Thank you, Veronica. I am *genuinely* grateful. Really."

"Given your recent promotion, however, I'm struggling to understand why you've come to this meeting. For irony's sake? Or did you just come to brag?"

"Those are both harsh accusations. Why would I swagger in here bragging when I've only just arrived at the starting line? Don't make me the subject of your petty suspicions," I said.

"Care to explain yourself, then?"

"I've been a regular at this pub for a long time. I wanted to see you all one last time, and I thought I should participate in at least one actual meeting. In other words, I'm here to make a memory."

"To make a memory? You—" Veronica's face turned bright red.

Wolf jumped in. "Hey, now, let's not fight. It's just about time for the meeting to start."

"Shut up, you brute. Beasts should shut up and sit down."

After that tongue-lashing, Wolf looked keen to protest, but instead obediently returned to his seat with his tail between his legs. He knew he wouldn't win this one.

"Ahhh...fine. Let the meeting commence."

There was no new information of note, and the meeting ended without incident. All the participants left the bar with satisfied expressions, as if they had accomplished something. I wanted to go straight home too, but there was something I needed to do.

"Wolf, Logan, how about a drink?"

"Why all of a sudden?"

"What do you want?"

They both looked at me with wide eyes.

"How about it? I can get a drink sometimes. No need to be suspicious," I said reassuringly.

They both looked suspicious but finally agreed.

"How about you, Veronica? My treat."

"No, thank you," Veronica answered without hesitation, then rushed out the door.

I shrugged and looked at the bartender. "Taisho, let us stay a bit. We'll just have one drink, then be on our way."

"That's fine, but make it quick. I've gotta get ready for the afternoon crowd," he said.

I nodded and he brought us three drinks. He already knew our orders without even asking.

Wolf examined my face as I sipped my wine. "So what is it? If you invited this butt monkey, then you aren't just looking to chat. I'm happy to have a drink with *you*, Noel, but this guy's making my booze taste bad."

"That's my line, you dumb wolf," Logan shot back.

"Stop fighting through me. I get quite enough of that," I grumbled, then downed the wine in my glass. "You guys are slacking off."

This prompted them to stare at me, mouths agape.

"Wolf, you said during the meeting that you dropped the ball on a big gig, right? Why did you fail?"

"Why? I-I mean, uh..."

"The target was a squid oracle, a beast with an abyssal depth of 5, right? I mean, that's strong, but nothing Lightning Bite can't handle," I said.

"Wh-wha..." He couldn't get a word out.

"You were unlucky? Nah. You lost because of your negligence as a leader."

"Urk!"

Next, I turned to Logan. "You too, Logan. Maybe you haven't failed any missions, but you don't have any results to speak of. Why don't you even try for any big gigs?"

"That's none of your business." His voice grew soft toward the end.

"It's not. I just can't believe you're that jacked, yet you have the courage of a flea. What are you so afraid of?"

Logan's eyes flickered with anger, but he looked away without a word.

I scoffed and looked between them again.

"Why haven't either of you taken even a single step forward while I was rebuilding my party? Why haven't you taken a lead? What are you doing?" I was outright scolding them now.

They stayed quiet and averted their eyes. I sighed, put the money for all our drinks on the table, and stood up. "If you're not even going to try, then why be a Seeker?"

That was what I had really come here to do. I turned on my heel and left the bar. I couldn't tell them what I heard from old Harold directly, but this would at least make them anxious. I wasn't criticizing them for fun; it was true that they had grown lazy. At this rate, their dreams of becoming successful Seekers would never come to fruition.

If a Valiant were to manifest, the nation would be in crisis, but it was also a chance for us Seekers to show our true mettle. If we remained weak in the face of this once-a-century opportunity, we would miss the biggest wave of our lives. My objective was to light a fire under their behinds so they would take advantage of this opportunity.

I would be at the top, above all other Seekers. It was what I lived for, and I would defeat anyone to get there, but I also believed that those with potential needed to grow. There was no glory in being the king if I were surrounded by nothing but pawns. Proving one's strength among notorious powerhouses was the true way to become a champion.

Of all the Seekers I knew, Wolf and Logan had the greatest potential. It was unacceptable that they were being so stagnant. If they were qualified to move up, they needed to. Needless to say, it was something they would have to decide for themselves.

"Dammit! That Noel just says whatever he wants and gets away with it!" Wolf slammed his hand on the table, thoroughly annoyed.

"And how will getting angry at him help you? You really are an idiot."

Wolf furrowed his brow, glaring at Logan. "I wasn't the only one he went off on, butt monkey. It doesn't piss you off?"

"That guy isn't someone who just sits around thinking of ways to berate people. He probably wanted to motivate us. I don't know why, though."

"Well, duh!" Wolf had known from the beginning that Noel wasn't dressing him down out of malice. But the boy's harsh words had rubbed salt in the wounds of Wolf's recent failure.

"I've made my decision," Logan declared before draining his glass of whiskey. "I'm going to take Veronica up on her offer."

"What? Veronica made her proposal to you too?" A few days prior, Veronica had visited Wolf's lodgings and made an offer. Maybe he had visited Logan for the same reason.

"Yes, she visited me, the 'butt monkey.' She is a shrewd strategist, but the proposal *is* appealing. We'll never reach Noel's level by conventional means."

"Logan, I really hate you. You're violent and arrogant and have zero redeeming qualities. But as a fellow party leader, I understand what you've been through. You're really going to throw it all away?" Wolf let his words hang in the air for a moment before continuing. "She wants to combine your parties, right?"

Veronica had told Wolf that merging was the fastest route to becoming a strong party. She wasn't wrong, but merging meant that the former parties would cease to exist. Everything would change.

"Unlike you, I have no intention of throwing everything away," Logan said as he stood up and turned away. "The merger would only happen on the condition that we form a clan. In that case, I can just become the master."

"You plan on fighting Veronica? You just said she's a strategist. The reason she even proposed merging like a know-it-all is because she has a plan to take us out. You know you can't beat her in a fight."

"Maybe not. But I've made my decision. It's that simple," Logan puffed up his chest and walked out, leaving Wolf alone.

"That idiot. If he loses, it's all over," Wolf muttered as he tipped his mug, draining the contents into his throat. "But going into a fight knowing that...he's a bona fide Seeker."

He had forgotten how to believe in such a character a long time ago.

"Okay, I got it. You're not suitable for the rear guard, Alma."

Alma sighed at the casual analysis from Lycia, the beautiful blonde elf. They were supposed to be friends, but Lycia didn't spare her feelings.

"You sure don't beat around the bush," Alma said.

"There's no point in just stroking your ego."

"That's true, but still."

After parting ways with Noel, Alma had met up with Lycia for a technique exchange in the forest near the capital. It was the place where Noel had once ordered her to catch killer rabbits. Now she and Lycia were having a productive afternoon, sparring and showing each other their skills.

Lycia was an excellent Archer. She was obviously proficient in her skills, and her judgment and maneuverability in battle was almost Rank B. Out of five sparring sessions, Alma had lost twice, even though she took the most victories. Lycia had quickly learned to completely read her movements.

That didn't mean Lycia was stronger. Had it been a fight to the death, Alma would have just slit her throat in the first instant. But when it came to reading the other's movements, Lycia was definitely superior. Now Lycia was telling Alma about the most important aspect of the rear guard.

"The main roles of the rear guard are commanding, as Noel does, throwing the enemy lines into disorder using large-scale attacks, and supporting the vanguard. What do you think these all have in common?" Lycia quizzed her.

"Tactical operations based on understanding battle conditions."

"Exactly. Tactical operations. There are very few people who can carry out the role of commander with unparalleled accuracy, so in general, the main roles are weakening the enemy line and supporting one's team. You'll naturally be the tailwind during attacks, and most importantly, it'll be your job to immediately create a situation where a teammate can recover if they're about to lose. Whether counterattacking or retreating, everyone has to be able to move together, or they're doomed. That's something the rear guard can facilitate. The vanguard is too busy taking on the enemy in close quarters, so they can't do it."

Lycia's explanation was thorough yet easy to understand. Her powers of observation were precisely why she was able to find Alma's weakness.

"You have Noel, so you can leave all the details to him. But what if he were to fall? Would you be able to fulfill the rearguard role?" Lycia asked.

"Piece of cake," Alma replied.

"Why are you lying? It's completely impossible! You get flustered too easily! If you can't control yourself, there's no way you can fulfill the rearguard duties!"

"Urk!"

As Lycia had pointed out earlier, Alma's weakness was that she got flustered easily. When Alcor had put her in restraints, she'd been unnaturally calm. But since breaking those chains, she had become extremely emotional, as if traumatized by the encounter.

"Okay, I'll let you have this one, Lycia."

"You don't have to *give* it to me. I'm right."

"If I don't move to rear guard when I move up to the next rank, there's a high possibility that we'll have too many vanguard types," Alma said.

Of the many classes a Seeker might be assessed into, the most common fighting classes were Warrior and Swordsman. Therefore, if Alma were to take flexibility of troop formation into consideration, the rearguard subclass of Chaser would be the optimal choice.

"You're right, too many front-liners is not ideal. But what I want you to think about is: If you decide on a rearguard subclass even though you're not suited for it, you'll just end up holding everyone back. Once you move up a rank, there are no do-overs," Lycia said.

"You're right. I guess Assassin is better in the end?"

"That's what I think. As long as you have Noel, he'll use you well."

As long as I have Noel... Noel was certainly an excellent commander. No matter what class Alma chose, he would make sure she fit.

After much deliberation, Alma nodded. "Okay. I'll do it."

"Heeey! Lyciaaa!" someone suddenly called from within the forest.

"I know that voice." Lycia's elf ears perked up to catch the sound.

Another elf woman ran out from the trees. Like Lycia, she was dressed lightly in a skirt and leather chest piece. Her strawberry-blonde braids fluttered behind her.

"Oh, it *is* you, Lycia!"

"Ophelia! It's been a long time!"

The elf called Ophelia stopped before her and Alma, raising her hand cheerfully and smiling. Just about every elf was beautiful, but Ophelia had especially enchanting facial features. Lycia was just as pretty, but Ophelia's eyes were unique. It was like gazing into a crystal-clear lake.

"Were you training, by chance?" Ophelia asked.

"Yes. We just finished. Are you on your way home from a gig?"

"Yeah, I just got back. It's faster to cut through this forest than to take the road. I've never seen your friend before. A new party member?" Ophelia asked, glancing at Alma.

Alma shook her head. "No, I—"

"This is my friend Alma. She's only just become a Seeker. I was teaching her a bunch of things." Lycia had cut her off for some reason. Alma thought it suspicious, but she trusted that Lycia had good reason, so she let her speak.

"I see! A newbie, huh? You're her superior, so make sure you take care of her, Lycia. It really is difficult for a newbie to get in the swing of things."

"I know that!"

"You two seem close," Alma commented. "Did you grow up together?"

The elves laughed and nodded. "Yeah, Ophelia and I are from the same town."

"We're close in age too. I became a Seeker first, though," Ophelia added.

So that was why they had similar scents. Standing next to each other, they looked just like sisters. Just when Alma felt she understood, Ophelia's male teammates showed up.

"Ophelia, stop running around by yourself. You scared us," said a Swordsman who seemed to be the group leader. He didn't look especially imposing, but of all the men in the group, his aura was the strongest. The man wore beautifully ornate, silver armor, but his face was gentle, as if he couldn't hurt a fly. His tousled blond hair made him look as though he had just woken up, emphasizing the "good guy" impression he gave.

While the leader looked gentle, the other two men had a ruthless air about them. The Lancer in black leather armor and wielding a spear was sharp-eyed, and the wolf-beast clad in white was rugged.

Ophelia turned to the blond fellow and said quickly, "Sorry, Leon. I just came across my friend here."

Leon smiled. "Well, then. Um, Lycia, right?"

"That's right. And this is my friend Alma," Lycia replied.

"A newbie, huh? I'm Leon Fredric, leader of the Winged Knights. Everyone else in the party is fierce, so I'm really just arm candy for them," Leon said humbly, scratching his head.

Alma did her best to not click her tongue. Leon wasn't putting on airs; he really meant it. However, it was clear to her that he was a level stronger than any of the others. She hated wholesome guys like him.

"Since we're here, let me introduce the others," Ophelia said, motioning toward the Lancer first. "This scary-looking Lancer is Keim."

"Hey, who are you calling scary-looking?" Keim chuckled as he stroked his bristly black hair. Perhaps because of this gesture, Alma didn't feel threatened. He had strong features, but he didn't seem like a bad guy. Next, Ophelia moved her hand toward the lupine demi-human.

"This furry fellow is Vaclav."

Vaclav didn't really say anything, just gave a little head bow. Evidently, he didn't talk much.

"And I'm Ophelia. It's nice to meet you, Alma," Ophelia pointed to herself last and smiled, baring her perfectly white teeth.

"Nice to meet you, Ophelia."

"If you ever have a problem, I'd be happy to help. We don't look like much, but we're pretty strong. Lycia knows how to get in touch with me."

"You're too kind."

"Seekers gotta help each other out. Especially since there are weirdos who've been running around doing whatever they want lately."

"Really?"

"Yeah, like that one Seeker called Noel Stollen."

With that, Alma suddenly knew why Lycia was acting so odd.

"He's the leader of a party called Blue Beyond, but they say he kicked out all the members who disagreed with him and made it his own personal party. To top it all off, he sold them into slavery. Can you believe it?"

Alma decided to keep her responses short. "That's awful."

"According to the rumors, he has ties to the mafia, and I heard that he sics gangs on anyone he doesn't like. He's really dangerous, so you should be careful, Alma," Ophelia said.

"Got it. I will."

Rumors really were frightening things. Alma could have gotten angry with her on Noel's behalf, but since at least half of what Ophelia said was true, she couldn't bring herself to get worked up.

"Ophelia, you shouldn't judge people based on gossip. You haven't confirmed any of it for yourself, have you? You can't go around spouting things you don't know are true or not to a newbie," Lycia chided her, but Ophelia shrugged.

"Where there's smoke, there's fire. Sure, I don't know if it's all true, but as a Seeker, it's good to stay on your toes. Especially if you're a newbie."

"Even if it *is* true, I don't gossip about people we don't know," Leon said firmly.

This time, Ophelia's long ears drooped down. "Urgh, f-fine. I'm sorry..."

Seeing Ophelia grow meek in an instant, Alma recognized Leon's ability to lead. He wasn't just strong; he also had the ability to govern the other members.

"We'll be going, then. Sorry to interrupt you." Leon smiled gently and started walking in the direction of the capital. Keim and Vaclav followed, and then Ophelia waved to Alma and Lycia and left after them.

"Bye, girls!"

Once the Winged Knights were out of sight, Alma looked at Lycia.

"They're interesting," Alma said.

"Right? I think you could tell, but they're really strong."

"Yeah. Leon especially was incredible."

"Leon is the strongest B-Rank there is," Lycia told her.

"I believe it."

"The others are strong too, but he's in a league of his own. The reason the Winged Knights were able to slay a dragon and become a famous party has a lot to do with Leon's exploits."

"Party? If they're so strong, why don't they become a clan?" Alma tilted her head to the side, confused.

Lycia laughed awkwardly. "Their motto is 'modesty and dependability.' They've already reached a high-enough level to establish a capable clan, but they've decided to not rush in to anything and take their time. I imagine they'll be forming a clan soon enough."

"Wow, so they're really serious." Alma wondered what Noel would think if he heard this. He'd probably scoff and make fun of them. To someone aiming for the top, the overly cautious might as well be dead. "The complete opposite of Noel."

†

When I finished my evening run, a lone figure appeared out of the darkness and approached me.

"Hey, boss. I did what you asked," said Loki, my informant. Trying to catch my breath, I motioned for him to move to a spot where no one could see us. The sky was already dappled with stars, but it was still too early to close the gates, so there were plenty of people in the city streets.

He handed me an envelope chock-full of papers. I looked at each sheet individually. He had really done a good job finding all the information I needed.

"Got it. Now for the payment." As I reached for my wallet, Loki shook his head.

"I can't take money from you, boss."

"You already paid me back for what happened. We're supposed to be even now," I said.

"I know, I just feel bad."

"I accepted your apology. You repaid me. So take your payment." I forced the cash into his hand.

Loki looked somber. "You're more straitlaced than I expected."

"No, I just know that you don't get anything for free."

"What?! Do you think I might betray you?"

"I'm not saying that. But relationships that are only sweet in one direction soon turn sour. That's all. As a professional, you should understand."

"Th-that's true, but still," Loki stammered. I gave him a sidelong glance and leafed through the papers faster.

"What sort of evil plan are you hatching this time, boss?"

"I don't have any evil plans."

"Bullshit. No one would ask me to gather information on all of the B-Ranked Seekers in the capital unless they were cooking up something nasty," Loki said, this time with confidence.

I chuckled. "Hey, Loki."

"What is it?"

"Is Leon Fredric really the strongest Rank B?" I asked.

"I mean, yeah, Leon is strong, but the entire Winged Knights party is really good too."

"I see. So the rumors are true, then," I said, coincidentally looking right at the Winged Knights page. The papers even had candid photos attached.

Keim Lazar, Lancer Class, Rank B, Warspear. 22 years old.

Ophelia Mercedes, Archer Class, Rank B, Hawk Eye. 40 years old.

Vaclav Rosegund, Wizard Class, Rank B, Summoner. 20 years old.

And finally, Leon Fredric, Swordsman Class, Rank B, Knight. 22 years old.

The party was small but capable. They'd already racked up more achievements than a regular party and were comparable to a mid-level clan.

They were excellent. Truly excellent.

"Y'know, you're denying it, but you have a really evil look on your face right now," Loki pointed out.

This prompted me to touch my own face. He was right. My mouth had twisted into a cruel grin.

†

"We'll be changing our bar starting today," I told Alma and Koga. "Our new spot will be The Rock-Hard Beak."

It was nighttime, when Seekers normally partied at bars. I'd called the two of them out to announce the change in our meeting place.

"The Rock-Hard Beak? W-wait a sec, Noel. Ain't that the bar where the best B-Rankers meet up?" Koga asked me.

"Oh, you know it? That's right." I nodded.

Koga's eyes went wide. "A-are you serious? Maybe I only just became a Seeker, but I know only the cream of the crop end up in a place like that. If I tried to go in, they'd kick me to the curb."

"Normally. But we have a loophole. Right, Alma?"

Alma, the key to that loophole, smiled and shrugged. "The regulars just have to recognize your abilities, right? Like when I pounded that monkey into the ground. But I don't think we're ready to take on a top B-Ranker right now. You and I just moved up to Rank B, and Koga is still Rank C."

There was no concrete difference between Ranks C and B, and under the right circumstances, a Rank C could easily beat a Rank B. However, as far as basic specs went, a Rank B with its augmentations was obviously superior. Even with a good command of tactics, if the opponent could make the fight a regular brawl, the Rank C would be defeated easily.

"So if we're gonna change bars, don't it gotta be one that fits us?" Koga frowned, looking worried.

I smiled and shook my head. "No, we don't need to settle."

"B-but we—"

"Just watch. Everyone will welcome me with open arms." I quickened my pace, and the others followed. When we finally reached the pub, I opened the door without a moment's hesitation. Everyone inside was obviously a veteran with a long list of achievements. That overpowering feeling made this a completely different world from The Orc's Club.

Almost all the eyes on us newcomers were sharp and full of hostility. Or perhaps they were looks of anticipation for what we might do.

"I've never seen you before, girlie. Whose Seeker are you?" A large man clad in black armor with a vulgar smile and a hooked nose approached us. The scars all over his face were proof of the many battles he had been through.

"I'm not a girlie. I'm a man."

"A man?! W-with that pretty face? Don't make me laugh. I don't care if you have balls hanging from your crotch; you're a girlie." The large man ostentatiously stroked the scars on his face as he looked down at me. Koga and Alma seemed ready to draw their weapons at any moment. I motioned for them to stand down.

"So I need a scarred-up face to be a man? In that case, you are extraordinarily masculine. Did your balls finally drop, ma'am?"

"What did you just—" As the man turned red with anger, I laughed coldly and raised my voice so everyone in the bar could hear me.

"Let me introduce myself. I am Noel Stollen, Talker and leader of Blue Beyond. We will be patronizing this bar from now on. Thank you very much."

There was a commotion at my announcement, which soon turned into an angry roar.

"Know your place, newcomer! Who do you think would let you come in here?!"

"Blue Beyond is that party with ties to the mafia, right?! You think you can bring that plague into our spot?!"

"A puny little Talker? Where do you get off?!"

"It hurts just looking at him. Get them outta here!"

Listening to the abuses spewed by *hoi polloi*, the large man grinned.

"The people have spoken. Now's your chance to get on your knees and beg," he said, certain that he'd already won.

"How savage. But I can't say I mind your simplicity."

"Is this a little Talker trying to act brave? Let's take this outside. I'll wreck all three of you." The man jerked his chin toward the door.

I took a step closer to him. "You're planning to take us all on at once? That's some confidence coming from you, Edgar. You're the leader of the chopped-up crew, War Eagle, huh? I can't believe the Seekers entrusted with running the clan were able to do their job under such sloppy supervision."

The man—Edgar—looked daunted for an instant, but he calmed himself down quickly.

"Hmm, you think that since you know me, your strategy is perfect? That's cute, amateur. If you think you're anywhere near my level, you—"

I interrupted Edgar's smug speech with a whisper. "If it's a boy, Bruno. If it's a girl, how about Kachua? Aren't they good names? They really ring with love."

"Huh?" The blood instantly drained from Edgar's face.

"You haven't told the rest of the team yet, have you? That the girl you're dating is pregnant? Congratulations. Let me be the first to say it," I told him, taking another step closer.

"H-how do you—"

"That's a trade secret. Anyway, the issue at hand is my imminent beating." I looked up at Edgar with a huge grin on my face. "If that's what you want, I'll fight you. But just remember one thing: if you're going to fight me, you'll need to put everything on the line."

"Y-you..." After I'd implicitly threatened his family, Edgar's expression took on a mix of fear and confusion. Obviously, I didn't have any intention of doing something so petty. But this sort of threat worked perfectly against idiots who saw fit to trample everyone underfoot. The ends justified the means.

"Hey, Edgar! What's going on?!" One of Edgar's allies sensed something was off and rose from his seat.

I really didn't want to deal with more people, so I spared no time in following up.

"If your friend comes over here, I'll take it as a sign to get started. Are you ready?"

"N-no need to come over! All is well!" Edgar said obediently. Nothing would stop me now.

"So it seems you want to avoid a fight with me. A wise decision."

"You're a demon."

"Demon? I like the sound of that. But I don't mean any harm. Actually, if our business is concluded, I'd love to take my seat. Would you mind stepping aside?"

"Ergh..." Edger gnashed his teeth and grumbled, but he didn't move. I shrugged, scoffed, and glared at him, bloodlust smoldering in my eyes.

"Move. Or I'll kill you."

"Eek!" Edgar let out a little shriek and jumped back. I moved along the now-cleared path and sat in an empty chair. Alma and Koga followed, disgusted looks on their faces.

Now that Edgar was out of the way, the other Seekers had no choice but to accept us. They probably hated us, but they understood that any careless moves would be dangerous. Edgar was distinguished and influential, even at The Rock-Hard Beak. Under normal circumstances, he wouldn't have backed down so easily—yet I'd forced him to step aside with just a few words. No other Seekers wanted to suffer the consequences of dealing with someone like me.

"Noel, I finally realized somethin' today. You're the scariest," Koga muttered.

"I hate to agree, but he's right. You are completely evil, Noel," Alma agreed.

I had to chuckle. "I don't know what you're talking about. I'm the nicest person in the world."

It was refreshing to eat and drink at a new place. I wanted to get on the owner's good side, so I ordered nothing but expensive alcohol and food, which also made Alma and Koga happy.

We'd made it in, but we still hadn't achieved my number-one objective. I kept my eye on the door while I drank my wine. When at last it opened, the group I was looking for walked in.

"The Winged Knights are here." I had never seen them before, but they were exactly as described in Loki's dossier. The leader, Leon, led the way, and his three teammates followed.

Now, how was I going to handle this? I considered a number of gambits, but in the end, it went in a direction I hadn't imagined.

"Oh, hey, Alma. Huh? I thought you were a newbie? Why are you here?" It was their elven member, Ophelia, who reacted to us first.

"Alma, do you know them?"

Talker skill: *Link*. I telepathically sent my question to Alma.

"Lycia does. I just met them once."

"Oh, Lycia." I remembered that her last name was Mercedes too. They must have grown up in the same town.

"Noel, be careful. That elf misunderstands you and thinks all the rumors are true. This might end in a fight."

A misunderstanding. Excellent. Just the ignition I needed. If I could rile her up, I would get an even better understanding of the party's true nature.

"Alma, is Ophelia your friend?"

"No. I told you, I only met her once."

"In that case, let's fight."

"That may be your worst quality, Noel. But at least you never disappoint." This time, Alma's voice in my head sounded excited.

It was definitely stupid, but I liked the fact that Alma was always down to play along.

"Good evening, Ophelia," Alma said, and Ophelia came up to the table.

"Are these two in your party, Alma?"

"Yeah. This is my party."

"O-oh... I've never seen either of them before. I'm surprised you didn't get kicked out."

"Everyone was really nice. They were very welcoming and even gave us snacks," Alma told her.

Ophelia frowned. It was obvious that Alma was blatantly lying. I could feel wariness and a little hostility emanating from her.

"Ah, that's right... I never asked your party name."

"You're right. I belong to Blue Beyond."

"Wh-what?!"

"I'm sorry, Ophelia. I should have told you." Alma giggled as Ophelia's jaw dropped.

"S-so that means...he's your leader?" she asked, pointing at me.

I nodded casually. It was pretty good that she could pick me out as the leader in an instant.

"Yes, I'm the party leader, Noel Stollen."

"Noel...Stollen... You're the..." She must have heard some really horrible rumors. Ophelia didn't even try to hide her resentment. Her disgust was so palpable that I expected she would draw her bow at any moment.

"Well, that's a scary look. Is there something you want to say to me?"

"No... If you're interested, why don't you touch my chest and listen for yourself?" she suggested.

I did as she said and put my hand on her chest, tilting my head to the side.

"All I hear is a regular heart beating."

"Is that how someone who sells his friends into slavery talks?" she shot back.

"Ahh, that. I got a good price for them. The mafia was able to resell them at a higher price. It really is important to have powerful friends."

"You...!" The moment Ophelia boiled over and tried to grab me, Koga kicked his chair away and stood between us. His hand was on the hilt of his sword.

"Miss Elf, you shouldn't get violent. This is my boss. Ya better think twice before ya move in on 'im," Koga warned her.

"You're a very loyal dog. Too loyal for a leader who'd happily put you on the market," she spat.

"Say whatever ya want about me. But ya better choose your words carefully. Don' make me draw my sword."

"Ngh!" Ophelia recoiled at Koga's threat. It was impressive that he could intimidate someone of a higher rank than him. Alma reacted at the same time, but she bonked her nose against Koga's shield and started bleeding. She looked up with tears in her eyes, trying to stop the stream.

"What's wrong, Ophelia?" Leon asked, coming over with a worried look on his face.

"Your friend here suddenly tried to grab me," I answered first. Ophelia's face turned red and she clammed up, unable to argue.

"Is that true, Ophelia?"

"I-I'm sorry... I got upset."

"I see." Leon looked back at me and bowed his head graciously.

"I apologize for my member's behavior. I'm really sorry."

"Nah, it's fine. But make sure you discipline her so it doesn't happen again. Even dogs can be taught not to attack humans. Your friend here is dumber than a dog."

"Dumber than a dog?" A frightful anger started to bubble up within him. Leon turned to me, his aura fierce—almost godlike. "Mind taking that back?"

"Are you trying to be threatening? That's some logic."

"Pardon my rudeness," Leon replied, ever polite. "I'm happy to apologize as much as you want, but that doesn't mean you need to insult Ophelia."

"So basically, you're trying to say we're both to blame? You sure you're not a Strategist?" I said sarcastically.

Leon frowned, looking uncomfortable. "You—"

"Leon, it's pointless to try to have a mature conversation," Ophelia cut in. "This is the infamous Noel Stollen. Apparently, the rumors are true."

Their leader blinked in surprise, then nodded. "I get it now."

"It's pretty childish to be so fond of gossip. Do y'all play house in your free time too? Or maybe play with dolls?"

"You're just insufferable. If you can't value your own friends, then you're not qualified to be a Seeker." Leon wasn't as polite this time.

His words set me off. "Actually, I've already got my qualification. Or are you saying I need your permission now? My bad, I had no idea. So you're not only the top Seekers, but you're also in charge of the entire Association?"

"That's fine. Live your life insulting others like that. But it will come back to bite you someday," Leon advised.

"So now you're a god? That's quite haughty. You should learn your place. Otherwise, it will come back to bite *you*."

Leon's shoulders were quivering with anger at the way I parroted his attitude back at him, but he didn't say anything else. He turned on his heel and quietly left the bar.

Ophelia ran after him. "Leon, wait!"

After that, the other two members of his party left too.

"Remember this, you two," I said, turning toward my own party members. "In the Seeker world, it's eat or be eaten. But the weak are not the ones who are eaten—it's always the arrogant ones. Showing your back to an enemy is the stupidest thing you can do. It's like you're begging them to kill you."

"So you mean...you're gonna use them for the plan?" Koga asked.

I nodded. "Results are always relative. They only mean something once compared to the results of other people. In other words, if we can just prove that we're better than other great Seekers, that'll boost our reputation. I can't control beasts with my Talker skills, but people are different. No matter how strong they are, they crumble in an instant. Once that happens, you can use them any way you want."

With a smile, I sipped my luxurious wine.

"The Winged Knights will be our stepping stone."

2 That Snake Has Wings

AFTER LEAVING The Rock-Hard Beak, Leon walked down the quiet streets in starlight. He needed to cool down. After that verbal assault, he didn't trust himself to remain calm. He wanted to remove himself from the situation before it got worse.

"Leon, stop! You're heading out of the city!"

He suddenly felt a tug on his arm. He turned to see Ophelia, her brow creased with worry. Keim and Vaclav had the same expression on their faces.

"Oh..."

He'd only meant to get some air, but he had ended up wandering around for a while. He felt bad that his friends had been following him this whole time.

Keim laughed awkwardly. "Feel better after your stroll?"

Leon dropped his head. "I'm sorry, everyone. I was lost in my thoughts."

"This isn't like you. I wasn't watching, so I don't know the details, but why would you fall apart just because of something an insolent little brat says?" Keim asked.

"Uh, well..." Leon mumbled.

Vaclav moved his snout in and took a whiff. "No sign of any mental abnormalities."

"So the problem is you?" Keim crossed his arms and tilted his head quizzically. "Tell us what happened."

"Fine."

Leon and Ophelia described what had happened in detail. While they were explaining their actions, Leon started thinking objectively and grew extremely embarrassed.

After listening to the whole story, Keim snorted at them. "I see. The problem was the two of you."

"Wha—why?! He's the one who—ow!" Ophelia tried to protest, but Keim stuck her in the side with the butt end of his spear.

"What kind of idiot takes rumors at face value and starts off posturing?"

"Y-you're right, that was my fault... But he, um, acknowledged it?"

"Dummy. If he was really ashamed of something, would he just acknowledge it in a public setting?"

"Huh, so it's a lie? Why would he lie about something like that?" Ophelia asked.

"I don't know. But it could be that he wants to use a bad reputation to his advantage? You know what they say: a bad reputation beats no reputation."

"What? Then—ow! Stop poking me!" Unable to take the pain

of Keim's consecutive pokes, she hid behind Vaclav's back. She stuck her face out, glaring at him hatefully.

"Even if it were all true, you don't go out of your way to get involved with someone who has nothing to do with you. Your sense of justice makes you too reckless, dummy."

"Ergh..."

He was absolutely right. No matter how just someone was, they needed to consider their surroundings. Ophelia could no longer protest. Tears started welling up in her eyes, and her ears drooped.

"You too, Leon."

"Yeah, I know."

"Whether he's qualified to be a Seeker and whether it's going to come back to bite him are irrelevant. All you needed to blame him for was insulting a comrade, right? If you give in to his provocation and then bring up other issues, any claim to being in the right goes out the window."

"Yeah, you're right. I was wrong."

What Keim said was painfully true and really struck a chord with Leon. He had no objections. No matter what Noel's intentions were, it was Leon who'd changed the subject. Leon was nothing but a Seeker; it wasn't his place to act so high and mighty.

"I'll apologize to him again. You can all go home—agh!"

Keim had grabbed Leon's collar, causing him to choke. "Wait, wait. If you go talk to him now, it will just make things worse. And if you apologize, then your standing up for Ophelia will be meaningless."

"But I..."

"If you're going to talk to him again, you need to know more about him first. That's what this whole argument was about, right? You want to just make the same mistake again?"

"Y-you're right." If he was going to apologize again, he needed to move carefully. Leon nodded and Ophelia raised her hand from behind Vaclav's back.

"I was wondering—how did Blue Beyond get the other Seekers in the pub to accept them? Normally, they would've just gotten kicked out."

"I wonder what happened before we walked in. If only we knew..." Keim scratched his chin, forcing a smile.

"Since we're so hated, there's no one we can ask," Vaclav said bluntly.

Leon and Ophelia sighed.

The Winged Knights were detested by the other Seekers. That was a cold, hard fact. But it was also a fact that they had never deviated from a just path and always did the right thing.

Once, in a newspaper article, a journalist had likened Leon and the others to wandering knights from a fairy tale, such was their emphasis on etiquette and honesty—hence the "Knights." The "Winged" part of the name came from the wings on Leon's shield. Their official name, the Winged Knights, originated from a nickname given to them by others.

At first, it had been cumbersome. They endured the heavy expectations and pressure. Since then, things had changed. The party's name was now a source of pride for Leon and the others. They all worked hard to live up to it.

However, the rest of the Seekers didn't see it that way. The Knights had no friendly relations with other parties, and Seekers always gossiped about Leon and his crew. But of course, since Seekers were mostly hooligans, the majority had plenty of skeletons in their own closets. From their perspective, the Winged Knights had a squeaky-clean reputation, which made them threatening and therefore offensive.

The Winged Knights had been assaulted in the dark more than a few times. Although they had always been victorious against these challengers, they hadn't found who had been ordering the attacks, so they would probably continue. Naturally, Leon didn't intend to just sit back and absorb the assaults. Eventually, the Winged Knights would settle the issue.

"Wait. Can't you get some information from Lycia? She's in a different party, but they used to hang at the same bar, right?" Keim proposed, looking at Ophelia.

"That's true... I didn't think of that," she said, her eyes growing wide.

"Are you serious? Lycia *must* have accurate information! Instead, you just go off these rumors!" Angry, Keim yanked Ophelia from behind Vaclav and jabbed her with his spear, just lightly enough so that she wouldn't be injured.

"Ow, ow, ow! I'm sorry, I'm sorry!"

"You two really are close," Leon mused. When he looked at Vaclav for backup, the wolf-man shrugged his shoulders a little.

After that, Ophelia and Vaclav headed home, while Leon and Keim decided to go to another bar they frequented. Unlike the

Seekers-only pubs, this bar was small and had a relaxing atmosphere—the perfect place to unwind after a mentally trying day.

"So what really happened?" Keim asked out of the blue as he sipped on his drink.

"What do you mean?"

"Why did you get so pissed off?"

"I don't know..."

The way Ophelia had been insulted was unforgivable, but he should have been able to respond more coolly. Instead, he'd ended up disgracing himself.

"I'm not even sure myself..."

"Jealousy, perhaps?"

"Jealousy," Leon repeated, cocking his head to the side. Keim nodded as he gnawed on a roasted bean.

"Noel is, what, sixteen? That kid showed up at The Rock-Hard Beak out of the blue and was acting all self-important. I can see how you'd be jealous. I'm pretty sure Ophelia lost control for the same reason."

"I see... I was jealous." When put that way, it made sense. Keim's guess was probably correct.

"Don't say anything to Ophelia, though. She overthinks things. If she realized that she was acting out of jealousy, she'd lock herself in her room and never come out."

"Heh, I know that. But if you're right, then I was being mighty self-absorbed... I'll never be able to apologize to Noel enough."

"Really? I think it's actually healthy. It's good to have a bit of a rivalry; it encourages growth."

"Even if you cause problems for the other party?" Leon asked.

"I'm sure Noel isn't even thinking about it. I think the Winged Knights and Blue Beyond can become great rivals," Keim told him.

Leon blinked, taking in his comrade's words. "Why would you think that?"

"Because neither of our parties fit in."

Leon couldn't help but laugh at the simple answer. "Ha ha ha, I see. You have a point there." He could feel his mood lifting. "I don't know much about Noel yet, but he must be something. He's really moving up fast despite being so young—and a Talker at that."

"Feeling jealous again?"

"No, I just respect him. He really is something," Leon said.

"They say acceptance is a virtue, but it concerns me how easily you're letting an opponent take the lead, Mr. Leon Fredric, twenty-two years old and single."

"Hey, you're no different there."

Leon and Keim had grown up together in the same village. Keim, slightly older, was first to aspire to become a Seeker. Leon followed Keim to the imperial capital, where they attended the training school together and then became Seekers.

Eventually, Ophelia joined them, and then Vaclav. Leon took command, but Keim was the natural leader. Even though they were equals, Leon always felt like the little brother.

"It's really been a long time since we left home, huh, Leon? Maybe we should take the next step soon. How about we set up a clan?"

Keim took a piece of paper out of his pocket and set it on the table. It was the exact same letter Leon had received that morning from the Seekers Association, urging capable parties to hurry up and establish clans.

"So you got it too?"

"I heard through the grapevine that other parties received it as well."

"Isn't it strange? Why do they suddenly want more clans? This has never happened before."

"I don't know. But there must be a reason, and I think it's a good opportunity. The compulsory insurance isn't so high either; we can pay it immediately. We don't have a clan house yet, but we can always use someone's lodging temporarily. What do you think, Leon?"

"Yeah..."

The Winged Knights had long since proven themselves eligible for clan status. The reason they'd held off was so that they could start from a superior position. If they could launch a clan and receive a positive assessment right away, it would be easy to maintain operations. That had been the party-wide consensus up until now.

"I think it's a good opportunity too. But we need to ask the others," Leon said.

"Ah, they already said it's fine."

"You talked to them before approaching me? When?!"

"Apparently, they also got the letter. We talked about it after the argument."

"I mean, I did sense I was a figurehead commander, but that's harsh..." Leon muttered, fed up.

"Don't sulk, man! I'm sorry!" Keim put his arm around Leon's shoulders and gave him a gentle shake, like when they were kids, but Leon just sighed.

Like the old saying goes, one should strike while the iron is hot. The next day, Leon visited the Seekers Association with Keim to apply for clan approval. Apparently, Ophelia and Vaclav had other plans and couldn't make it.

They told a receptionist their business and were shown to a waiting room. Normally, parties needed to make an appointment for the interview at least a few days in advance, but there may have been a reason they were being seen immediately.

After they waited for a bit, a white-haired older gentleman dressed in a tailcoat finally entered. "My name is Harold Jenkins, and I am the third inspector of the Seekers Association," he said. "I hope to be of some assistance."

"I am Leon Fredric, leader of the Winged Knights."

Once the introductions were over, Harold smiled gently. "I've been hearing about the Winged Knights for some time. We're very pleased that the best party in the business has finally decided to form a clan."

"Well, we still have a lot to learn."

"No need to be modest. After all, the Winged Knights have succeeded in slaying a dragon. That is an impressive feat even for a mid-level clan, and you achieved it as a quartet. That is something to be proud of. I may have to construe your modesty as sarcasm."

The Winged Knights had technically slain a dragon in that they'd defeated a dragon-type beast. Dragon types were the strongest of beasts, and even mid-level clans had their hands full when fighting them. For that reason, slaying one was a huge achievement for a Seeker.

Leon's party had slain a beast known as Aiatar, with an abyssal depth of 7. While it couldn't fly, Aiatar was a formidable opponent. It spewed venom, had an unbelievably tough hide, and could turn invisible. Even so, they had managed to conquer it. It had been almost exactly a year since their battle with the beast.

"Let's get down to it, then. With your reputation and excellent results, your clan formation normally wouldn't even merit an interview. Were circumstances different, I would have given you my wholehearted approval. However..." Harold paused for a moment and frowned. "The Seekers Association unfortunately denies the Winged Knights' clan application."

This was the definition of a bolt from the blue. Stunned into silence for a few moments, both Leon and Keim cried out in disappointment.

"What do you mean 'deny'?!"

"Denied?! Why?!"

"I understand your confusion. I will explain, but please promise me one thing. What I am about to tell you must not leave this room. Can you promise me that?"

The party members exchanged glances and nodded.

"Yes, we promise."

"Now, I'm going to be very frank. A Valiant will be manifesting soon."

"A Valiant?!"

"Yes, that's right. Therefore, the Seekers Association is reducing the number of clan approvals. By reducing the distribution of orders, we can improve the fighting strength of individual clans."

"In other words, the government doesn't think our party is worth training?" Leon asked, his voice shaking.

Harold nodded. "That's right, Leon. Your party is unmistakably strong. However, there is doubt regarding your future prospects. Why didn't you apply for clan approval a year ago, when you defeated the Aiatar and became renowned as dragon-slayers? I think that would have provided you with sufficient capital and the chance for even better results."

"We planned to establish our clan once we were in prime condition," Leon replied quietly.

"It's good to be cautious, but your excessive wariness concerns us. Once your party becomes a clan, will you grow stronger than you are now? Or will you choose stability over aiming for the top?"

"B-but…"

The Winged Knights had never imagined that their delicacy would backfire. Leon felt all the blood rushing from his face.

"Wait a second! You're the ones who asked us to apply to be a clan, and now you're denying us? What's the big idea?!" Keim yelled, flinging the letter onto the table.

"What is that?" Harold asked, picking it up. He read over it carefully and cocked his head to the side. "This didn't come from the Seekers Association."

"That's absurd! Then who sent it?"

"I have no idea. Perhaps it's a prank?"

"A...prank?" Keim's shoulders drooped. If Harold was telling the truth, then it had to be some sort of practical joke. But who would do something so cruel?

"Anyway, your application has been denied. Thank you very much for coming all the way here. Please excuse me," Harold said politely, then turned to leave the room.

Leon stood straight up and called out to stop him. "Please wait! Won't you give us a chance?" He knew he was being irrational, but he didn't want to leave things like this. He bowed low and cried, "Please! Approve us as a clan!"

Harold sighed, slowly facing them once more. "Fine. I will give you a chance."

"Really?!" the two Winged Knights shouted in unison.

"Yes. Instead, you will take a test."

"A test?"

"In addition to the normal requirements, you will also defeat a beast designated by the Association. If you succeed, I will approve your clan application," Harold told them.

"What beast is that?"

"There is a beast that is currently manifesting as we speak. It is a Dantalion, with an abyssal depth of 8."

Leon gulped. "Eight...?"

That was even stronger than the Aiatar they had defeated. Could they win? While he was going over it in his head, Keim put a hand on his shoulder.

"Leon, don't think about it too much. If we're going to continue as Seekers, we must fight stronger enemies. There's no reason to hesitate."

Feeling reassured, Leon nodded. "Fine. Harold, we accept this test."

"Understood. However, there is more to the test than defeating a single beast. You will also compete against another party."

"We'll be competing against someone?"

"Yes, they were also dissatisfied with the denial of their clan application. They begged for a chance. It would only be appropriate to accept one of your applications," Harold went on, eyeing the door that connected the waiting rooms. "He is waiting in that room over there. I'll call him." Raising his voice, he shouted, "The Winged Knights have agreed! Enter, please!"

The door opened, and a young man with beautiful, feminine features walked in with steady steps.

"Hey, it's been a whole day since I last saw you, Winged Knights."

"Noel Stollen..."

"I will now explain the rules," Harold announced. "The winner must defeat the Dantalion, which recently manifested with an abyssal depth of 8. Incidentally, do you know about Dantalions?"

"They can read human minds," I answered. "They generally grow to be over four meters tall—so they're medium-sized beasts. A Dantalion looks much like a large monkey with a third eye in the middle of its forehead, which is the source of their telepathic abilities. They are highly intelligent and understand human speech. They are both crafty and cruel. There are even historical records of Seekers, who—after failing to defeat a Dantalion— were tortured by the beast for ten days before they died. Beasts are generally violent, but the Dantalion is the most brutal of them all. If you fail, I recommend taking your own life while you still can. The main strategy is—"

"That's enough, Noel," Harold cut in. "Thank you for your description." He cleared his throat. "The target is as Noel described. The Winged Knights and Blue Beyond will compete to slay the beast."

"How can that be a competition?" Leon tilted his head to the side inquisitively. Harold smiled.

"It's just as it sounds, Leon. Once we reach the site, I'll give you the signal to start and mediate the mission. That's when you will both launch your assaults against the Dantalion. Whichever party succeeds in defeating the beast first wins."

"I understand that," Keim said, frowning. "But it sounds like you're telling us to take out Blue Beyond before taking out the Dantalion. I'm sorry, but we don't murder people. Even if we came across bandits, we would apprehend them and turn them over to the military police. If you're ordering us to kill each other, then we will concede."

Leon nodded in agreement. "We appreciate the opportunity, but I'm sorry; we can't kill people. That's where we draw the line."

They won't kill people, huh?

It sounded like lip service, but their conviction was bolstered by their deeds. Naturally, apprehending a criminal was much more difficult than just killing one and getting it over with. Most Seekers formed parties with the idea of taking out bandits and other ruffians, but the Winged Knights were different. According to Loki's findings, Keim was right; the Winged Knights had never killed a person before. They had taken down eight bands of thieves. Some were particularly large bands, but the Knights had captured every last thief alive. Their noble principles were truly befitting of their name.

"Don't worry, you two. I am not ordering you to kill each other." Harold continued with his explanation of the rules, but the Winged Knights were now on the defensive. "As this is a competition, we will allow interference from the other team. However, murder is against the rules. I will be monitoring the Abyss using my skills the entire time. I will be aware of all actions. For example, you will not be able to kill someone and then blame it on the beast. Any party violating the rules will be immediately disqualified."

Leon's hand shot up. "What is the limitation on 'interference'?"

"I want to say you can do anything short of murder, but that's too vague. Let's do this. Once the opponent is down, any further attacks are forbidden. Anything after that will be construed as intention to kill."

"Can we use restraints?"

"Yes. However, only in locations where there are no beasts nearby. Leaving a restrained person in a dangerous area will be construed as intention to kill."

"Fine. Then we have no problems," Leon said with a sigh of relief. Then he looked at Keim and smiled.

It was easy to tell what they were thinking. They just planned to tie us up as soon as the test started. If they did that, they would be able to concentrate on defeating the beast.

"Oh, one more thing. Interference will only be allowed once both parties are in the Abyss. Anything outside of that will result in disqualification. Dropping out before the test even starts defeats the point; I want to avoid that. Any more questions or objections?"

The other two shook their heads, but I raised my hand.

"I want more clarification on the regulations for interference outside of the test area," I said.

"What do you mean?"

"You will only be monitoring us during the test, right? So you won't know about any behavior outside of the test? The other day, I was nearly attacked by Ophelia, a member of the Winged Knights. The Winged Knights have a reputation for good manners, but apparently their true character is like that of any other hooligan. I'm quite concerned for my safety. If I'm not careful, they might even arrange a sneak attack." I laughed.

Leon shook his head, looking distraught. "Noel, I am very sorry about that night. We were in the wrong. Please forgive us. We won't cause you any more problems."

"You think I can believe that?" I shot back.

"Ergh... Fine, then what you say is correct. Harold, will you please do as Noel says? We will comply."

With Leon's consent, Harold nodded.

"Now then, Noel, please tell us your request for restrictions. However, understand that we cannot impose any rules that put you at a clear advantage. Even if Leon were to agree, that would defeat the purpose of the competition."

"I know. My request is simple. Instead of just prohibiting any interference before the test, change the conditions to: 'All members must be present and in prime condition on the day of the test.' If even one member is absent, regardless of the reason, the test will be postponed indefinitely until all members are present. How is that? It doesn't put anyone at a disadvantage."

It didn't just avoid a disadvantage; it was a provision that affirmed the safety of both parties. There was no reason to refuse it. The Winged Knights nodded, and Harold looked at me.

"It's true that this provision doesn't cause anyone disadvantage, but we can't allow an indefinite postponement. If not managed, the Abyss will continue to grow, so only two postponements will be allowed. If the test cannot be conducted even then, both parties will be disqualified."

"Fine with me."

"Same here," said the Winged Knights.

Now that the matters were settled, Harold looked at us again.

"Finally, this is not a rule, but a condition for participation. This test is a special measure. Do not think that it will happen again. Therefore, in order to confirm that you are prepared for this test, I ask that the losing party disbands. You will be allowed to continue working as Seekers, but the Seekers Association will not recognize activities of the party members under a new name. If you violate this, your Seeker qualifications will be immediately revoked. Do you understand? If you agree, I'd like each leader to sign this pledge." Harold set the document in question and a pen on the table. I signed it first. Leon conferred with Keim before signing his own name.

"All right, that's agreement from both parties. The test will take place at noon, three days from now. I will send you letters with the details this evening. Make sure you are prepared on the day of the test."

After that, Leon stood and came over to me.

"Noel, I'm sure it sounds arrogant, but as far as abilities go, ours far surpass yours. Under normal circumstances, your party wouldn't stand a chance. But you seem special. You have skills that defy conventional wisdom. Therefore, we will not be holding back, and we'll fight at our full potential," he declared and held out his large right hand. I didn't try to hide the expression on my face as I shook his hand.

"Let me teach you something," I offered.

"What is it?"

"Talkers have the highest intelligence augmentation of all classes. Now that I've increased my rank and chosen the subclass Strategist, I can even predict the future using my exceptional statistical abilities."

In actuality, I could only predict things up to two seconds into the future. Anything beyond that was pointless. However, I was sure that this bluff would work well. "I can see it now. After losing, you'll awkwardly come crying to me."

Leon winced at my provocation for a moment, but he quickly changed his expression to a smile. "We look forward to the test, Blue Beyond."

"First of all, may I say that was impressive."

The Winged Knights had left, and only Harold and I were left in the room. He continued, partially sighing and partially complaining.

"You did well in luring such a virtuous party onto the battlefield. Normally, trying to use another party as a stepping stone would just result in them ignoring you. I tip my hat to your trickery. If it hadn't been for this..." Harold held up the fake Association letter. "Well, I didn't think you would go as far as to forge an official document. It certainly was effective in nudging the Winged Knights into applying for clan status. But it was going too far."

"Going too far?" I scoffed. "You agreed to go along with my plan."

"I followed your script because it was advantageous to me. I did not agree to fraudulent use of the Seekers Association name." Harold was stern, but as a co-conspirator, he couldn't publicly denounce the act. That had also been part of my plan.

The only reason the Winged Knights's clan application was denied in the first place was because I told him to deny it. In order to use the Winged Knights as a stepping stone, I needed to draw them into an officially recognized battle. Just a surprise attack on them wouldn't improve my results. In that case, a competitive battle with clan approval on the line, mediated by a Seekers Association inspector, was the optimal place to judge which party was superior. Above all else, it'd make us famous.

Harold had no obligation to follow my instructions. However, the Seekers Association *was* temporarily reducing approvals. Even without Loki's research, it was easy to assume he'd comply, considering the situation. Rather than dispersing orders among many clans, picking a few to train would be the optimal battle strategy.

Thus, my proposal was convenient for the Seekers Association. If the Winged Knights—the strongest party of their level—were denied their clan application and took a test, everyone else would have to comply as well. After that, parties would probably have to pass strict Association examinations in order to register as a clan. Until now, the compulsory insurance and whether the group had a house had been the basis for approval.

"Noel, you think that as your accomplice, I have to let this go, don't you?" Harold asked me.

"Yeah, I do. So?"

He heaved a deep sigh. "You really have no endearing qualities at all." His expression turning deadly serious, he said, "Noel, my cooperation ends now. From here on out, your abilities as a Seeker will be tested. Sure, if you beat the Winged Knights in the competition, you will be revered. However, can you win? The Winged Knights are currently capable of beating a beast with an abyssal depth of 8. Are you?"

I stood up from the sofa and smiled. "I will win. That's the way I learned to fight from Overdeath."

Keim, vice-master of the Winged Knights, had grown up right alongside Leon. His abilities as a Seeker were inferior to Leon's, but he was the team's moral support. However, he had no friends outside of the party, and no private life. He was a regular at one bar, where he drank alone. Leon was the only one who ever joined him, but Leon didn't have a particularly strong tolerance for alcohol, so Keim usually sat by himself.

When I showed up at his favorite bar, Keim eyed me warily. "What are you doing here?"

I ignored him and took the seat next to him, ordering wine.

"I said, 'What are you doing here?'" Keim mean-mugged me, and I snorted.

"Don't bother threatening me. You remember the competition rules, right?"

"You don't think this is interference? It doesn't matter what your objective is; stalking your opponent is crazy. It's impossible for me not to be suspicious."

"Hey, did you forget the non-interference stipulation? All members of both teams have to be in prime condition. Just coming in contact with you doesn't violate the rules."

"Is *that* why you made that request?"

He was right. I'd requested that we tweak the rules so that reaching out to Knights wouldn't count as interference, and that this conversation wouldn't lead to me being disqualified.

"Heh heh, you're even more interesting than I thought," Keim said. "Fine, I'm listening. Tell me why you're here. Entertain me."

"I only have one objective: I want you to betray the Winged Knights."

When I said this, Keim laughed loudly. "Ha ha ha! Are you trying to kill me with comedy?!"

"That's not my intention. If I were to kill you, that would violate the test," I said frankly.

"Hmph, so you're serious. Interesting... Go on, tell me. What do I get if I do? Money? Power? Or maybe a fine woman?"

Keim was joking around, but I could tell that he was steadfast on refusing any bargaining chips I might offer. His loyalty to Leon, his lifelong friend, was even stronger than his connection to the rest of the Winged Knights. No offer of money, promotion, or women would convince him.

But I knew something Keim wanted so bad, he could taste it.

"Freedom. I'll give you freedom."

"Freedom?" Keim cocked his head to the side.

"I looked you up in the newspaper. In every single article, your party is praised for its magnificence. But the only name mentioned in them is Leon's. Sometimes a third party might be mentioned, but only as a side note."

"He's the leader. That's normal."

"No. It's because Leon, and only Leon, is special. As his lifelong friend, I'm sure you know that better than anyone."

"Well..."

"Why did you give up the leadership position to the guy who's basically your kid brother? Or did you have no choice? The answer is clear. It's because Leon is by far your superior."

"You... How do you...?" Keim was caught off guard by my knowledge of their past.

"The Winged Knights are unbalanced. Even if you were to become a clan right now, the rest of you wouldn't be able to keep up with Leon's abilities. When that happens, what despair awaits you? Do you really plan to continue like this? Just working yourself to death doesn't mean it will pay off. Keim, it's time to be free," I said softly. "This is your last chance."

Eyes downcast, Keim replied, "You're right; we are unbalanced. At some point, we won't be able to keep up with Leon. He really is a prodigy. Still..." Keim lifted his head slowly with a sad smile. "I want to support him. I don't wish for freedom. My only wish is for my lifelong friend to succeed at being a Seeker. My role is to help make that happen."

"And you're really okay with that?"

"Naturally. Maybe it's hard for a kid like you to understand." Keim put his money on the counter and stood up to leave. It seemed his mind was made up. As he walked toward the door, I could sense his resolution to continue on this path with no reward.

But it didn't matter how resolute he was; it was not going to be effective against me.

"If you don't betray him, Leon will betray you first, you know?" I called out after him.

Keim stopped and turned around.

"What did you say?"

And just like that, the third member fell neatly into my trap.

Our clan application test held by the Seekers Association, the Dantalion competition, took place on the scheduled date. It was held in a sea of trees at the base of the highest free-standing peak in the empire, Gustav Mountain. Abysses formed frequently in this forest, which was thick with mana and regularly managed by the Association.

The area currently corroded by the Abyss was a circle with a diameter of about five kilometers, projecting outward from the forest entrance. The surrounding area had already been closed off by Association staff, and there were armed guards at each crucial point so that the general public couldn't get in.

"Winged Knights and Blue Beyond, thank you for gathering here today. It seems everyone is prepared," Harold said, looking at both teams. "I will explain today's test once more. Both parties will enter the Abyss from the front and start the search, then defeat the Dantalion lurking at the core. This is a competition. Interference is allowed, as long as you do not kill each other. Whichever party defeats the Dantalion first is the winner. The winning party will be approved as a clan, whereas the losing party must disband. Are you ready?"

We all nodded. Standing face-to-face with the Winged Knights, I could feel their ferocity—they were battle-hardened Seekers. If they fought seriously, we wouldn't stand a chance. They could crush us.

"Before the test begins, I ask that each leader step forward. Shake hands and swear to a clean and fair fight."

Leon and I stepped forward and shook hands as we were told.

"Noel, as I said before, we will not be holding back."

"Yeah, yeah, good luck to us all," I said flatly, then went back to my team.

That ritual done, Harold raised an arm.

"Now, let the test begin!"

When his arm fell, the Winged Knights started moving at once into the forest. On the other hand, we in Blue Beyond set our bags down on the ground, with no sense of urgency to speak of.

"I'm going to lay the sheet out here, so you guys clear the ground of stones."

"Fine."

"Got it."

Koga and Alma moved all the stones out of the way and I laid out the blanket we'd brought.

"How's this? Shall we eat?"

We sat on the blanket, pulled lunch boxes out of our bags, and started to eat. The lunch boxes were filled to the brim with sandwiches, a meat dish, and even dessert featuring seasonal fruits. It was made specially by the head of the Stardrop Inn.

"Noel, what exactly are you doing?" I looked up to see Leon standing there, confused.

"Oh, Winged Knights. Shouldn't you hurry on in there? This is a competition, you know?"

"That's what I was going to ask you. Seriously, what are you up to?"

"We're eating lunch."

Leon's face twitched at my response. "I have no idea what you're trying to say. Why do you have to eat lunch here?"

"Can't fight on an empty stomach."

"This is a competition! You don't have time to just be loafing around!"

"Haven't you ever heard the phrase 'More haste, less speed'?"

"Why, y-you...!" Leon glared at Harold, his shoulders shaking with anger. "What is the meaning of this, Harold?!"

"Honestly, I have no idea." Harold approached us, looking just as puzzled as Leon. "What are you playing at? I gave the signal to start."

"I told you, we're eating lunch."

"Hmm? Are you abandoning the test?"

"Of course not! I would never," I told him.

"Then please stand up. Otherwise, you will be presumed to have forfeited the test."

"I don't remember hearing such a rule. There's no reason for me to oblige."

"That's true, but..."

As Harold's lips drew thin, Leon shouted, "Stop messing around and get serious! Stand up! Stand up and fight!"

"No. If we wait too long, the sandwich bread will dry out."

"I thought you wanted to register your clan?! If you lose the competition, you won't just lose the chance to be a clan—your party will have to disband!"

"I know that."

"In that case—"

"But I have no intention of rushing. You're welcome to go on ahead," I said.

"You...!"

The furious Leon reached out to grab my collar, but it was Keim who stopped his hand.

"Stop. Let's go."

"B-but...!"

"Leon, don't lose sight of the objective." Keim lowered his voice and whispered in Leon's ear. "Listen, talking to this guy will only make us look bad. Remember why our clan application was denied."

This startled him. Without thinking, Leon shot a sidelong glance at Harold. The reason the Winged Knights' application had been denied was because Harold had assessed that the party's prudence would lead to stagnancy in the future. In order to revise this assessment, the Winged Knights needed to not only win against Blue Beyond but also demonstrate dauntless courage. If they didn't, their poor showing would hurt them even if they were ultimately approved as a clan. Just like Keim said, they didn't have time to stop. They needed to defeat the Dantalion as soon as possible.

"Fine." Leon took one last look at me and then turned on his heel. "Noel, I'm disappointed in you."

Leon and his party left to carefully search the Abyss.

Using her detection skill, Ophelia found that the Dantalion—the core of this Abyss—was two kilometers into it.

"There are about five hundred underlings. Oh, wait a sec," Ophelia said, moving her ears and checking farther away. "A vanguard of two hundred are heading this way. I wonder why they're starting upwind, where we can detect their smell. But they're moving slowly, so we'll intercept them in about five minutes."

Leon looked around and thought for a moment. "Okay, let's wait for them here in this clearing. Once we defeat the vanguard, we can advance again. Everyone, prepare for battle."

Keim and Ophelia brandished their weapons and took their positions according to Leon's directions. Only Vaclav stood his ground and instead raised his hand.

"Leon, can I talk to you?"

"What is it?"

"I don't know if this is the right time, but I think I need to tell you before things get busy. The other day, Noel Stollen came to see me."

"Huh? What do you mean?"

"He came and asked me to betray the Winged Knights."

Leon was immediately taken aback. Keim and Ophelia were also too surprised to speak.

"I said no, of course," Vaclav told him. "Everything he said was just miserable lies. But when I think about it, he may have gone to see other members. I don't want to believe that someone here would betray us, but I want to make sure right here and now." Vaclav looked at each of the other members one by one. Leon had no idea what he was talking about; he shook his head almost mechanically. But Ophelia timidly raised her hand.

"He came to see me too..."

"What?!"

"O-obviously, I turned him down! I could never betray you!" Ophelia pleaded her case desperately. Leon didn't doubt her, but he was in complete shock.

"Actually, me too." Once Keim admitted to the same thing, Leon felt a chill run down his spine.

"So...Noel tried to cajole everyone except for me?"

"Because you're the leader, Leon. He probably figured he couldn't convince you. I mean, it's silly to think he could target any of us either, but..." Keim shrugged his shoulders, smiling wryly.

Ophelia let out a sigh of relief. "I was actually worried! I thought there might be a traitor among us too. Oh, b-but just a little! Really!"

Leon finally relaxed. "I know. The Winged Knights aren't traitors."

"Honestly, I didn't really understand what Noel was saying. He said that I would get freedom in return, but it just sounded like lies," Vaclav recalled, cocking his head to the side.

"He said the same thing to me! What does that even mean?" Ophelia asked.

Keim nodded. "Same here. Hmph, what a joke." Apparently, Noel had used the same words to deceive everyone.

"How did that conversation go?" Leon was genuinely curious.

But everyone clammed up, their faces betraying a certain discomfort at the question. Even though all three of them said they didn't know what Noel had meant, they all seemed to feel the same fear and anxiety.

"A-anyway, let's forget about Noel. None of us are going to betray you. Maybe he just wanted to make us all suspicious of one another so we would be distracted. He wants us to be thinking about it," Keim said.

At last, Leon understood why Noel wasn't rushing into battle.

"I bet he thought we would argue and turn on one another," Keim suggested.

Noel probably planned to take his time, wait for that opportunity, and then rush in.

"I see...he does have interesting ideas."

In the end, his plan didn't work. While Leon couldn't approve of his behavior, he was somehow glad to know that Noel also planned to fight seriously. Thinking back, the Winged Knights were always alone. There were no parties with which they could have a friendly rivalry, and all they could do was encourage one another. As Keim had pointed out, Blue Beyond's sudden arrival harbored the possibility of a good rivalry.

Now that Noel's plan had been foiled, the Winged Knights would win the competition. Once the test was over, Blue Beyond's fate was disbandment.

Leon thought it unfortunate. "Hey, guys, let me ask you something. After this test is over, why don't we invite Noel's team to join the Winged Knights?"

The other three gaped at him, surprised.

"They have a promising future. I'm sure we could work well together. The conditions said that the losing team cannot reform under a new name, but if we ask Harold after we win, he'll probably agree to it. What do you all think?"

Honestly, he thought they would all be against it. No matter how promising Noel was, his behavior was hardly praiseworthy. But the reaction was better than he expected.

"I think it'd be fine." The first to agree with Noel was Ophelia, whom he had been sure would dispute him. "I asked Lycia, and she said that Noel's friends betrayed him and stole their shared funds. He sold them into slavery to get the money back. I still don't agree with it, but at least there was a reason. Most of all, I think Noel's hunger to reach the top would be a good motivator for us."

Vaclav nodded. "It's fine with me too. Either way, once we become a clan, we'll need more members."

"I agree too," said Keim. "But first we need to complete this test." All the while, his gaze was elsewhere.

"Leon, the vanguard has picked up the pace," Ophelia announced. She generated a magic arrow with one of her skills and nocked it. "They'll be coming all at once."

"I'll move in first. You guys take care of the leftovers." Leon gripped his sword and shield and braced for the fight.

Before long, countless small lights appeared from deep within the forest. They were the shining eyes of the Dantalion's underlings. The white-haired magic monkeys attacked in a group so dense, it was like a wall coming down on the Winged Knights.

The Dantalion was a mind-reader and shared this ability with its underlings. If the Seekers tried to dodge or counterattack, the monkeys would know and respond instantly. Therefore, even the underlings were assessed as having an abyssal depth of 6. Even with a party composed of B-Rank Seekers, defeating such beasts would be no mean feat.

Also, there were two hundred of them.

"Keeeyaaah!" The monkeys' howls were torture on the ears. Thirty of them were in the first wave. The sharp claws and fangs flew at Leon and the others, trying to tear them apart. However, these magic monkeys smacked right into a wall they couldn't see.

Knight skill: *Holy Shield*. This was a defensive skill that erected an invisible wall. Knight was a vanguard role that specialized in defensive skills to protect the team and healing skills to keep everyone up and moving.

However superb one's skills, they mattered not, since these beasts could read and react before they could be activated. The monkeys had only been caught off guard by the barrier because Leon was using his skills in the very same moment he thought of them. There was no room for the enemy to react.

For most Seekers, the thought and action could not occur in tandem. Leon's natural powers were more fluid than those of normal Seekers, so he was able to attain high-speed activation of his skills. This was a skill of its own, unique to Leon Fredric: *Angel Wings*.

Leon decapitated the monkeys that were held back by the barrier in one blow. As the monkeys waiting behind them were struck dumb, Keim's spear, Ophelia's arrows, and Vaclav's heat rays shot through, reaching the enemies in a heartbeat.

Two hundred of these beasts, with an abyssal depth of 6, were annihilated in under a minute. Each movement was simple and thoroughly elegant. The strongest in their league, the Winged Knights fought without wasting a second.

"Let's move," Leon said. "The moment we reach the Dantalion, clear out the riffraff with a ranged attack. Kill the Dantalion immediately."

"Got it," his party replied. After exterminating the enemy vanguard, the Winged Knights proceeded deeper into the forest.

"Are you sure this is okay...?" Koga muttered uneasily, just before he bit into a sandwich.

It had been about thirty minutes since the Winged Knights had crossed over into the Abyss. If we listened carefully, we could hear the sounds of battle. However, we remained where we were, eating the entire time. Alma, who always burned a lot of calories in battle, was so focused on eating that she barely spoke.

"If the Winged Knights take down the Dantalion while we're out here, it's over, y'know? I'm so nervous..." Koga shuddered.

"Don't be so pathetic," I told him. "You don't have to worry; they're an equal match for the Dantalion. There's definitely a possibility they'll beat it."

"Huh?! Wh-what do you mean?! If the Winged Knights can beat it, then what are we sittin' around here for?!"

I took a sip of tea and shook my head. "No, they'll win. But—"

"Then we'll lose?! Our party will be disbanded!"

"Listen to me, you idiot. The Winged Knights are capable of taking down the Dantalion, but there are conditions. Conditions the team can't meet."

"Conditions?" Koga cocked his head to the side.

"They'll have to make a last-ditch effort. Leon is an extremely capable commander. He isn't just a great fighter; he's also skilled at party tactics. There are very few people in the entire capital who can successfully command from the rear, let alone the vanguard. However, there are times when excellence is a burden. In other words, he will only have his eye on a sure victory."

"What's wrong with a sure victory?"

"The Winged Knights will show you soon enough. Believe me, Koga. We *will* win. No doubt about it."

Koga reluctantly accepted it and settled down in his spot on our blanket. "Well, I'm Noel's sword. If ya say 'Believe me,' I gotta believe ya. Yeah, 'cause I'm not that bright. I dunno anything."

"Stop sulking. It's sickening. I've already planted the seeds; our victory is guaranteed."

"Did you do something bad?" Koga asked in a low voice, leaning toward me with his eyes on Harold. Harold, whose eyes were shut, must've been using his long-distance sight skill to watch the goings-on inside the Abyss.

"I haven't done anything bad."

"That's bull. What seeds are ya talkin' about?"

"All I did was tell everyone except Leon what was sure to happen," I said.

"What's that mean?"

I looked in the direction that I assumed the Winged Knights were currently fighting in and twisted my lips in a grin.

"The Winged Knights will collapse. Leon will betray them."

†

Simply put, beasts were strong. Although their complex abilities seemingly put Seekers at a disadvantage, it was easy to destroy them with the right strategy. The Dantalion, which could read minds, was truly well-rounded. It was strong, fast, and intelligent, and it wouldn't be harmed by ordinary weapons.

Another beast of comparable strength—that is, with an abyssal depth of 8—was the Black Dragon. They were both highly dangerous, and in some circumstances, the large Black Dragon was more dangerous. When it came to challenge, however, the Dantalion was leagues beyond the Black Dragon.

"Keim, take care of Vaclav—he's injured! Ophelia, help Keim!"

The Winged Knights were clearly struggling. The Dantalion was stronger than Leon and his team had anticipated.

"Toys... Toys... Lots... Lots of toys to play with..."

They had been battling the Dantalion for an hour. The forest had been visibly scarred by all the attacks and retreats; trees had snapped and collapsed, and great gouges had been dug in the earth.

Although Leon and the others had started to tire from the struggle, the Dantalion's stamina was limitless, and it had breath enough to ridicule the party's fighting skills in their own human tongue.

At the beginning, the Winged Knights succeeded in clearing out the peripheral beasts with a wide-range attack. However, after cornering the Dantalion, they hadn't dealt so much as a scratch to its hide. Even though the party was stronger overall, they weren't able to cooperate with the beast reading their minds.

Leon used his healing and barrier skills continuously, immediately repairing the shield when the Dantalion damaged it. As soon as Vaclav's injury was healed, he summoned a fire giant. The giant's blazing arm swung at the Dantalion. The beast easily dodged the blow, but it shifted into range of Keim's spear and Ophelia's arrows. The sharp projectiles fell like rain upon the Dantalion—or rather, where it had stood a moment before.

"It's useless."

The Dantalion had suddenly disappeared. They looked up. Despite its massive body, it had flown up like a shuttlecock, taking refuge in the air for a moment. Surprise attacks didn't work on the Dantalion because it could read minds.

However, the party had known that from the beginning.

"Eee-gee!"

For the first time, the Dantalion opened its mouth in surprise. After dodging the attack, it found Leon atop its head.

Though the beast could read his mind, Leon could move at the very speed of thought, thanks to his *Angel Wings*. A true Seeker endeavored to improve during battle. Amid the back and forth,

Leon was finally able to suss out how the Dantalion was moving at a seemingly ungodly speed.

A holy light flashed across Leon's sword as he swung it down.

Knight skill: *Divine Impact*. This skill converted magic power into a superheated ball and launched it. It also had the added holy attribute, which was a weak point for almost all beasts. When Leon hit the beast, the blow cut all of its abilities by 20 percent for about five seconds.

It was only five seconds, and the beast would soon develop a tolerance to the skill, so it couldn't be used continuously. But Leon was sure that the Winged Knights could defeat the beast in that narrow window.

A small ball of light as bright as the sun flew from Leon's sword. The Dantalion twisted in the air, dodging it. Leon was about to shoot another, but he sensed something was off and called out to his friends on the ground.

"Everyone, move!"

The Dantalion they'd thought was at a loss flashed an evil smile in midair. It was holding countless rocks in its hands. Leon generated a barrier just as the beast loosed the rocks.

Like stars hurtling through the sky, the missiles obliterated anything they hit. The thunderous sound was deafening, and a cloud of dust coiled up. Leon leapt to the ground and swung his sword through the air, summoning a gust of wind that blew away the dust. Once he could see again, he frantically searched for his teammates. Keim was unharmed. Vaclav was scratched up, but he could stand on his own. But Ophelia—

"Dammit! Everyone, retreat! I'll fight!"

Ophelia was on the ground, her right arm completely gone. Leon had been able to mitigate the force of the attack with his barrier, but some of the rocks had still punched through, and one had taken Ophelia's arm. Keim put Ophelia on his back and started to retreat with Vaclav. The flaming giant that Vaclav had summoned was destroyed with a single swing of the beast's arm.

Leon charged the Dantalion to cover the retreat.

Knight skill: *Holy Shield*.

Knight skill: *Iron Will*.

Iron Will doubled his strength. The shield held back the Dantalion's violent assault, but just barely. Blood started pour from Leon's eyes and nose due to the impact.

"Toys, strong... But only you...really strong," the Dantalion said, putting pressure on Leon's shield from above with its sturdy arm, an eerie smile on its face.

"I can see fear, fun... You guys...not my enemy. Toys... Toys... Hee hee..."

Through his debilitating pain, Leon scoffed. "Such cheap provocation. They may call you a beast, but in the end, you're just a chimp."

"Hee hee... No act strong, useless... I can see your mind... You can't win... You know it..."

"You're right; we can't win right now. But Seekers don't give up. We may lose once, but we will win. You're the one who's going to lose here!"

Just then, Leon's shield emitted a burst of bright light.

Knight skill: *Invincible.*

This defensive skill perfectly reflected any attack once. Hit by its own power, the Dantalion was flung far back into the woods. Before it could recover, Leon rushed away. It would be twenty-four hours before he could use *Invincible* again. Ophelia was seriously hurt, and he had already played his *Invincible* trump card. They had lost the initiative.

But he planned to win yet. They still had a chance.

However, in order to defeat the Dantalion, he would have to sacrifice one of his teammates...

"Hey! Where you? Hey! Hey! Hey..."

No longer able to detect the Winged Knights, the Dantalion kept calling out, searching for them, but to no avail. Vaclav had set up a perimeter to obscure their presence from the beast. As long as the party remained inside that perimeter, the beast wouldn't be able to smell them, hear them, or even read their minds.

However, this perimeter was extremely fragile, so they couldn't use it for cover during a surprise attack, nor could they prepare any attack skills, without the ripples of magic destroying it. It also consumed an immense amount of power, so Vaclav couldn't maintain it for long. There was the risk that the furious Dantalion would initiate a sweeping wide-range attack, as it had moments before.

"I did what I could. Can you move your arm?" Leon asked.

Ophelia tried moving her reattached right arm and nodded. "Yeah. It's a little numb, but it's fine. Thank you, Leon."

Vaclav had retrieved Ophelia's arm, so Leon was able to reattach it immediately. Even so, Ophelia lost a lot of blood, she was extremely pale, and her breathing was unstable. Her voice filled with regret, she uttered, "I'm so sorry, Leon..."

Leon smiled and shook his head. "Don't worry about it. We haven't lost yet." Despite his words, the situation was abysmal. The time had come for him to make an executive decision. Having made up his mind, he began, "Hey, everyone—"

Keim raised a hand to stop him. "I have a plan. Will you hear me out?"

"What plan?"

"We can't win at this rate. But if we don't, we have no future. I want to put everything on the line," Keim explained.

"Everything? You don't mean..." Leon couldn't hide his surprise. However, he could tell that Keim had fully come to terms with the idea.

"I'll be the decoy and draw him out. When I do, use *Seraphim's Blade*. That's our only shot at winning."

Knight skill: *Seraphim's Blade* was Leon's strongest attack. It consumed all of his magic power to combine divine attributes with flame attributes and emit a massively powerful heat ray. Surely, that would kill the Dantalion. The attack had another major drawback, however: its area of effect was so wide that there was a risk of striking his teammates as well. If Keim was acting as a decoy, he couldn't use the skill.

"We can't! I'm completely against it. It's too dangerous!" Leon protested, but Keim quietly shook his head.

"This perimeter is keeping the beast from finding us, but if we use a strong attack skill, the perimeter will fall. We can't launch a surprise attack from here. If we're going to succeed at a surprise attack, we need a decoy."

"B-but still...!"

"Leon, I'm not suicidal. There's plenty I want to do, and I don't plan on dying here. It'll be fine. I'll time it so I can escape the blast. Trust me," he said firmly.

Leon believed that Keim wasn't planning on dying, but the plan was nevertheless a deadly one. Keim was essentially prepared to risk death so that Leon and the others could win. It looked like Ophelia and Vaclav sensed the same thing, but they understood Keim's resolution. They kept quiet, grim expressions on their faces.

"It's true; if we want to win from this situation, we have to sacrifice someone. I understand that too. But I still can't allow it," Leon said.

"Then what? There's no other way. If we retreat, we lose. The Winged Knights will be disbanded, and we'll be forced apart."

"No, there is one more possibility. We can join forces with Blue Beyond. If we work together with them, we can fight without sacrificing anyone."

"Wha—?!" Keim was dumbfounded.

"W-wait a second, Leon! If we do that, what happens to the test?" Ophelia cut in, flabbergasted.

Leon let out a sigh and spoke honestly. "Let's just forget the test. There's no way Blue Beyond can beat the Dantalion on their own. *No one* can win this test. Let's work together with Blue Beyond to defeat the Dantalion so that we don't lose our reputation. We probably won't be approved as a clan, but there won't be any winners or losers, so if we talk to Harold, we can probably avoid being disbanded."

This was the most just way to proceed without any sacrifices. Leon thought his party members would understand. Instead, the three of them looked bewildered—even downright terrified.

"No way... It's just like he said..." Ophelia muttered in disbelief.

"Oh, that's what he meant," Vaclav said.

Leon tilted his head to the side, puzzled.

Keim grabbed his shoulder. "Leon, are you serious? You really want to give up on the test and fight alongside Blue Beyond? They're our enemy! We have to beat them!"

"I know. I know that, but—"

"No, you don't! You don't know anything! Trust me, Leon! I'll do it! You can win! It's a sure thing!"

"Keim, calm down. What's wrong? You guys are acting strange."

"I am calm! I'm thinking of the Winged Knights, but you're saying you trust Noel Stollen over me?"

Leon unintentionally averted his eyes in the face of Keim's ghastly accusation. But as a leader, he couldn't go back on this decision. He had to harden his heart.

"Yes. I do trust Noel more than you. Right now, you're not thinking clearly. How can I trust you in such a state?" Leon didn't hate Keim. It wasn't that he didn't trust Keim. He just didn't want to sacrifice anyone.

Keim removed his hand from Leon's shoulder and backed away. He was crying, his face screwed up in frustration. Leon had never seen his friend make such an expression.

"I see... So that's your answer."

"Keim, let's talk after the battle is over. At any rate, right now—"

Suddenly, Keim embraced Leon and whispered in his ear: "That bastard was right. You were the traitor."

"Huh?" Leon felt a sharp pain in his abdomen. He dropped to his knees and brought a hand to his flank. When he pulled it away, it was covered in bright red blood. "K-Keim, what...?"

When he looked up, he saw Keim wielding a bloody knife.

"Don't worry, you won't die. But the knife was covered in a strong paralytic. You won't be able to move for a while."

"Keim, what are you doing?!" Ophelia tried to dash over, but Leon held her back.

"Vaclav, get the elixir from my pouch! Hurry!"

"O-okay! Just a sec!"

Ophelia and Vaclav started to treat Leon for his injuries, panicked by the sudden reversal of fortune. His consciousness hazy, Leon looked at Keim and moved his mouth, trying to ask what happened.

"I've always been jealous of you, Leon. I hated that you were more talented than me. But you're my friend—you're like my little brother. I thought you trusted me, so I always stuck by your side. I wasn't even afraid to die for you..." Keim fell to his knees. "But I can't anymore... It's over. I...want to be free," Keim admitted, sobbing.

Leon's eyes filled with tears. He had no idea. He didn't know how much pain Keim had been in. He thought he knew everything.

"Found you! Found you! Toys, found you!"

Just then, they heard the gleeful voice of the Dantalion echoing around them. Leon tried to gather his strength, but something was wrong. The Dantalion hadn't found *them*.

Instead, a young boy in a black coat appeared at the end of the beast's line of sight. It was Noel Stollen, leader of Blue Beyond. He shouldn't have been able to see them through Vaclav's perimeter, but Noel looked toward Leon and the others, bowing politely.

"Winged Knights, good work getting this far."

✝

All of the Winged Knights were excellent fighters. But there was only one true talent among them, and that was Leon. He wasn't just noticeably superior; he was on a completely different level.

Leon was a great Knight. He could also play the role of commander while also setting up barriers. As a bonus, he had even acquired a non-standard skill: *Angel Wings*.

The "Winged" part of the name "the Winged Knights," bestowed upon the group by a certain reporter, came from the decorative wings on Leon's shield, which represented his unique skill. It was often said that his Knight's sword moved like it had soaring wings.

To put it plainly, Leon *was* the Winged Knights. Any of the other three members could be replaced, and the party could still be called the Winged Knights, so long as Leon was among them. Conversely, even if the other three members remained, the party wouldn't be the Winged Knights without Leon.

No matter how hard they worked, the others would never be more than accessories to Leon. Personally, *I* wouldn't have been able to live with that. No one with even a lick of pride would. Keim understood the imbalance and had tried to correct it with his own devotion. It was true that the bond within the Winged Knights was strong. But their bond was barely kept intact because the other three members ignored the lump of jealousy toward Leon that they kept inside.

Had they confronted it themselves, they never would have been able to put up with it. That was precisely why they were the perfect teammates for Leon, and so desperate to keep going. In the midst of that desperation, they had no need to be aware of the depths of their own minds. They were no better than migratory fish, which would die out if they ever stopped swimming. They were lying to themselves.

In one way or another, the party would have collapsed eventually. Those lumps of jealousy would have swollen over the years, eventually bursting forth from their chests. I had approached each of the members except for Leon and told them to betray him, but that wasn't what I really meant. Even if the three of them were able to keep up the pretense, there would come a time when Leon wouldn't be able to trust the abilities of the other three.

Ultimately, he would no longer deign to treat them as equals and, in the end, he would forsake them. My small suggestion had grown into their accusations of betrayal. Alongside it sprouted the idea that escape was freedom.

From the beginning, I'd known that the battle with the mighty Dantalion would be such a struggle that the Winged Knights would be forced to sacrifice one of its members, but Leon would never agree to such a strategy. I hoped that, when that happened, one of the other three would realize their own powerlessness and awaken to their jealousy, then denounce Leon as a traitor and attempt to eliminate him.

Had they been thinking rationally, the situation could have easily been avoided. However, bonded parties sometimes lose their cool. It doesn't take much to manipulate someone's emotions. Like the saying goes, a small leak can sink a great ship, and just a small crack in the wall of someone's heart was more than enough. You just had to wait for the wall to crumble. Under intense stress, the three Winged Knights would no longer be able to repress their feelings, and they would be overwhelmed by hateful emotions. The only path left for a member driven by overactive emotions and trying to escape the pain of it all was to eliminate the leader—the traitor, Leon—thereby freeing themselves from the prison of their party structure.

My bet had been on Keim, with Ophelia as a backup and Vaclav as a last resort. Not that I cared who broke first.

Once the sounds of battle subsided, I'd come to see what was happening, and it seemed to have gone exactly as I planned.

The Dantalion was alive and well, and the Winged Knights were nowhere to be seen. They were probably using a perimeter to hide themselves somewhere. They were no longer in a state to continue the battle.

I looked around, found a place where the grass was lying unnaturally flat, and politely bowed in that direction.

"Winged Knights, good work getting this far."

Actually, since the Winged Knights had taken care of all the underlings in one fell swoop, there were no obstacles between me and the Dantalion. Naturally, I had planned for that too. This test was a battle competition, but I never had any intention of fighting the Winged Knights head-on. I knew well that if we fought them, we would lose.

The battle rules I'd arranged through Harold were to draw the decidedly un-homicidal Winged Knights into battle against me, making them overly sensitive to the fact that they were aiming to defeat *people*. Leon and the others understood that their clan application had been rejected for their practice of being too careful, which meant they would have to be even hastier. In the end, the Winged Knights had rushed in first and thankfully taken care of all the minions for us.

There were no more onerous underlings, and their party had already been rendered unable to continue the battle. Now our team could savor the main dish without anyone getting in the way.

"Toys! Toys! New toys!" the Dantalion said, clapping its hands over its head when it found me. It really did just look like a monkey, but I couldn't let my guard down. I knew very well how crafty and troublesome this beast was from past battle records. Had he been less dangerous, the Winged Knights never would have lost.

But this wasn't my battle. I laughed, genuinely comfortable with the situation.

"Nice to meet you, Dantalion. My name is Noel Stollen."

"Noel! Noel! My toy!"

"Unfortunately, I'm not going to be your toy. Instead, I'm going to kill you. In order to do that, I'm going to utilize everything from your pelt to your meat and bones, from your guts to every drop of your blood. Sorry, not sorry."

"Bwa ha ha ha! Useless! Die, Noel! Die!"

"Is that what you think? Then I'll have to show you. Okay, then. Fight to the death, monkey man."

Sensing my bloodlust, the Dantalion charged at me. But by then, I had already given orders.

"Koga, do it."

Tactics skill: *Battle Voice*.

Tactics skill: *Tactician*.

Since I had moved up to Strategist, some of my Talker skills had been upgraded to Tactics skills. With the upgrade, *Battle Voice* and *Tactician* had also both increased from 25 percent to 40 percent support value.

Empowered by my voice, Koga attacked the Dantalion from a tree above its head. Completely unable to detect him, the Dantalion was caught unawares and sprang away from the attack. Koga's sword missed and only grazed the beast's nose.

"Eee? You... Why? Why that?" The reason the Dantalion was so confused was because it couldn't read our minds.

The only person who could use the *Angel Wings* skill perfectly was Leon, who was endowed with that unique gift. However, through training with my *Link* skill, our party could achieve a close facsimile through sensing one another's intentions. Instead of thinking faster than we acted, we could act without thinking. We called this *Angel Wings: Zero*.

"Koga, *Clear and Serene*."

"Ready!"

When I gave the next order, Koga closed his eyes.

Longswordsman skill: *Clear and Serene*. This skill could only be activated when his eyes were closed; it doubled the acuity of all senses besides sight. It also tripled the user's attack speed and power.

The rock-solid arm of the Dantalion swung down on us. However, Koga's sword intercepted the intense blow. The Dantalion's attack was deflected, and its great iron arm swung wide of its mark. Though Koga was a teammate, his divine skill frightened me. It was even more terrifying because he was still only C-Rank.

"Gee gee gee?! Geh-geee!"

Panicked, the Dantalion flailed about, but Koga artfully dodged, prioritizing counterattacks. Counters didn't require thought, just response, and involved no sensory information beyond the visual. Between this and *Angel Wings: Zero*, the Dantalion wouldn't be able to overtake Koga, even with its mind-reading skill. But the beast was far more powerful than Koga, and it could withstand the counterattacks. Koga was hunting, in a state that nearly transcended thought, for a mighty killing blow. The Dantalion sensed this and swung its fist hard. In that instant, I dove onto its chest, whipped out my silver flame, and fired a Garmr bullet.

Refined from the bone marrow of a beast with an abyssal depth of 9, the Garmr bullet was lined with a magic-conductive essence of near-perfect purity and a non-attribute explosive magic skill. When the bullet hit the target, the essence would absorb the target's magic power and explode.

The Garmr bullet hit its target. The Dantalion's torso quivered, then tore itself to pieces. Just as the explosion was about to reach me, Koga grabbed me and ran just out of range.

"Eee... Gaaah!" The Dantalion was in agony, spewing bloody foam. There was no hole in the actual abdomen, but its meat was exposed and blood was pouring out.

"Ha ha, that's what you get for 10 million fil per bullet." I'd prepared two bullets for this battle. I laughed at the projectile's overwhelming power. It was even greater than I had expected.

I kept my eye on the Dantalion as it writhed in pain, debating whether I should fire a second time. It was the perfect opportunity, but the beast could still counterattack. I had only one Garmr bullet left, and with no augmented firearm skills, I couldn't be reckless with my shot.

"Koga, can you get through?" I asked.

"Nah. It's too hard. My sword ain't gonna cut it."

Through our training, Koga had full knowledge of all my skills. Even with the support effects of my strongest skill, *Assault Command*, he wouldn't be able to deal damage.

"Okay. Let's follow the original plan."

As I made that call, the Dantalion stumbled to its feet. A wounded animal was frightfully violent, and a wounded beast was far worse. The three eyes of the raging Dantalion smoldered with a horrifying hatred for me.

"You, why... Not like that, boy... Can't read, thoughts, heart... Why? Eee... Eee... Gaaah!"

"I want to say it's a trade secret, but I'm having such a great day, I'll be generous and give you a hint. We're compatible, you and me. I'd say we're great together."

It was me who had chosen the Dantalion after all. I was the one who'd told Harold to use this beast for the test. Really, I could have chosen a ghost-type beast so I could use *Exorcism*, but there were no Abysses forming with apparitions at the core. Regardless, the Dantalion was an easy beast for me to fight, as I was able to completely nullify its ability to read minds.

My Talker class allowed me to think at incredible speeds. Even if the Dantalion could read my mind, I was able to think faster than it could interpret my thoughts. Not only were my tactics incomprehensible to it, but the beast couldn't even sense that I'd been aiming to jump upon its chest.

"Turns out you're *my* toy," I said, provoking the beast.

"Kill you kill you kill youuu!" Hackles raised, the Dantalion picked up a stone from the ground and wound up.

"Koga, *Crazy Cherry Blossoms.*"

Longswordsman skill: *Crazy Cherry Blossoms.* This skill transformed one swing of the blade into thousands of slash attacks. The stone the Dantalion threw collided with Koga's endless slashes in midair, and Koga's sword smashed it to smithereens. Using the resulting cloud of dust as cover, the Dantalion rushed us.

"Way ahead of you," I said, already aiming my silver flame. But if I fired now, the beast would probably just dodge it. I changed my high-speed thinking to high-speed parallel thoughts.

"Eegaah?!"

The Dantalion clutched its head in pain. For him, it was like a crowd of people was screaming into his ears all at once. He probably could have handled it had he been prepared, but he wasn't.

"We really are compatible," I said, pulling the trigger on my silver flame.

The Dantalion jerked and dodged, but the second Garmr bullet penetrated its right arm and blew it off at the shoulder.

"Gaaah! Arrrrm!" A fountain of blood was spewing forth from the steaming stump. "You... You pay... You paaay!" As the Dantalion cursed me, it stuck a finger into its third eye and gouged it out. "N-now...head no hurt... Hee hee hee..."

"Oh, I see."

The bloody Dantalion wheeled around and stormed toward us. "Diiie!" It had cast away its ability to read minds, so my psychological attacks were useless. But now I could bring my other skills to the fore.

Talker skill: *Link*. This was a telepathic communication skill that allowed allies to share thoughts. When I'd been using high-speed thoughts, I risked giving the rest of my team brain damage, but now there was no possibility of our minds—or strategy—being read. I could give directives to my heart's content.

"Prepared. Order: Alma, shoot it to death."

I gave Alma, who had been waiting at the entrance of the Abyss, an order.

"Accel—Duodecuple!"

I couldn't hear Alma's voice, but that was what she must've said, because a flying object traveling faster than the speed of sound zoomed over my head. The ball of force was barreling straight toward the Dantalion.

Alma's promotion from Scout to Assassin had not only increased her physical ability correction; it had also strengthened her skills. She could push her *Accel* skill to the limit and launch surprise attacks from outside an opponent's range of perception.

In other words, she was a human cannonball.

Assassin skill: *Accel*.

Assassin skill: *Quick Attack*.

As an Assassin, Alma could now boost *Accel* by twelve times and add the *Quick Attack* skill to multiply that damage by her speed. My buffs provided a further multiplier.

Tactics skill: *Tactician*.

Tactics skill: *Assault Command*. A Strategist skill, *Assault Command* could increase the value of attack skills by ten to fifteen times. Alma could now kill a beast with an abyssal depth of 8 with a single strike.

The Dantalion had already noticed Alma and turned to bat at her with its remaining arm, but it was a futile gesture.

Assassin skill: *Phantom.* This was a new skill that Alma had acquired from a skill guide when she moved up to Assassin. She could only use this skill once every twenty-four hours, and the effect lasted for a mere three seconds. It turned the practitioner intangible, like a spirit.

Alma activated *Phantom* at the optimal moment as determined by my high-speed calculations. Alma kept slipping out of the Dantalion's iron-handed grip, so it was as if he were trying to squeeze smoke.

That was the moment our victory was sealed.

After escaping the beast's attack, *Phantom* expired, and Alma stabbed the beast in the throat with her knife. She dug deep into its neck and spine and sent the beast's head flying.

The Dantalion's head fell to the ground, and its massive body collapsed right after.

"*Battle, complete.*"

When I gave the final directive, Koga and Alma sank down to the ground. Alma, who was experiencing the after-effects of *Assault Command*, was especially exhausted. Just when I was starting to feel sympathy for what I'd put them through, Koga suddenly yawped.

"Woohoo! Rank up!" Koga sprang to his feet and held out the back of his right hand, which bore an emblem of a sword.

Defeating the Dantalion had earned him enough experience to rank up.

"Oh, nice. Congratulations."

"Yeaaah!" Koga jumped around, his exhaustion forgotten. It must have been rough on him, being the last C-Rank in Blue Beyond. He was acting like a giddy little kid. Exasperated as I was, I mustered a smile.

"Noel, you..." came Keim's voice.

The Winged Knights had dispelled their perimeter, and I could see that Leon was injured, just as I'd anticipated.

"From the very beginning, you..."

Upon seeing the Dantalion's corpse at my feet, he'd realized that I had been working with Harold to set all this up. "You...!"

The agitated Keim started to rush me, but Harold—who'd been watching it all from outside the forest—dropped from the sky and landed between us.

"Good work to both of you. I observed the entire battle from start to finish. I would like to announce the results." Harold looked around at each and every one of us and all but bellowed, "The winner is Blue Beyond! This party's clan application is approved! The losing team, the Winged Knights, will immediately disband as pledged!"

Keim looked bitter about the results but couldn't say anything. He just stood there, his head hanging low. It was true that I'd conspired with Harold. I had him set up the test to my advantage. But the Winged Knights had their own chance to win. It was their own fault that they couldn't pull the trigger. The Winged

Knights had already lost their heart. They probably didn't even have the will to seek revenge against me.

"Noel," Alma said. I hadn't even noticed her come to my side. "This has given us the results we needed. Now all we need is strength."

"I know. It's all part of my plan," I answered, *sotto voce*.

Alma frowned. "Do you...really plan on making him part of our clan?"

I brushed her off. "We've been over this."

"I'm not complaining. If he's on our team, we'll be stronger. But would he even join us? After what you did to him?"

"Of course he would. We targeted the Winged Knights because they were the strongest party of the bunch. They had Leon Fredric, the Angel Wings." I laughed as I glanced over at Leon, who was struggling to breathe.

"He'll join us. There is no doubt."

When Lycia picked up the morning paper delivered to her lodging, the front-page headline caught her eye. It was so shocking, she couldn't help but put her hand to her mouth.

"No way... The Winged Knights disbanded? What?"

The Winged Knights were the strongest party in the capital and the one to which Lycia's childhood friend, Ophelia, belonged. They were both busy, and Ophelia was ranked higher than Lycia, so it wasn't as though they got to spend a lot of time together, but they still always made sure to meet for lunch once a month or so.

Numb from the news, Lycia scanned the page, then returned to the headline. There was another shock in store for her.

"What?! The Winged Knights were forced to disband after losing to *Blue Beyond*?!"

The headline and subhead read: Fallen Wings! Winged Knights disband after upset by Blue Beyond in Association-sanctioned Contest!

Having no idea what that meant, Lycia read through the article and finally got an idea of the facts.

There'd been a sudden change in Seekers Association policy. Until then, clan applications had been approved unconditionally for parties who could pay the 20-million-fil compulsory insurance and secure a base. However, going forward, no applications would be approved without passing a rigorous examination. For that reason, the applications of both Blue Beyond and the Winged Knights had been declined. Both parties had strongly objected and were thus offered a combined test—with only the winning party's clan application to be approved. Furthermore, any losing party would be compelled to disband.

The test was a race to defeat a beast designated by the Seekers Association, a Dantalion with an abyssal depth of 8. Blue Beyond proved victorious. Then, according to the pledge, the Winged Knights disbanded immediately as instructed by the Seekers Association.

The article included quotes from each of the members, some

speculation, and the like. There was far too much harsh criticism of the losers, the Winged Knights, prompting Lycia to throw the newspaper to the ground. After praising the Winged Knights so much when they were active, the media had brazenly turned on them. Lycia felt a renewed hatred for newspapers.

"Still, Noel beat the Winged Knights... I can't believe it. There's no way he could be advancing so quickly."

Blue Beyond was excellent. Everyone in the party except Noel was new, and they hadn't racked up any big achievements as a group, but both of the other members were so strong that it was unbelievable they were still lingering at C-Rank. The common analysis was that the current Blue Beyond was just as strong as the previous Blue Beyond. Even so, they were all rookies. She didn't believe that they could win out against the mature Winged Knights. On top of that, they'd been pitted against not just the Winged Knights, but a formidable Dantalion as well. No matter how much she tried to imagine it, Lycia couldn't picture a scenario where Noel won.

"Well, I guess it *is* Noel they're talking about."

Noel Stollen, leader of Blue Beyond, was an extremely special Seeker even in Etrai, the heartland of Seekers. Although he was a Talker, widely understood to be the weakest of all Seeker classes, he had a gifted mind and exceptional command, which had earned him the nickname "Rookie Giant-Killer." He was highly regarded as strong by those in the know.

In the past, he had resolved an issue that Lycia was dealing with in an instant with that brain of his. That was when Lycia had decided to always keep an eye on Noel. Allegedly, he had even stymied the strongest mafia gang in the imperial capital, the Luciano family. It had happened right when Lycia was out on a gig, so she hadn't seen it with her own eyes, but Alma was horrible at keeping secrets and had told her everything.

"He must have found a weak point and used it to win. Ophelia and her team are strong, but they seem like they'd really fold if he found their weakness... It must have been a bad match."

She didn't know what method Noel had used, but it must have been frustrating for Ophelia and the others to fall into Noel's trap. She couldn't help but sympathize. However, for Seekers to complain about below-the-belt punches was nothing but an excuse. Victory or defeat were the only two options in Seeker life. If you lost, no matter how frustrating, you had to admit to the loss. You could even say that the Winged Knights were lucky to be alive.

"Unfortunately, that is the life of a Seeker," Lycia said to herself, letting out a deep sigh. Just then, she heard a knock on the door. When she opened it, she saw a familiar face.

"Ophelia?"

"Yeah..."

With such a short and negative response, Lycia could guess why she was there.

"Hey, are you going to quit being a Seeker?"

"Yeah."

She'd expected that. She had probably come to say goodbye to Lycia. Lycia debated whether she should try to stop her. Ophelia was a very capable Seeker. Even if the Winged Knights disbanded, some other group would take her in. But if Ophelia was this emotional, maybe it was better to let her go.

While Lycia was trying to decide what to do, Ophelia muttered in a nasal voice, "We worked so hard for so long, and I thought we were strong... But I wasn't strong at all. I'm so tired... I don't think I'm cut out to be a Seeker..."

And with that, Ophelia's presence in the hallway completely disappeared. Lycia panicked, opening the door to find that Ophelia was gone. All that remained was her perfume hanging in the air.

Lycia knew that she probably went back to their childhood village and that going home was the best way to heal the soul. Nevertheless, it saddened her.

"The Seeker life sure is rough."

Vaclav was part wolf. Hybrid beasts combined characteristics of both human and animal. In the case of wolf-men, they looked human but seemed to wear a fur coat made from wolf hide. Alternatively, you could say they looked like bipedal wolves. Even among hybrid beasts, some had more prominent animalistic features than others. Therefore, they often suffered unwarranted discrimination and defamation and were scorned by other species, even in the highly diverse capital.

Vaclav's tribe lived in the desert, where humans rarely ventured.

Perhaps because of their unfavored position in society, the race was clearly unsociable, pessimistic, and fatalistic about the future. Vaclav had hated his tribe from the time he was a child, but part of him wanted to give his people a future. One way to do that was for a wolf-man to achieve a significant position in society, in spite of the discrimination. To him, that meant becoming a Seeker and honing his body. That was why Vaclav had come to the capital.

At first, he had been anxious. He didn't even know if there'd be any Seekers willing to work with him in the first place. But once he met Leon, his anxiety had disappeared. The Winged Knights was a wonderful party. It wasn't just strong; it adhered to a code of ethics, which made it the perfect vehicle for Vaclav's goal of improving the lot of the wolf-men. He knew, however, that the relationship would be a long one. The more missions they took on, the more the Winged Knights were seen as Leon's personal property. Vaclav was nothing but an accessory for Leon. He would never be able to achieve his goal with a career as a third wheel in a long-standing party.

Thus, he was hardly shocked when the Winged Knights lost to Blue Beyond. Either way, he had planned to quit sooner rather than later.

"Welcome, Vaclav! We've been waiting for you!"

When he went to The Orc's Club, Veronica Redbone, leader of Red Lotus, greeted him with a huge smile. It was still early morning and before opening, so no one was there except Vaclav, Veronica, and the owner.

It had been more than a month since Veronica had tried to recruit Vaclav. Veronica had sensed that he wanted to continue work as a Seeker but wasn't satisfied with his current situation. She had invited him to her party and offered attractive benefits. He'd promised that if he decided to take her up on the offer, he would notify her by owl post.

The night the Winged Knights disbanded, Vaclav had sent his owl flying. She'd responded quickly and invited him to The Orc's Club the next day.

"I take it you've accepted my proposition," she said. Her tone was stern and impatient, but he did appreciate that she didn't beat around the bush.

"Yeah. I'd like to join." Vaclav put his two fists together in front of his chest in a classic wolf-man bow.

Veronica immediately let out a cheer. "Woohoo! Now all I have to do is get the dumb wolf and the stupid monkey to agree! Then we'll be a massive party—no, a massive clan! You watch, Noel! You'll never boss me around again!"

It seemed this woman hated Noel too. Now that he was in her party, Vaclav planned to obey Veronica, but he did not want to fight Noel again. He'd learned that lesson firsthand. That incarnation of evil had no rival among humans.

"Keim, why don't you go home?" the bartender said to Keim as he drank.

"Just let me drink a little longer..."

"How many drinks has it been since you started saying that?

I know you're down, but don't drown yourself in booze. You're still young; there are plenty of other paths you can take."

"No, there aren't... It's all over for me..."

It had been two days since the Winged Knights broke up. After the test, they went their separate ways without any significant conversation. Keim hadn't stopped drinking since. When he tried to sober up, he couldn't stop shaking.

"I can still feel the knife in my hand, when I stabbed Leon... I've done something horrible. Somewhere inside of me, I wanted to be free... But that was completely unnecessary. I didn't even try to talk to him...I just prepared that knife with the paralyzing agent..."

The more he thought about it, the more he felt he was in the wrong. In his cowardice, he'd repressed his emotions rather than face them, and he'd come to the twisted conclusion that he had to commit that atrocity in order to be free. Even if Noel had come and made that suggestion to him, the fact that Keim had lost himself was his own fault.

"I really said terrible things... He was just worried for me. I should've never even brought up the term 'traitor.' I was the true traitor... I'm the worst piece of crap..." Unable to bear it, Keim dropped his head down on the table, letting out a sob. As he was crying out all the pent-up emotions, the bartender gently patted his shoulder.

"Look, you did something you can't take back, but are you really ready to give up? Do you think sitting here and drinking yourself to oblivion will redeem you? Of course it won't. There is something you need to do."

"Something...I need to do?" Keim looked up, and the bartender nodded.

"Set Leon free."

"He already is free... The Winged Knights have disbanded..."

"That's not what I mean. You haven't seen Leon since that day, but I'm sure he's hurting just as much as you are. He must be tossing and turning over not being able to trust you in the end. He thinks of you as his big brother."

The bartender was right. That was the Leon he knew. Leon had a strong sense of responsibility, and whenever his teammates struggled, he tended to blame himself.

"Well, maybe... But what can I do? I'm the one who hurt him... I literally stabbed him with my own blade."

"Even if there's nothing you can do, you need to talk to him. I've been watching you here for a long time. That's how I know. If you talk to each other, you'll both understand."

"And if it doesn't work?"

"Then it's just another way for you both to become free."

"I see... Yeah..." Keim nodded and made up his mind.

He would face his own weakness...and Leon.

A heavy rain began to fall from the cloudy sky. It was cold and soaked him to the core, but Leon continued walking without an umbrella.

His beloved Winged Knights had broken up. They'd had so many chances to win, but all were wasted because of Leon's own cowardice. He hadn't seen the rest of his erstwhile party.

He'd divvied up the party funds and wired them their shares, so hadn't had the chance to see them. And none of them had responded to the letter he'd sent by owl.

No matter how sorry he felt, it wasn't enough. The Winged Knights was a part of Leon. After losing that part of him, he felt that his life was over. He was just wandering the streets now without purpose, like the walking dead. Passersby either ridiculed him or shot him pitiful looks. Either way, Leon was no longer the figure they had once admired. Now he was inferior, nothing but a failure.

Just when he was thinking that, a young boy ran up to him, out of breath.

"Leon, please! Help me!"

"Huh? What is it?"

"My sister slipped and hit her head! Now she's bleeding... But we don't have any money so...she'll just... Ngh!" The boy let out a wretched sob.

Seeing him lit a fire inside Leon that he thought had gone out. "Don't worry! I'll save her! Don't cry!"

"R-really?"

"Yeah, really. Healing is my specialty. Now, take me to your sister."

"Okay! This way!"

The young boy left the main road and turned into a back alley. As a byproduct of accelerated development, the back alleys in the capital were positively labyrinthian. Leon needed to keep up with the boy showing him the way. He followed carefully so as not to lose the boy among the complicated turns and doglegs.

"This way! Here!"

Finally, they came to an open space that felt out of place between two buildings. It was as if a third building had either been demolished or the lot's owner had abandoned it. He wasn't sure which, but there were spaces like this here and there throughout the capital.

"Is your sister here in this clearing?" Leon asked, looking around. Suddenly, he sensed the presence of a large number of armed people. It was a trap. By the time Leon realized it, he was already surrounded. The boy who'd led him there stuck out his tongue and then ran away. In his place stood about twenty armed ruffians with vulgar smiles on their faces.

"I sure didn't think it would be so easy to trick you. I guess the Angel Wings really have fallen," came a man's voice. The speaker, a large man with a hooked nose, stepped forward.

Leon knew the man. "Edgar... You're the leader of the chopped-up crew, War Eagle."

"You remember me? How flattering."

"What do you want with me?" Leon asked.

"It's no big deal. It's just that I've always hated you. I'm keen to see you suffer a little bit."

"You used a little boy for that? What is wrong with you?" Leon shook his head in disbelief.

Edgar's expression turned dark. "A genius like you probably wouldn't understand. Do you know how much we've been ridiculed while you were getting nothing but praise? One of the newspaper articles said, and I quote, 'Compared to the Winged

Knights, the perfect model of a Seeker party, War Eagle is nothing but a bunch of punks. They peacock their clan title even though they are nothing but foot soldiers with no results to speak of.'"

"Sounds like a fine observation to me. I think you're proving all of that to be true right now."

"No. It's all your fault, Leon. If it weren't for you, no one would be making fun of us. You're nothing but a pretender and a media darling. It was such a huge relief when I heard that you lost to Blue Beyond and your party broke up. Mask's off, finally."

Hearing his ridiculous speech, Leon felt anger welling up inside of him. At the same time, something had clicked into place. Edgar must have been behind the attacks on the Winged Knights. "So it was you who ordered the thugs to attack us..."

"You finally figured it out? It took you long enough. We were only at the same bar every day," Edgar scoffed.

"You're insane," Leon said, glaring at him with quiet anger.

Edgar just shrugged his shoulders. "Yeah, maybe. But what about you? It was awesome seeing you just shuffle around like a zombie. You've really hit rock bottom."

"Shut up."

"The days of glory of the Winged Knights are a thing of the past! Now that you've failed and lost your senses, the only thing left is for you to die as a loser. You would look great in the slums!"

"Shut up!" Furious, Leon brandished his sword, but at the same moment, he was hit hard in the head. He didn't lose consciousness, but since he was caught off guard, he found himself facedown in the concrete.

"Die! Die, Leon! How dare you draw another breath! Die, right here!"

Edgar and his entourage quickly moved in on Leon. He calmly and objectively understood that he would die right there. But he also believed he was worthless. Perhaps this was all for the best...

"Aaagh!"

Just when Leon had decided to give up on everything, the Seekers surrounding him started crying out, one after another. When he looked up, he saw the goons losing fingers and armor being torn through as if sliced by steel wire. Every last one of them had dropped their weapons and were writhing about in agony.

"Er, wh-who's there?! Show yourself!" Edgar yelled out, desperately gripping his bloody, mutilated hand. Then he heard slow footsteps clacking on the cobblestone as someone approached from an alley.

"This looks fun. Let me join you," said a demon clad in a black coat.

✝

"Blue Beyond..."

Once we showed ourselves, everyone's malicious expressions melted into fear. It was a splendid reaction. It was best for a Seeker to be feared by other Seekers.

Lying there on the street, Leon was proof that once they stopped respecting you, it was all over. No matter how great a Seeker you were, if you showed weakness, you'd be victimized.

Even the Winged Knights, a class act that never caused anyone trouble, was practically begging to be attacked this way. This violent industry was really about nothing but blood. Thus, it was very comfortable and easy for someone like me to get ahead in the world.

"Wh-what are you doing here?" Edgar asked us, quivering.

I sneered. "Why, we're just taking a walk. Right?" I glanced at my comrades.

"Yeah, a walk," Koga said.

"Walkity-walk," Alma joined in.

Koga and Alma played along nicely.

"D-don't be stupid! Why would a little stroll bring you here? What are you playing at?!" Edgar yelled, holding tight to his now-fingerless right hand. He was still trembling, but he was starting to regain the wherewithal to check for his fallen battle-axe and the condition of his crew. He was clearly grasping at threads to try to stage a counterattack. But I wasn't about to let that happen.

"Edgar, bow your head to me."

"Wh-what did you say?"

"You have some nerve talking to us when we're so much more powerful than you. I don't like it. Yeah, I don't like you. Or would you rather just die right here?"

"Wha—you th-think you're better than me?!" Bright red from my jab at his pride, Edgar picked his battle-axe up with his left hand and roared, "Raise your weapons, fellas! Or are you gonna let them talk to you like this?! It's gonna rain Blue Beyond blood!"

Edgar swung his battle-axe valiantly overhead. However, rather than answering Edgar's battle cry, his comrades tried to talk him down.

"C-calm down, Edgar..."

"Blue Beyond beat the Winged Knights, man."

"And they took out a Dantalion with a team of only three!"

"We can't beat them..."

They were all petrified. Finally, one of them turned on his heel and ran away as fast as he could with a delightful "Aiieee!"

Seeing that, the rest scattered like baby spiders.

"Wait! Don't run! Come back here!" Edgar called out desperately, but not a single one returned.

I predicted this would happen. Had they actually hung together, they might have stood a chance. We were prepared to defend ourselves, but Edgar had strength in numbers. Instead, his friends had overestimated us based on reputation alone and convinced themselves that they could never win. Flight was the only alternative left to them.

"Oh, Edgar, you're not very popular, are you?" I took a step forward, and Edgar took a step back.

"L-Leave me alone..."

"Leave you? Are you giving me orders now? You have so much to learn. Who is in charge here, right now? Me? Or you?"

"Ergh..."

"Answer me! I'll kill you!"

"Eeek! W-wait! I surrender! Please, forgive me!" Edgar couldn't take it anymore. He tossed away his weapon and knelt before me.

"Lower. Are you trying to offend me?"

"N-no! It's a misunderstanding!" Edgar pressed his forehead on the ground. He had transformed into someone quite obedient after all that distorted pride. People really did have fragile hearts.

I stepped up close to Edgar, grabbed a fistful of his hair, and yanked his head up to look him in the eye. "So sorry for making you grovel, but I still don't like you. What to do? What do you think I should do?"

"P-please... Let me go..." Edgar pleaded.

I forced a friendly smile.

"Oh, I got it. I don't like this nose."

I swiftly drew my knife from its hilt and cut off Edgar's beaklike nose.

"Oaah!" He held his now nose-less face with both hands and thrashed around in agony. I grabbed his head and held it in place right in front of mine.

"Look at me. I said, *look at me!*"

"Ah, eee... P-peeh fuhguh muh..."

"If you want me to forgive you, heed this. Never act like such a pompous prick again. If you break that promise, I won't come just for you—I'll come for your friends, your family, your neighbors. I don't care if they're women or elderly, I'm going to get a good start on my Noses of the Capital collection. Got it? Hey! I said, 'Got it?!'"

"Uh guh iii..."

"Go. I won't say it again."

The second I let go of him, Edgar scrambled to his feet and sprinted off down an alleyway. Once he was gone, I turned to smile at the dumbfounded Leon.

"Now, Leon. Let's talk business."

"Business?" Leon sat up and shot me a dubious look.

"That's right, business. I want you to join our clan."

"What?! Are you joking?!"

Judging by how quickly he refused, it seemed he still hated me. That was understandable. But his emotional state was a trivial matter.

"If you join us, you'll be vice-master of our new clan. We're a fast-growing team. It's not a bad offer, huh?"

"I would never join your team!"

"Why not?"

"You guys—no, *you*, Noel. You destroyed the Winged Knights!"

He wasn't going to hold back. Luckily, it was easy to understand the mind of someone backed into a corner.

"Just like Edgar," I muttered. "Do you understand what you're saying?"

"I'm nothing like him! I know you were scheming with the Seekers Association!"

"It's true that I was working with Harold. I'll admit it. But we gave you a head start. You had plenty of chances to win."

"I also know what you said to my teammates! That's why Keim went and... When I think of how he's suffering, there's no way I could forgive you!" Leon punched the ground, tears of frustration spilling down his cheeks.

I couldn't help but laugh.

"What's so funny?"

"It's strange. If you know how Keim is suffering, then why don't you go reconcile? I'm the one at the root of all this evil. Even if you can't work together as Seekers anymore, you can still be friends and hang out as much as you want."

Leon didn't answer me.

"You're not going to talk to Keim because you're scared, right? Because this lifelong friend, who you thought you understood completely, was deeply jealous of you. But if you'd thought about it, you would have noticed right away. You didn't recognize that there was a problem. That was a significant dereliction of duty. I'm very disappointed in you, from one party leader to another."

"What would you know? You know nothing..."

"I know quite a bit. I'm in charge of people too. As a leader, you're responsible for all problems in the party. In return, you get all the party's glory. Leon, you weren't fulfilling your responsibilities as leader. You overlooked the fact that the world was only praising you for the results the party garnered. A party like that can't last."

Leon was excellent. But because he was *too* excellent, he couldn't understand the weak hearts of others. As a result, the other three were constantly exhausted.

"I knew it deep down... It was all my fault. Even if you hadn't targeted us, we wouldn't have had a future. But if we admitted that, all our work would have been for nothing. I couldn't stand that," Leon sobbed, his shoulders convulsing. I was standing directly in front of him.

"Leon, let me return the favor. Stand up. Stand up and fight!"

"Fight for what? I'll never get back what I've lost..."

"You will."

"Huh?"

"The glory of the Winged Knights is a thing of the past," I said matter-of-factly. "The world is cruel. The glory is gone, and only the tarnished name will remain. Even that tarnished name will soon disappear. After six months, no one will even remember the Winged Knights."

"Yeah, probably."

"But if you, the former leader of the Winged Knights, can still cement a legacy as a Seeker, the Winged Knights name will live again."

"That's why I should fight? Just for that?" Leon's lips twisted in self-derision, but I nodded.

"Yep. Fight on. Fulfill the responsibilities you neglected before. Create a legacy that future generations will remember. That's the only path to redemption for you."

"But if I join your clan, I really will be a traitor..."

"Be a little selfish, Leon. Cast aside your superficial feelings; they won't save you or your friends. If you truly want to treasure your memories forever, then you have to be prepared to throw everything else away. In this cruel world, you can't get anything for free."

Leon remained quiet for some time. Finally, he opened his mouth, as if he had decided. "Noel, what do you want? Why are you a Seeker?"

"I want to show this world that I am the strongest Seeker in it," I answered without hesitation.

Leon's eyes widened. Then he slowly stood up. "Can I truly trust you? If you're lying, I will never forgive you..."

"Ha, that's a silly question." I laughed, holding out my hand. Leon grabbed it, a wry smile on his face.

✝

A few days after Leon joined our group, we visited the Seekers Association again.

"It looks like your machinations paid off in the end. You're the talk of the capital," Harold said by way of greeting. He flashed us a smile but awkwardly diverted his eyes from Leon before addressing him directly. "Leon, what I did to the Winged Knights was horrible. But I have no intention of apologizing. This is reality. It may be frustrating, but you could have carried on and won, or worked harder so that you could win in the future. You were excellent. But you're also lacking in some ways."

"I know... I'm not here to complain to you." Leon's voice was placid, not betraying his obvious inner turmoil.

His smile now for Leon alone, Harold said, "Still, I can understand if you're angry. So, if you don't mind me as the target, you are welcome to punch away until you feel better." He tapped his own cheek with his finger.

Leon looked surprised at Harold's offer. He thought for a moment, but then slowly shook his head. "No thank you. I've no interest in hurting an old man on the brink of death," Leon said, smirking.

Harold shrugged. "Just because you're going to become Noel's vice-master doesn't mean you need to start talking like him." With a chuckle, he picked up the newspaper next to him. "But my goodness, the newspapers sure do get word fast. The fact that you two joined forces was already common knowledge throughout the capital the next day. Noel...you leaked it yourself, didn't you?"

"Of course. I had to use the newspapers to boost our popularity."

It wasn't just me. All the top Seekers understood the value in manipulating information. Seekers couldn't just be strong; they need to understand popular opinion and utilize it to progress. Once the public abandoned you, you'd just end up like the Winged Knights.

"You're very scrappy, but whether you'll survive in this world depends on you." Harold tossed the newspaper aside and took out the Association's official stamp. "The Seekers Association officially approves your clan application form," he said, emphatically imprinting the seal on the application.

"First of all, I will pay your bounty for defeating the Dantalion. The fee for completing the mission is 20 million fil. The proceeds from selling materials were 80 million fil. A total of 100 million fil will be wired to your clan's designated account today. Here is your payment slip." Harold set the slip on the table, and Alma and Koga gazed at it in wonderment.

"A-a hundred million..."

"Wow."

I understood their surprise. It was an amount that most people would never see in their lifetimes. Only Leon, who had a long history as a Seeker, kept his cool.

"And, upon assessing your achievements and reputation, I would like to issue you a suitable mission. The target is a Garmr with an abyssal depth of 9 that is currently manifesting in the Quartz Valley. The Association-issued reward for this job is 30 million fil. The current estimate for materials is approximately 120 million fil. Naturally, you will be granted all rights to the sale of the materials. The deadline to defeat the beast is one week from today. Do you accept?" Harold asked.

I frowned but nodded. "Understood. We accept your offer."

On the way home from the Seekers Association, the four of us walking together prompted a lot of whispers in the street.

"Look, it's Noel and Leon..."

"So they really did merge and form a clan... This is gonna be big..."

"They don't have many members, but they're carrying over the past achievements of the Winged Knights. As soon as Blue Beyond becomes a clan, they'll be ranked high."

"Blue Beyond sure is powerful."

"Wait, I heard that they tossed out the Blue Beyond name when they became a clan. Now that they've merged, their name is—"

Harold was right when he'd said we were the buzz of the city. I was glad I asked the informant Loki to spread information about us throughout the capital. Not only would improving our reputation lead to higher assessment by the Seekers Association, but we would also be able to secure financing from the bank. Everything was going according to plan. As I chuckled to myself, I suddenly heard someone calling my name.

"Noel Stollen! Demon!" I turned around to see Keim, looking enraged with his spear in hand.

"Hey, Keim. It's been a while. I haven't seen you since the test."

"It's your fault! Die!" Keim sprinted toward me. Alma and Koga stepped up to block him, but Angel Wings—Leon—was the one who took the blow with his shield.

"Keim, stop! This will not end well for you. Put down your spear!"

"Shut up, traitor! Why are you wagging your tail at this jerk who set us against one another?"

"Yes, I am a traitor! So I won't let you kill Noel!" Leon declared, sending Keim reeling. It wasn't that Kiem had seen the error in his ways and retreated; he was merely backing up to make room for his next charge. Keim regripped his spear and expelled a barbaric yawp. "In that case...I'll have to kill you first!"

Keim charged again. He had momentum enough to split Leon's shield in two, but Leon sidestepped and punched him in the jaw. Keim flew through the air and landed hard on his back.

"D-dammit! You won't even draw your sword! How weak do you think I am? I'll see you in hell, traitor!" Keim spewed insults at Leon from his spot on the ground.

Leon didn't engage and instead turned his back on his former friend. "I won't argue. I truly am a traitor. That's why I'm going to follow my own path," Leon said as he returned to where we stood.

"Good luck, Leon..." Keim murmured. Leon's eyes turned bright red, his lip quivered, and he started to turn around.

"Don't turn around!" I shouted. "Don't turn around, Leon... Leave your brother a shred of dignity."

Keim hadn't come to kill me. He hadn't even come to confront Leon. He came to test his little brother's resolve. And he came to tell him good luck.

"Let's go," I said.

Leon wiped away his tears and nodded. "Yeah. Let's go, Master."

The clan house I'd bought was a five-story brick building with fifteen rooms, formerly used as communal housing. It was built relatively recently and contained the latest anti-seismic technology, so it wouldn't easily collapse even in case of an earthquake. Pretty good location too.

But there was a reason why I'd been able to acquire it so cheaply. It was an absolute bargain; I just had to buy it. I wanted to move in immediately, but due to various circumstances, the entire building had to be gutted and remodeled, so we couldn't set foot on the premises yet. We went to check out the exterior.

"It's a great building. We really can't go in?" Koga asked, looking the clan house up and down.

I shook my head. "It's still being remodeled. It would be better not to."

"I can't wait," he said, an innocent smile on his face.

Next to him, Alma was cocking her head to the side, looking confused. "You really bought this building for cheap?"

"Yeah. I was lucky to find such a good deal." I still had to pay it off, but once the money for taking out the Dantalion came in, that would take care of it.

"How much?"

"Huh? About this much..." I held up two fingers to Alma.

"Two hundred million?"

"Not 2 billion. Two hundred million, right?" Koga chimed in.

Alma furrowed her brow and started yelling. "Shut up! You know nothing about real estate! You couldn't buy a building like this for 200 million! Die!"

"Y-ya don't hafta get so angry..."

After snapping at Koga, Alma turned on me with a glare. "Tell the truth. You didn't borrow money from the mafia, did you?"

"O-of course I didn't! I wouldn't put us in debt!"

"Okay, then, how did you get your hands on 2 billion fil? Oh! Maybe you provided some services to some rich old man..."

"Are you high?! I'll kill you!" This vile woman even made someone as tolerant as me murderous. "You're both misunderstanding. It wasn't 2 billion or 200 million fil... It was 20 million."

"Twenty million?!" they both blurted out at the same time. After their initial shock, their expressions grew dubious.

"What the hell?!"

"You have to be lying!"

What a pain. I racked my brain for an adequate excuse.

"I-I just remembered..." Leon muttered in a shaky voice as he looked up at the building. All the blood had drained from his face, and he was pale as a ghost. "This used to be an execution site..."

Alma and Koga suddenly grew stiff.

"I heard that ever since, bad luck has come to anyone involved with this building. Come to think of it, a year ago, a rich man whose check bounced had orchestrated a murder-suicide, taking out his whole family in their own home, and I think something similar happened here too..."

Suddenly, a sharp scream came from the building.

"Aaagh!"

When we looked in the direction, our hearts hammering in our chests, we saw hundreds of crows loitering around. The voice we'd heard was just a cawing crow. It was strange; all of the crows were gazing at us. A warm breeze blew down the block. I cleared my throat to break the long silence.

"Ahem! Now, if you'd just let me continue—"

"Wait a minute!"

This time, all three of the other members cried out with anger and fear.

"Noel, you're joking right?! C'mon! This is too cruel, even for you, Noel!"

"Wh-who do you think we are?! This is hell!"

"Are you insane?! To make a tainted property our clan house?!"

All three of them spoke over one another to protest. I shook my head and let out a loud sigh.

"Calm down. You're supposed to be Seekers, not Cowerers. People have died everywhere. If you're afraid of that, you can't live anywhere."

"Y-yeah, but... Wait, what?" Dissatisfied, Koga looked at Alma and Leon, who were both wagging their heads so hard that I thought they might fall off. They were trying to insist that this was something to be afraid of.

"We all fight beasts for a living; what could possibly be scarier about ghosts?" I asked.

"Beasts aren't scary, but I *hate* ghosts. It's the same as thinking that beetles aren't scary but cockroaches are. I hate them on a conceptual level," Alma said, and I chuckled.

"Relax. There are no ghosts in this building. It's already been purified by a priestess. Even if a ghost does appear, I can expel it with my skills."

Talker skill: *Exorcism*. I could use that skill to annihilate ghost-type opponents—and only ghost-type opponents—in an instant, so long as I was ranked higher than them. I could even purify human spirits, and quite easily.

"So it won't be a recurring thing. Okay, end of discussion." When I forced the conversation to end, the other three nodded, but they weren't in agreement at all.

"Back to the topic at hand. I brought you all here to give you this." I pulled three pendants from my pocket. They were all the same shape: a snake with wings. "They're platinum. I had them specially made. This is the symbol of our clan."

They each took a pendant in turn and examined it. First was Alma, the first member, then Koga, and finally Leon.

"Since ancient times, the snake has been a symbol of prosperity and immortality. But they are also feared as evil beings and the deceivers of men. I think that contrast describes us. Good and evil, light and dark. We'll use all our differing attributes to make it to the top."

The other three stared, nodding.

"Our clan has been approved. We are not Blue Beyond or the Winged Knights. Like I told you before, this will be our new name."

I looked at each of them in turn.

"We are Wild Tempest."

3 An Honest Scheme

NEARLY SIX YEARS PRIOR, a Seeker prodigy had become the talk of the town. His name was Hugo Coppélia, and he was eighteen years old.

Hugo's class was Puppeteer. It was an extremely rare class and widely considered to be the strongest of them all. He had the ability to create various types of puppets, and by controlling them, he could counter any strategy. His body was well proportioned and fit perfectly into his sophisticated suit. His handsome features gave him an air of intelligence and refinement. His bright-green hair, always kept short and neat, was perennially in fashion. The glasses he wore to correct his astigmatism accentuated his cultured look.

He had both talent and good looks, so it was no wonder that he caught the attention of others. However, Hugo preferred his own company to that of others. He liked being alone. Hugo was thorough in his individualism and, although he was a Seeker, he opted for mercenary work over joining a party. Mercenaries were common enough, and there was even a system for it. Seekers like Hugo, who didn't rely on any organization at all, were rare.

There was one specific battle that really set Hugo apart from everyone else. He was hired by a major clan with over twenty members, and while he contributed greatly to this victory, the clan had reprimanded him after the battle was over.

"Just what are you trying to do?!" the clan master yelled at the mercenary. "Why didn't you listen to my orders?"

"Well, I mean..." Hugo cocked his head to the side, his face devoid of expression.

Hugo had defied an order during the battle against a dangerous beast with an abyssal depth of 10. One tiny mistake in their coordination could have spelled death for the entire clan. In the end, they'd succeeded, but one of the clan members had been severely injured. Of course, the clan master was furious.

"It could have ended a lot worse than it did! If you have something to say, then say it!" the master barked, wagging his finger.

Hugo's expression was docile as he nodded. "Had I followed your orders, there was a high possibility that everyone would have been annihilated. I know that when we are on the battlefield, you are the master and what you say, goes. However, my contract with you clearly states that I have the right to protect my own life. I do not feel it is necessary to explain which I will prioritize, when I must choose between following your orders and preserving my own life. It is all laid out in the contract you signed when you hired me. Have you forgotten?" Hugo kept his voice even.

The clan master was dumbfounded, but his face gradually started to redden. "Such insolence! Are you trying to say my orders were mistaken?!"

"Yes, that is what I'm saying. Was it not clear?"

"You ingrate! Thanks to your disobedience, one of the most important members of my clan was gravely injured!" The clan master gestured toward a female Seeker, who glared contemptuously at Hugo. Her clothes were ripped at the right shoulder, and her white skin was exposed. She had been healed, so there was no visible wound, but moments earlier, a bone had been poking through the skin.

"She suddenly ran into the ray. Had she obeyed your orders, she wouldn't have been there. I recommend disciplining her."

"L-Liar! Don't be ridiculous!" the female member snapped. Objectively, it was clear who was lying. However, too angry to think straight, the clan master took the side of his comrade.

"That's enough of your bunk! How do you plan to compensate us for this?!"

"It is I who has had enough. There is nothing more tedious than conversing with someone who is one or more standard deviations of intelligence below me," Hugo said, exasperated.

"Wh-what did you say?!"

"Shall I use simpler words?" Until then, Hugo's face had been expressionless, but then his eyes grew sharp behind his glasses. "You and your clan were inadequate for the task set before you. None of you have the skills to be a Seeker. You were victorious only because of my intervention. Were it not for me, you would all be dead."

A deafening silence fell. Then, the clan master roared, "This, coming from a friendless mercenary! Are you ready to back that up?! Do you think you can take us all on by yourself?"

"Why, yes, of course," Hugo said, pushing his glasses up his nose. He started walking toward the clan master just as naturally as taking a stroll through the park. "I deplore violence. But when it comes to self-preservation, I have no qualms."

At first, the clan master recoiled, but then he laughed cruelly. Although Hugo had told him he didn't have the skills to be a Seeker, the clan master was A-Ranked. He was no ordinary Seeker; he was the best of the best. The other clan members were mostly B-Ranked. The clan was an extremely capable one. If the clan had been weak, it never would have been assigned the task of dispatching a beast with an abyssal depth of 10.

Although Hugo was also an A-Rank, he stood alone. Still, there was no doubt that the Puppeteer was a threat. Every puppet he created was the equivalent of a B-Rank Seeker. And he could create scores of them at a time. Hugo was alone, but he was by no means outnumbered. Though his dolls were effectively B-Ranked, they had fewer skills and were weaker than humans— they were still just dolls. The clan master knew that he held the advantage.

"Fine. If that's what you want, I'll bring you to your knees. Team, don't hold back! We're going to crush this man and his little dolls!" The clan master sounded almost happy.

But then something unbelievable happened.

"N-no way..."

Though the clan had flocked around Hugo in a flurry, the clan itself was now surrounded by an army of armored dolls. The Puppeteer, Hugo Coppélia, had created over two hundred automatons to do his bidding.

"I would recommend surrender. As you know, each one of my dolls has power equivalent to a B-Rank Seeker. They are also very sensitive to an opponent's intentions. If you make even one wrong move, I can't guarantee your life."

Hugo was a Puppeteer Grandmaster, which meant he could control three types of doll soldiers. The first category specialized in close-range combat using weapons such as swords, spears, and battle-axees. The second was long-range combat specialists, like archers, sharpshooters, and magic-wielders. The third consisted of support staff: healers, defenders, and transporters. The skill that allowed him to create any combination of these types was the Grandmaster skill *Legion*.

The myriad doll soldiers that Hugo created had enveloped his enemies, the clan master included. There were four spears pointed at his neck, one from each cardinal direction.

"I thought you could only generate twenty dolls at once..."

Had Hugo's skill been limited to twenty, the clan could have easily won. However, with two hundred, the clan could not possibly survive the battle.

"I don't remember ever saying that. I generally just preserve my magic power. Puppeteer skills consume massive amounts of magic power. When confronting a beast in the Abyss, I am always sure not to spread myself too thin. There was no reason to use all my power against a beast with a mere abyssal depth of 10. Incidentally, this manifestation represents about 20 percent of my power. If normal battles are a walk in the park, this is but a light jog."

"T-twenty percent?" the clan master stammered, the color draining from his face.

He had heard Hugo was a capable mercenary, hence why he'd hired him. The Puppeteer lived up to his reputation, but the clan master hadn't realized that battle was nothing but playtime for Hugo. How could he possibly have predicted that Hugo could overpower their entire clan and compare it to a jog? The clan master, who had been praised as a prodigy since childhood, felt total defeat for the first time in his life. He was also in serious danger of wetting himself.

Hugo tilted his head to the side. "It is as I said—you lack the skills to be a Seeker."

Skill assessment was always relative. Hugo Coppélia was so far beyond everyone else that he considered the genius clan master to be nothing more than a jumped-up chancer.

"Remember this: I choose not to associate with clans because I've no wish to be put in the same category as conceited weaklings like yourself. That's why my only dealings with clans are simple business transactions. Feel free to contact me anytime about a gig, for as long as playing Seeker interests me anyway."

Hugo snapped his fingers, and all of the puppets disappeared in an instant. Having lost the will to fight, the clan members fell to their knees, thanking God for the preservation of their lives. Hugo left quietly and without giving any of them a second thought. No one was so bent on dying as to attack him from behind. On that day, the Seeker mercenary Hugo became a household name.

Then, two years later, Hugo suddenly retired at his peak. That was when he started his life as a dollmaker. Hugo became the most successful dollmaker there ever was, but two years after that, he was trounced by the goddess of fate, framed for a bizarre murder, and tossed into hell.

It had been two years since his arrest. Hugo Coppélia was twenty-four years old, locked away in a dark prison.

"He has what you would call a 'difficult personality.'" As I told the others about Hugo in the carriage on the way to fight the Garmr, Koga stroked his chin as if unsure what to think.

"Well, puttin' aside whether he wants to join our clan, ya wanna do somethin' about his bein' falsely accused," Koga concluded, satisfied.

Next to him, Leon nodded vigorously in agreement. "If he really *was* framed, I want to help him. Once he's out, he can decide whether to join us. I don't think I could survive being locked up for two years..." Leon shivered as he imagined himself in jail.

Alma yawned, looking bored. "You definitely want him in the clan, right, Noel? So whatever you want to do is fine. Oh, but we don't need Koga, so if you could just fire him right away, that'd be great."

"What?!"

Alma gave a peculiar laugh at Koga's reaction.

"Okay, so no one objects to releasing Hugo?"

I'd wanted to make Hugo Coppélia my ally ever since I'd first heard of him. I didn't have enough power to get him released before, but I soon would. First, I needed to make sure the entire clan was on the same page. In our enclosed carriage, I wouldn't have to worry about anyone eavesdropping. I even told Alma, who was terrible at keeping secrets, that I would seriously kill her if she leaked it, so I figured it would be okay. Probably.

"Nope," Koga said.

"Me neither," Leon agreed.

"Same here," Alma added.

With their unanimous approval, I could proceed without any concerns.

"But to think that he can create two hundred doll soldiers with B-Rank abilities... Puppeteer must really be the strongest class, as they say," Leon mused.

"There is definitely no mistake: Puppeteer *is* the strongest class. But no matter how strong an individual is, the world runs on power. We can't forget what happened to Hugo the Puppeteer. True strength is never falling under the control of another person," I told them.

Hugo wanted to be a lone wolf, and I didn't want to invalidate that. But in the end, his failure to make friends who he could trust meant that when he got locked up for a crime he didn't commit, he had nobody to save him. He wanted to live on his own terms so badly that he didn't take time to understand the risks.

"People should use others more," I went on. "Society is built on mutually beneficial relationships; it's a key aspect of human intellect. But since most people insist on their own principles and positions, someone has to lose for another to gain, lest the independent types be robbed of their rights and their dignity." I then hammered home one point in particular: "No matter how strong you are, a lone wolf will always get picked off."

"You mean by someone like you?"

Leon's question stung, but I nodded with a snicker.

"You've been paying attention. Yes, that's right."

With that, I changed tack and made the final checks before we headed into battle. "We'll be arriving soon. Koga, you've only just moved up in rank. Any problems?"

"I feel good. I'll show ya the power of a Samurai."

After the battle with the Dantalion, Koga was able to move from Longswordsman to Samurai. His skills were stronger, and his physical augmentation was worlds above what it had been when he was C-Ranked.

"Alma, are you in fighting condition?"

"I had a lot of meat, so I'm good." Her smiling face was fearless, and she was in high spirits. Her skin had a healthy glow. Alma would have to really push herself in this battle, but she looked like she would be fine. "I have to admit, though, my butt's in rough shape. I hate carriages. They have a railroad in the Republic of Rodania next door, right? I wish they would build one in this empire..."

"If they could, they already would have. You'll have to put up with your sore butt. Mine hurts too," I told her.

A railroad involved laying tracks and running engine-powered vehicles upon them. It was a groundbreaking innovation that allowed for mass transport of trade goods. Magic engines made from beast materials were sturdy, and train lines could easily be built with technology that existed in the empire. The problem was that Abysses occurred much more frequently in the empire than in other countries. There was a high possibility that sooner or later, an Abyss would manifest atop a major rail artery.

The empire had cultivated their magic-engineered civilization from the fruits of the land. Ironically, this same land kept us lagging behind other countries in many ways.

"Leon, I know you're not used to our team yet, but would you say you're ready?"

"Yeah, I'll give you everything I've got. I will help you claim victory."

The deadline for this beast was only a week, which was quite short, so we didn't have enough time to refine our teamwork. Regardless, Leon was really excellent. His abilities spoke for themselves, and since he'd served as the leader of the Winged Knights, his understanding of directives was frighteningly better than the other two. While Alma and Koga acted according to my directions, Leon read my directives first and moved with them; he could anticipate what I needed him to do without being told. With the addition of Leon to the group, our battle speed had improved dramatically.

"The Garmr is a strong opponent. We're all Rank B, so we wouldn't ordinarily be able to beat this beast with a team of only four. However, vanquishing a seemingly impossible opponent is the essence of being a Seeker. It's evolution. In order to take great leaps, we need to train appropriately."

That was precisely why I used an intimidating voice to give orders to my team.

"We will survive the Garmr, and move beyond it. This is our destiny. We will defy death."

We came to a magnificent valley, where the exposed stone cliffs on either side sparkled with amethysts. Normally, such a profoundly beautiful sight would take our breath away, but this place had turned into an Abyss and was currently connected to the Void.

The valley was *filled* with skeleton knights. They brandished swords and battle-axees, spears and mallets, and every one of them wore jet-black armor. The bony infantry came in all different builds and sizes. The smallest was roughly the height of an adult human and rated at an abyssal depth of 5, and the largest was nearly six meters tall with an abyssal depth of 7.

Bringing up the rear was an enormous dog.

It had jet-black fur, as if its pelt were made of night sky. Three pairs of shining red eyes peered at us from afar, and emerald flames dripped from its maw. That was our target, the Garmr. With an abyssal depth of 9, it was an extremely dangerous upper-level beast. Even major clans would be hard-pressed to defeat it.

Raising its snout to the sky, the Garmr howled. Its cry was a signal for the skeleton knights to march forward. This beast had the innate ability to summon and command skeleton knights.

"You who have strayed from the laws of nature, thou hast no life, and no sin!"

Talker skill: *Exorcism.*

I could use this skill to annihilate ghost-type opponents of a lower rank than me. Even high-ranking opponents would falter and be weakened by my skill. The moment I uttered the word "sin," a third of the army was annihilated. The remaining two-thirds were significantly weaker, and their march slowed. Without a moment's delay, I gave orders to support my teammates.

"Koga, use *Crazy Cherry Blossoms* to clear out the front lines! Leon, use *Divine Impact* to take care of the bigger ones! Alma, mop up any stragglers!"

"Got it!"

"Roger!"

"Understood!"

Samurai skill: *Crazy Cherry Blossoms.* Koga drew his sword and sent countless slashing arcs flying across the valley. His strikes had multiplied immeasurably and were far more forceful than before. A wall of swirling cherry blossom petals filled the valley and reduced numerous skeleton knights to unmoving heaps of bones. Some of the larger skeleton knights held on, enduring the occasional tear in their armor or loss of limb. Five of them—with abyssal depths of 7—remained. Just as they were upon us, weapons held high, Leon began to glow.

Knight skill: *Divine Impact.* The skill reduced opponents' power, but only for a few seconds. But that was plenty of time. Alma rebounded off the surrounding stone walls like a ball smashing against the sides of a court, decimating the skeleton knights' joints as she flew back and forth across the valley. With their knees and ankles shattered, the final five knights collapsed like buildings in an earthquake.

That took care of all the soldiers. Now all we had to do was take out the Garmr, the core of the Abyss...

Or so I thought.

The Garmr howled again, and a dense shadow spread from its feet, carpeting the valley. A second skeletal army emerged from the darkness, this one twice the size as the previous muster.

"Er, I knew it could resummon the army, but I didn't know it would be *this* fast."

As long as the Garmr had magic power, it could continue to summon skeleton knights. According to past battle records, the only way to defeat the Garmr was to overwhelm it with attacks faster than it could summon. I clicked my tongue. As if the Garmr could hear me, the corners of its mouth quirked up.

"That bastard is laughing..."

Beasts with high intelligence were generally cruel, and this Garmr was no exception. Just like certain humans, these beasts delighted in closing in on their prey.

"Awaiting *Exorcism* and further orders, Master!"

"I know! You who have strayed from the laws of nature, thou hast no life, and no sin!"

At Leon's coaxing, I executed *Exorcism* again. This time, far fewer knights collapsed into dust. Not only was this army larger, but it was stronger as well.

"Koga, clear 'em out! Leon, support Koga! Alma, engage the Garmr! You're the only one who can get close to it!"

All three of them sprang into action. Koga kept the army at bay with wave after wave of *Crazy Cherry Blossoms*. Leon erected a barrier around Koga and picked off individual skeletons with long-range attacks.

"Accel—Duodecuple!"

While the battleground was in chaos, Alma ran along the cliff face to reach the Garmr, then rushed the beast at maximum speed. However, the Garmr easily dodged her attack.

"Dammit! Missed!" Alma desperately rushed in with another attack, but she didn't even graze it. It even dodged a hail of steel rods from Assassin skill: *Perfect Throw* at the last second, leaving them embedded in the wall.

The Garmr was able to move faster than its large body would suggest. Maybe its thought processes were developed to the point of anticipating attacks before we launched them. It had matched me thought for thought, prediction for prediction. No—it hadn't matched my processing speed. It was faster.

Regrettably, the Garmr didn't retaliate. If it would just launch an attack of its own, it would be vulnerable. The beast was probably trying to exhaust Alma, then tear her apart before she could resist; that was how a true predator would proceed. In spite of its overwhelming advantage, there wasn't a speck of haughtiness to its actions. It would kill us, and it would take no chances.

"This is bad... We can't keep this up much longer!"

The situation was deteriorating by the moment. Alma was tiring; her speed would peter out soon. Koga and Leon were on the verge of being overwhelmed by the army of skeleton knights.

"We've got no other choice... New plan! Koga and Alma, cover Leon! Leon, raise a barrier, then prepare to initiate *Seraphim's Blade*!"

Knight skill: *Seraphim's Blade*. Although the skill consumed all of his magic power, Leon could flood the entire valley with a heat ray worthy of a solar flare. No matter how fast the Garmr was, surely it couldn't avoid that.

"Master, *Seraphim's Blade* may not work!" Leon shouted, his expression grim. "And if we can't win with *Seraphim's Blade*, my power will be depleted—no more barriers, no one to heal the rest of you. Reconsider!"

"Comply! If we do nothing, we'll be defeated anyway. Our only play is to go all in!"

"I know that! But—"

"That's enough! This is your clan master's order!"

Leon reluctantly nodded. "Fine... Everyone, please lend me your support!"

After raising a barrier to protect us, he switched his sword to the other hand and crouched low. He was ready for *Seraphim's Blade*. Noticing our change in tactics, the knights rushed Leon, but Alma and Koga fought them back. I also had my silver flame ready to protect the unarmored Leon.

As Leon focused on his sword, it began to glow red. Without regard for timing, a wave of heat snaked across the valley like flowing lava, melting all in its path. We were protected by Leon's barrier, but the heat was still too much to bear.

"Prepared! Awaiting signal!"

The moment Leon asked for orders, the Garmr tried to flee from the valley.

"Don't let it get away!"

I shot a thunder bullet, which hit the Garmr in the head. The thunderous shock spread like a spider web, and the Garmr lost its escape route.

"Leon, release!"

"Seraphim's Blade!"

Tactics skill: *Tactician.*

Tactics skill: *Assault Command*, engage.

Leon swung his sword and released *Seraphim's Blade*. Strengthened by my support, a heat ray spread rapidly throughout the entire valley. Everything in its path was incinerated in an instant, annihilating the skeleton knights and changing the very topography of the valley.

"Did it work?"

It was hard to see through the wall of smoke and ash. Even squinting, I could see no better. But I heard something—a bestial howl.

With the Garmr's third cry, the ash-laden valley filled again with an army of skeleton knights.

"Dammit..."

The Garmr was unscathed, even after a direct blow from Leon's *Seraphim's Blade*. With its massive magic power, the Garmr had raised a barrier of its own to absorb the attack. But we had scored a hit. The third army was fewer in number, so we had clearly hurt the beast and forced it to expend some of its reserve magical power. Still, it had taken all four of us exhausting our *own* power to get this far.

The strain of *Seraphim's Blade* and *Assault Command* sent Leon into a swoon. Even if I were to pour an elixir down his throat, he would be unable to fight.

"This is it... Retreat! Alma, carry Leon and evacuate! Koga and I will distract the beast!"

We waged battle for three kilometers, but then the balance was broken. Koga stopped the wild swing of a giant skeleton's longsword with his blade, but he couldn't handle the force and was thrown against one of the cliffs.

"Koga!" I called out, and Koga fell to his knees, spitting blood.

"I-I'm sorry, Noel... I'm finished..." He clearly had broken bones and punctured lungs. Only Alma and I could still fight.

"Noel, watch out!" Alma rushed to me and knocked me aside as a large skeleton cleaved the spot where I'd been standing with its long sword. But Alma couldn't stop her own momentum and went careening into the same wall that Koga had just been slammed against.

"N-no..." I was the last one standing. Koga and Alma were too injured to move, and although Leon was conscious, he still couldn't stand. As I stood there, speechless, the skeleton troops suddenly parted, making a path. From the far end of the valley, the Garmr slowly marched toward me.

120, 119, 118, 117...

"Battle, you." The beast spoke in a monotone facsimile of human speech, like a machine. He stopped before me and lowered his snout. "Amusing. But you, you miss."

100, 99, 98, 97...

"Why did you call off your army?" I asked it. "What is your goal?"

"You. Your special brain. I eat it warm, gain its power. Human child, my food."

The Garmr opened its big mouth, baring its ferocious teeth.

"Wait, I surrender! I'll jump right into your mouth if you like. But I have one question."

"Ask." Sure of its own victory, the Garmr turned its ear to listen.

"Do you know of a humanoid beast lord with a horned head? He might be wielding a battle-axe made by a human. Can you tell me if you know of such a beast?"

"Why...?"

"I want to avenge my grandfather. The lord fled back to the Void to heal the wounds my grandfather dealt it, but it still lives. I want to kill it."

"Vengeance. Petty," the Garmr said, twisting its mouth in a sneer.

75, 74, 73, 72...

"I kill you, or lord does. No need answer you."

So it wouldn't answer me. Well, that was fine; I hadn't really expected it to. What I needed was another way to keep the conversation going.

62, 61, 60, 59...

"Now I eat."

"One more thing. How about making a deal with me?"

"Deal?" The Garmr cocked its great head to the side, interested.

"If you let us go, I'll tell you something you really wish to know. I promise it'll be significant—and useful to you."

"Information about Seekers? Pitiful! You are no infantry. Repent in hell, dirty child!"

The second the Garmr let out its furious howl, I took out a silver pipe from my coat.

"Don't freak out. I don't plan on selling out other Seekers. What I want to tell you is about this bottle."

"What...is that bottle?" Evidently intrigued, the beast sniffed at the jar. Its guard was completely down, probably because it could sense I had no bloodlust in me. Had I betrayed any kind of hostility, it would bite my head off in an instant.

"This is a sprayer. Fill it with liquid, flip the switch, and out comes a mist. It has a pretty good range too. Watch."

I flipped the switch and sprayed out a couple puffs of mist.

35, 34, 33, 32...

"Hmph. How is that useful?"

"You don't know? Well...sounds like a personal problem for you," I snorted. Sensing a change in my demeanor, the Garmr took a step backward, wary once more. I still wasn't hostile, but that only confused the Garmr.

"What...did you do?"

"Well, I guess it's only natural that you don't know. The only reason you approached me in the first place was because you determined that I'd lost the will to fight. Had you perceived any intention to counterattack, I'm sure you wouldn't have come near me."

"What are you talking about?! What are you saying?!"

13, 12, 11, 10...

The Garmr took another step back. I was ripe for the taking, but the intelligent beast was weighing the risks and couldn't just attack me outright.

"It's not that hard. You're right; I'd lost the will to fight. I still don't want to. But you must understand: I have no will to fight with you because I've already won."

5, 4, 3, 2, 1...

"Zero. Exactly two minutes."

At that moment, the Garmr's legs buckled under it, and it collapsed to the ground, coughing up foam. It desperately tried to gulp in breaths as it sputtered.

"Impossible? Is this...poison?! I dodged all attacks!"

"No, you didn't dodge all attacks. We set up these sprayers all over the valley in advance. Naturally, there's deadly poison inside. Poison you've been breathing in all along. In other words, the moment you manifested here, you lost. That's why I'm not interested in fighting you."

"Agh, im...possible... Then you...poisoned too..."

"This poison is only effective against beasts. Humans and elves are immune. Right, Alma?" I looked over, and Alma was sitting up and nodding.

"It is colorless, has no odor, and aerosolizes quickly. The red blood cells start to melt in the blood about two minutes after exposure. You're dying, Garmr, of oxygen deficiency. Since it's synthesized from my blood, we don't have a lot, but it is definitely fast-acting," Alma explained.

Assassin skill: *Blood Poison.* In exchange for sacrificing several liters of blood, Alma could make about a liter of poison. While she could supplement her blood supply via transfusion, the process was draining both literally and figuratively, so she couldn't use the skill often.

"So, now do you understand?"

"Ergh... Skeleton knights! Kill that human!" Gasping for breath, the Garmr ordered its knights to attack me.

It was all in vain, obviously.

"You who have strayed from the laws of nature, thou hast no life, and no sin!"

The knights were annihilated by my *Exorcism.* Their summoner, the Garmr, was on the verge of death and largely drained of magic power, so this batch was probably far below my rank. There was nothing left to fear from the skeleton knights. Without his army, the beast snarled in frustration.

"You fled...to lure me here... It was an act..."

"It was a pretty good act, right? I wrote, directed, and starred— I'm a triple threat!. But it wasn't *all* an act. We did have to fight with everything we had in order to exhaust your energy reserves— whoops, looks like you're trying to heal yourself, but you can't because you're out of magic power, right?"

Considering the magic power the Garmr had used to shield itself from *Seraphim's Blade*, and the amount it used for three rounds of summoning, there was no way it had enough magic power left to regenerate. If we had tried poisoning it from the start, it would have healed itself right away and then been on guard against such attacks. Not that we had enough poison to repeat the same strategy. Instead, we'd fought with all our might, getting the Garmr—which could think even faster than me—to let down its guard and fall into our trap.

"I know it was all a part of yer strategy, but we took some real big hits. The way things was goin', following yer orders to put on an act was really tough... But that made it work." Koga rose to his feet, wiping away the blood on his mouth. His whimpering had been an act, but the injuries were real.

Leon and Alma tried to stand up as well, but I motioned for them to stay put. Everyone fought well. I could handle the rest.

Rising on shaky legs, the Garmr turned to face me. Then it used every last ounce of remaining strength it had to charge, but I pulled the trigger on my silver flame before those claws and fangs could reach me.

The Garmr bullet hit the target in the neck and exploded. As the Garmr's shredded head flew through the air, its voice rang out loud and clear: "Soldier, impressive!"

The head of the Garmr dropped to the ground, a satisfied and smiling expression on its face.

"Instead of whining or bearing a grudge, it praised us. I'm surprised that even beasts can have dignity."

I tucked the silver flame back in its holster and gave my final order.

"Battle complete."

"I confirm defeat of the target and purification of the Abyss," Harold said, grinning. In order to prevent damage to the surrounding area, Abysses with beasts of depth 8 or higher were managed directly by the Seekers Association. Harold had been encamped at the site.

"Taking down this beast will definitely boost your reputation."

"This was a cakewalk."

"Is that modesty? Or arrogance? Well, either way, all I care about is the result." Harold was in a great mood and removed a cigarette from his breast pocket. Taking a puff, he said, "Ahh, and that's become famous too." He gestured at the pendant I wore around my neck. It was the symbol of Wild Tempest, a snake with silver wings.

"Every clan has its own nickname, and in your case, people are calling you the snakes because of that symbol. By now, just saying 'snake' in the capital refers to you, Wild Tempest."

"The snake is a symbol of prosperity and immortality," I replied. "Doesn't it fit perfectly?"

"Wow, I just thought you chose the snake because of the way you acted."

"Huh? What are you trying to say, you old fart?" I glared at Harold, who looked away and blew a smoke ring.

"Noel, I'm done speaking with the supporters. They'll start

working now," Leon said as he came up next to me. Behind him, I could see the staff members from the Support Association who were hired to take the Garmr back to the capital. Supporters handled logistics, battlefield cleanup, and the harvesting of materials. They were in charge of dismantling and transporting the beast. It would have been impossible for us to transport the Garmr on our own, so we'd arranged for a large crew.

The supporters, who had been waiting outside the Abyss, skillfully dismantled the Garmr and loaded it onto multiple wagons. Technique was important because the longer the corpse stayed on the battlefield, the more the materials would deteriorate. Alma and Koga were excited by the efficiency of the Supporters and watched, wide-eyed, like children.

"Noel, Can I talk to you?" Leon nudged his head, gesturing to a point a few meters away. I nodded and walked with him into the shade of some large stones.

"What do you plan to do next?" he asked, leaning against the rock with his arms crossed. His face was stern. "I admit that you are amazing. You're the reason we were able to take down a Garmr at this level. Without you, we never could've beaten such an enemy."

"It was a team victory. Every one of us was vital to our success."

"You're right. Wild Tempest is a good team; we have the potential to go much further." Leon frowned as he chose his next words. "After this battle, I'm certain we cannot become part of the regalia in six months by conventional means. Even if we were able to release Hugo, and even if he joined our clan, we would still lack

combat skills, a proven record, reputation, and most of all, cash."
Leon paused again, then continued with a grave look on his face.
"Becoming part of the regalia means taking a slot from a current
regalia clan. As the vice-master, I want to know what your scheme
is for doing that."

There were always only seven positions in the regalia. Unless
an existing clan was removed, there would be no space for us.
Just as Leon said, even if we continued improving at this rate,
we wouldn't be able to enter the regalia. We just didn't have the
experience.

"Noel, answer me. You vowed to me that you were going to
become the strongest Seeker."

"I do have a plan. Think about it the other way: in what ways
do we *beat* the regalia?"

"Ways we beat them, you say? Do we have something like that?"
Leon cocked his head to the side, looking doubtful. I laughed.

"Of course we do. It's money."

"Money?! We don't have that kind of money! The regalia has
massive funds! One of the privileges of the regalia is permission
to own an airship, but that means having the funds to build an
airship is one of the qualifications. The minimum required for
building an airship is—"

"Eighty billion fil, right?" I cut in.

Leon nodded. "That's right, 80 billion. The reward for defeating this Garmr, which nearly killed us, is 150 million fil, including
the sale of materials. Even if all of that went straight into the clan,
we would have to win more than 530 battles just to afford an

airship. There's no way we can do that in six months. Moreover, we can't just keep battling like this without taking breaks in between. Our bodies couldn't handle it."

"That's right. But you need to be more open-minded. Just because we're Seekers doesn't mean that defeating beasts is the only way we can make money. First of all, I plan to get a sponsor."

There were plenty of rich aristocrats keen to sponsor famous Seekers. By doing so, they raised their own reputations and acquired a platform for launching new businesses. In economics, money attracted money. The same was true when it came to the relationship between Seekers and sponsors.

"It's a good idea, but I really don't think it'll be possible to reach 80 billion fil... Just one or two sponsors would be a drop in the bucket."

"Yes, we'll need dozens of sponsors."

"H-how?"

"Hugo Coppélia."

Leon's eyes opened wide when he heard the name. Then he bubbled over with anger. "So that's why you want to help him— it has nothing to do with his powers. You're going to turn his false conviction into a show and gain the support of the people, right?"

I was grateful Leon caught on so quickly. That was precisely my plan.

"People are always looking for a hero. What is a hero but someone who slays the beasts that prey upon the people? The evil Department of Justice, which threw an upstanding citizen in prison on false charges, is nothing but a monster. Everyone wants the hero to come and slay the monster," I explained.

"So basically, once the hero has gained the support of the people, the plan is to use that reputation to attract even more sponsors...?"

"Exactly!" I snapped my fingers and smiled brightly. "That's part of the plan. Once we've gone through all the stages, we will be the top Seekers. Undoubtedly."

"I see." Leon quietly looked at me, then turned to leave. "I'm relieved. You were exactly the man I expected you to be," he said, voice cold. Leaving that hanging in the air, he walked off.

I called after him, "Leon, you are who you are. You don't need to pander to me. You do you. Live what you believe. I don't want a yes-man for a vice-master."

Leon stopped and dramatically let out a big sigh.

"I know, you don't have to tell me... I won't be objecting to your plan, that's all. People should use each other more, right? That's really a wonderful concept."

His empty agreement oozed with dissatisfaction. He understood the logic, but he couldn't accept it on an emotional level. I couldn't blame him for that. Besides, Leon had an important role to play.

"Wait. I'm not done talking to you. Leon, I have a job for you."

Leon looked back at me over his shoulder. "A job?"

"Yeah. I think you'll like it."

I gave a half-smile, and Leon scowled at me with open disdain.

✝

After defeating the Garmr, we gained a reputation not only in the capital but throughout the entire empire, thanks to the newspapers. It was just what I wanted. If we could use our new-found notoriety to our advantage, our chances of success would skyrocket.

Just before noon, I heard a knock at my door at the Stardrop Inn.

"Noel, are you here?" came a lisping voice from the other side.

It was Marie, the innkeeper's daughter. They should have been busy with the lunch rush, but for some reason, Marie didn't sound hurried at all.

When I opened the door, little Marie looked up at me with a gentle smile. "You are here. That'sh good."

"What is it?"

"There'sh someone here to shee you. Can I let them in?"

"Might that be the reporter from the *Modern Opinion* newspaper?"

"Yesh, yesh. A newshpaper reporter. So you're expecting them?"

I nodded. I'd been asked to do an interview.

"Will you send them here to my room?"

"Fine. But...he's not very handshome."

"His looks have nothing to do with it."

"But it's sho much better when two handshome men are to-gether. If you're going to have a man up here all alone, I'd like it better if he wash good-looking!" she whined.

"I'll be absolutely frank: I have no interest in that."

"Huh?! You're joking, right?!"

"Why, you..." This brat was just getting worse and worse. If she was already like this at ten, then what kind of adult would she grow into? I didn't even want to think about it.

"Noel, you don't have to be afraid. God shays good-looking guysh should be together. That'sh the natural order."

"What kind of malevolent god do you worship? Marie, you need therapy. Or should I find someone to drill a hole in your skull and tweak your brain?"

"I'm not wrong! The world ish wrong!"

"That is quite a declaration, you little brat. Maybe I should kill you now in order to save the world."

"Ahh! Ahh! I'm againsht violence!"

I watched the tiny girl run off and then let out a deep sigh.

"Seriously, what kind of woman is she gonna grow up to be?"

A smart-looking older man with glasses stepped into the room. "Nice to meet you. I'm Thomas from *Modern Opinion*." We sat down at opposite ends of the table. "Thank you for taking time out of your busy schedule for an interview today."

The conversation went smoothly, but I noticed that Thomas seemed very concerned with his watch. He probably didn't realize, but he'd checked it five times over a ten-minute period.

"Are you late for something?" I asked.

"Huh?! Oh, no, ha ha ha…" Thomas bowed his head apologetically. "I'm sorry to act like that during our interview. You see…the Seekers Association is going to make a big announcement after this, and I need to head over there too."

"Oh, so that's why."

The announcement was definitely going to concern the Valiant. The manifestation of a Valiant dangerous enough to cause massive disasters would have a significant impact on the economy. They couldn't keep it under wraps forever. The timing was perfect; I planned to take full advantage of it.

"The Association will announce that one year from now, a Valiant will manifest within our borders. There's your scoop."

Thomas's eyes grew wide as saucers. "Is...that true?"

"Sure is. I heard it from the inspector in charge of us, so there's no mistake. He told me to keep quiet, but as they're announcing it today, I'm sure it's fine to tell you. The new policy for testing parties applying for clan status was implemented to focus Association resources on only the most powerful Seeker groups," I explained.

"I-I see. Then it *must* be true. But a Valiant a year from now? The entire empire will erupt in panic..." Thomas crossed his arms, deep in thought.

I leaned across the table and smiled. "Thomas, I have a proposal for you. What if we held a symposium?"

"A symposium?" He looked at me inquisitively, so I continued.

"I'm sure all the citizens of the empire are interested in how the major clans will approach a once-in-a-century threat like a Valiant. Each of the clan masters can discuss it at the symposium, and you can get an exclusive article. It's guaranteed publicity."

"Th-that's a good idea. Yes! It's a wonderful idea!" Thomas pushed his glasses up his nose and sat up in his seat. "Please, let *Modern Opinion* take that on. We will do whatever you need!"

"Okay, then, you arrange the venue and make the preparations.

Let's make it a grand event to get the most viewers possible. I don't want to invite just Seekers; we need the rich and famous to be there too."

"Understood. Leave the venue to me. Can I leave the invitation list in your hands, Noel?"

"Yeah, I'll take care of that."

"Do you *really* think the other clan masters will participate?" Thomas asked, looking understandably worried. I was a new master who had just recently established a clan—there probably wasn't anyone interested in an event run by someone so young. That was why I needed him.

"It won't be a problem. We'll hold it using a different Seeker's name."

"Which Seeker?" Thomas asked, prompting me to grin.

"Zeke Feinstein, vice-master of Supreme Dragon, the strongest clan in the capital."

After Thomas left, I hopped on a fast horse and traveled to a dangerous, rocky mountain located about an hour's ride away from the capital. The bare rocks were sharp, and there was no suitable path for hiking to the top. It made for an awkward climb, despite my being in tip-top shape. The air at the peak of the mountain was thin, and the ice-cold wind licked painfully at my cheeks. It wasn't exactly an environment amenable to human life. However, according to Loki, it was a place that Zeke frequented. While I was surveying the area and looking for him, a freakish sight lunged at me.

"The mountain…is moving."

To be exact, some of the bare rocks were moving up, then down. As I moved closer to see what it was, I was too surprised to speak. There, a man was lifting up a small mountain of rocks—a mass that must've weighed tons. Furthermore, the man was squatting them. His strength was undeniable; it was as if he were divine.

"So this is what a true EX-Rank can do," I marveled.

Finally, the man—Zeke Feinstein—threw the pile of rocks away. The impact when they hit the ground shook the earth and echoed like thunder.

There was steam coming off Zeke's bare torso. He pulled a towel out of his bag to wipe his sweat. Even with his superhuman strength, there was no sign of hypertrophy. Zeke was actually quite slender.

After wiping down his hair, he looked over at me and smiled, though he was clearly surprised. "I sure didn't expect to see *you* here," he said.

"So you actually are a hard worker. I never would've guessed you had such an aberrant training regimen. I have newfound respect for you."

"I'll take that as a compliment. But I don't particularly like being thought of as a hard worker," Zeke said, taking a swig from his water bottle. "I'm sure you of all people understand, Noel. There is no glory in the word 'effort.' The only thing we need is results. I actually find it embarrassing to be covered in sweat like this. If I had my way, I would do away with all the fluff of effort and just keep the results."

I laughed and nodded. I really did understand.

"I can definitely agree with that. Results are the only thing that matter in this world," I agreed.

"So what do you want? You came all the way up here to see me. That means it's something we can't discuss in the capital, right?"

"I have a request for you. Will you hear me out?"

"I seem to remember you saying some pretty harsh things to me... But then again, I'm an adult. It's water under the bridge. I can't make any promises, but I'll listen."

"I appreciate it. I want you to let me use your name."

I explained the symposium I was working on with *Modern Opinion*. After I finished, Zeke stroked his chin, looking intrigued.

"That sounds pretty interesting. So your goal is to search for sponsors during the symposium?" he asked.

I nodded. "Yeah, that's right. I need money."

A wicked smile spread over Zeke's face. "But once you open your mouth as a new clan leader at a symposium, you'll probably lose all hope of a significant sponsor. Is that why you're trying to twist the Bloody Taxidermist's false arrest to pad your own reputation?"

"Oh, you know about that?"

Just as I had Loki to feed me intel, Zeke seemed to have his own sources of information. I'd figured as much, so it wasn't much of a surprise.

"Well, Supreme Dragon had our eye on Hugo's talent too. I still know a lot about him. In the end, we had to give up on getting him released because of the cost."

"The cost? Didn't you just lack the resources to get him out?" I said, snorting. Zeke shrugged.

"I won't argue with that. But can you really do it? If you want to use Hugo, first, you have to get the false conviction dropped. You can't do that simply by gathering evidence. The authoritarian Department of Justice won't easily admit to a mistake. One wrong move, and you'll be in jail for treason."

"Have you forgotten my class? This is my specialty," I said.

"Heh, that's some confidence. I hope to get front-row tickets to your appearance," Zeke said, a cold smile on his face. "You're competition, Noel. There's nothing in it for me if your plan goes well. My clan won't like it one bit. So why should I go along with your little request?"

"Well, I plan to express my gratitude."

"Oh, and what could the likes of you offer me?"

"I'll let you fight Leo," I declared, and Zeke's face went blank.

There were two extremely strong Seekers in the imperial capital, the heart of the Seeker world. One was Zeke Feinstein, the guy standing right in front of me. The other was the master of regalia clan Pandemonium, Leo Edin.

Supreme Dragon was ranked higher, but in the capital, the two were treated as equals. Zeke, however, was too proud to accept this. He wanted to prove once and for all which of them was stronger. I'd gotten a glimpse of his frustration when we'd met on the street not too long ago. Zeke and Leo were both in positions of power; they would never be allowed to hold a private sparring match to establish superiority. I'd sussed out that he'd been convincing himself of that fact for a long time.

"You want to fight with Leo, right? I can make that happen."

"I do. I want to finally show everyone who's the strongest. But I have my position to consider. Risking my life in a private fight is not allowed," he said.

"That's why I'll give you a place to fight that everyone will accept—a place where you won't have to worry about dying."

"How?"

I didn't give him the answer first and instead decided to explain my plan from the top. "Wild Tempest will be part of the regalia within six months."

Zeke didn't respond to my declaration. I couldn't tell if he thought it possible or not, but at the very least, he didn't laugh and say it was impossible. This was the vice-master of the strongest clan, after all. Since Zeke was silent, I continued.

"The regalia is a title granted by the emperor, so naturally, we'll meet with him. When that happens, I'll make a proposal to His Imperial Majesty."

"What proposal?"

"Why, a fighting tournament that all Seekers are allowed to join."

"What?!" Zeke's eyes bulged in surprise.

"I'm sure you already know, but a Valiant will be manifesting in the empire. It'll take a massive show of power to put the people's worries at ease, which is why the emperor will accept my proposal. The event will be held in the emperor's name, so Seekers who have already made a name for themselves *and* the unrecognized ones who want to show their stuff will sign up. The regalia—the clans that are to fight the Valiant directly—will have to participate."

When the Valiant manifested, the regalia clans would be on the front lines, and a supreme commander would be assigned from among them. Considering past results, Victor, the master of Supreme Dragon, was most qualified. However, Victor was too old. It would be impossible for him to both fight and command.

With Victor excluded, every other master in the regalia had a shot. A tournament would be the best place to determine the nominee—the winner would become the leader. Naturally, it would be best for me as well.

"Uh-huh... Yes, I see! I wouldn't have thought of something like that. If killing the opponent is against the rules, then I'll be able to fight Leo. Plus, if the emperor approves, it won't be a problem for both of us to enter." He was getting it.

"Precisely. I'm still thinking about the rules, but I plan to allow duels between Seekers even of different ranks, so it will be open for anyone to win."

"That's an interesting idea too. But aren't you worried about blabbing this to me? I could steal the idea and host the event myself. If I killed you right here, no one would know that it wasn't my idea in the first place. This also happens to be a pretty isolated place."

I guffawed at Zeke's transparent threat. "You shouldn't joke about something you don't have the guts to carry out. I think it's easier for you to allow me to build the tournament rather than doing it yourself. Most of all, can you ask Leo directly to fight you?"

"You sure know how to pour salt on a man's wounds... Pride really is a pain, isn't it?" Zeke looked glum and turned away from me. "Fine, I'll go along with your plan. You can use my name, so as soon as you join the regalia, make sure to get the fighting tournament started."

"Got it. I swear on the name of my grandfather, Brandon Stollen."

With that, I had everything I needed. When I started to turn to leave, Zeke spoke up again.

"Noel, I want to ask you something. Who do you think is stronger, me or Leo?"

"I've never met Leo in person ... But if I were to go by his battle record, I would say he's stronger than you. As far as brute strength goes, Leo is definitely superior."

They were both Rank EX, and Zeke had superhuman strength, but I still believed Leo to be the stronger one.

"I see. I think I'll trust your analysis. In other words, I'll be the underdog. Me, against him... It's pretty exciting."

Zeke's magnificent zest for battle was palpable. He was facing away from me, so I could only see his back, but I was sure he had a big grin on his face.

"When you're like this, you're not so bad," I murmured, but the cold wind carried off my words before Zeke could hear.

✝

"Ahh! I can feel it flowin' through my tired body!"

Koga, sitting next to Leon, praised his water as if he were drinking top-shelf sake. The brilliant noonday sun poured down on them. The two men had volunteered to come to the capital's outer wall to repair it.

A protective barrier incorporated into the wall kept enemies from infiltrating the capital. It was a large-scale mechanism to protect the city in case an Abyss manifested nearby. The wall used cutting-edge technology, but it was ultimately just another stone wall, so the parts that had crumbled from age had to be repaired regularly.

The wall was tall and encircled the whole city. There weren't enough masons and engineers to maintain it, so a large labor force operating under their instructions was needed. Most of the people who came to work there were day laborers. However, there were plenty of volunteers as well. It was common for people to want to work for the city they loved. Leon and Koga weren't there out of love for the capital, however; they'd come because Noel had ordered them to.

"I can't believe Noel sent us here fer this. When he told us to come do volunteer work 'cause it'd be good for the clan's reputation, I wanted to punch him. Who does he think ruined our reputation in the first place? He did." Koga grumbled continuously about Noel during their break, fingering the snake pendant he had around his neck.

Leon smiled wryly, nodding in agreement. "It's not a bad idea, though. The work isn't terribly interesting, but if people besides other Seekers see our faces, our status will improve. If our clan's reputation is good, then it will be hard for other clans to interfere with us."

Seekers were always trying to drag one another down. They would spread defamatory rumors or try to off them in a fight. As a general rule, Seekers were ruthlessly competitive. However, it wasn't as if *every* clan dealt with sabotage. Highly recognized clans were no easy targets. A careless attack on one of them could destroy the perpetrator's standing.

With that in mind, doing volunteer work to get in the public's good graces could be extremely effective. Indeed, Leon and Koga had left a positive impression on the other volunteers. The common folk were seeing a different side of Seekers—who were notorious for their penchant for violence—and had to reevaluate the opinions they'd developed from the media.

"Here, you two. My wife made honey lemon slices."

"It's so good of you to take the time to do this, even though you have your Seeker work. You fellas single? I could set you up with my daughter."

"Such respectable young men. With Seekers like you, the capital's future is in good hands."

The other workers expressed these sentiments and more, and if they went and told their friends about their day, Wild Tempest's reputation would further improve. The saying went that making an enemy of a clan that was popular with the people meant making an enemy of the people. Unless they were a complete idiot, or someone with overwhelming societal influence, no one would touch a popular clan.

"When Noel asked me to do this, I was worried about what sort of evil plot I'd be partaking in this time, but I don't feel bad about doing work people are grateful for," Leon said with a bright smile, squeezing a lemon slice. Of course he was thinking about it. In a way, Noel was always telling Leon that he was lacking when it came to public service work. Back when Leon was in the Winged Knights, he never even considered volunteering. His party had donated money to an orphanage, but it wasn't a means to an end; it was just a whim. Other Seekers were probably the same.

"He really is excellent," Leon mused. "He understands what a society needs in order to function."

"Yeah, he's the best, but why ain't he here? He's the most important guy."

"Ha ha ha. Apparently, he has his own preparations to take care of."

"The symposium, right? Just another trick..." Koga muttered.

Leon laughed, completely in agreement. Then something dawned on him. "Koga, why did you decide to work under Noel? I heard it was an odd situation. But I imagine you don't agree with Noel all the time, let alone Alma."

After working with the new clan, Leon could tell that Koga was a good person. He was friendly and sociable, so he could have worked anywhere instead of under Noel. It wasn't as if he'd entered into a business agreement with Noel, like Leon had. That was why he found it so strange.

"'Cause he's special. I'm sure of my sword, but it's nuttin' but a sword. If ya want value in this world, ya gotta have a sharp mind and some real grit."

"So that's enough for you to ignore any discontents?"

"I accept it. That's the most important thing, ain't it?"

"Yeah... That may be true."

At that moment, the site supervisor came over.

"Ah, there you are. The materials are delayed, so today's work is off. You can go home now."

"Understood. We will be back tomorrow." Leon stood, and Koga followed suit.

"Today's volunteer work is done?"

"Well, the work here finished early, but we said we'd go to the orphanage in four hours. We're volunteering to watch the kids while the nuns get some work done."

"So we're gonna play with kids? Sounds easy," Koga said.

"It does. For now, let's get something to eat and kill some time."

Leon and Koga chatted amicably as they headed to the shopping area.

"Raaagh! Dieee!"

"Owww! Ow, ouch!"

Leon and Koga had found themselves surrounded by—nay, covered in—children, and they both howled like monkeys. All they could do was scream as the kids yanked their hair, taunted them, and beat them with poles.

"This what you'd call easy, Leon?!" Koga yelped. "Blech, don't put sand in my mouth!"

"D-don't ask me! H-hey, stop trying to take off my clothes! Stop it!"

The ruthless children were having their way with the two Seekers. There was only so much the men could resist, since they had to be careful not to hurt the kids. They were forced to suck up the abuse and resist the urge to dropkick the little urchins over the city wall.

"My, my. You two are popular," the nun said, looking on with what must have been glass eyes. She belonged to the convent attached to the Holy Cross Church, which ran the orphanage.

"Wh-when will this hell end?"

"W-we have three more hours..."

"Are you joking?! I'll never make it!"

Leon and Koga were practically preparing themselves for death.

"Hey! What if we said that thing?!"

Suddenly, they heard a threatening voice. Looking over, they saw the nun arguing with a couple of thugs.

"Hand over the deed to this land, now!"

"I-I've told you many times, we can't..."

"Stop messing around! Hurry up and go get it!"

As far as they could tell, the thugs were land sharks. They probably wanted to redevelop this area. They went around threatening landowners who wouldn't sell. The nun talking to them was shrinking with fear.

"Hey, Leon..." Koga nudged him, and Leon looked over.

"Yeah, I know."

The children had also noticed the land sharks and grown quiet, looking at the nun with concern. It didn't have anything to do with him, but Leon couldn't just ignore someone being harassed like that.

"Hey, you, what's going on here?"

Before Leon could step in, a young blond fellow stepped between the nun and the thugs. Judging by his collar, he was a priest. He was young and thin, and his gentle-looking face was dappled with freckles. "This house belongs to the church. You'll not commit violence here," he said, spreading his arms in an attempt to protect the nun.

"Well, well, Father. You've come at the perfect time," one of the thugs said, flashing a leering smile. "You tell her to give up this land to us too."

"Why would I—"

"Why? You sure are dumb for a priest. Our boss is Andreas Hooger of Hooger Commerce. Even someone as ignorant as you must know how much money Andreas donates to the church?"

"W-well..." The priest floundered, unable to make a comeback.

Leon clicked his tongue. "This is bad. They're backed by Hooger Commerce."

Hooger Commerce was a distinguished enterprise, even in the capital. Although it had only seen rapid growth very recently, it had wide influence in a number of fields. Many wealthy and powerful people were shareholders, and it had deep ties with not only aristocrats, but the mafia as well.

The authority of the church was absolute. However, in the end, it was an organization of self-interest. Surely if they had to choose between a fat cat like Andreas or a rundown orphanage, they would support the former. The priest had no power here.

"It would be easy to save them, but it would be a mess if we made it worse..."

"How can ya say that?! I'll go!"

"H-hey, Koga!" Leon tried to stop him but couldn't.

Koga inserted himself into the argument. "You, dun' get carried away."

"Huh, who are you?" One of the thugs turned on Koga, his eyes fierce. "Stay out of it! I'll kill you!"

"Go ahead 'n' try."

Leon stepped up next to Koga, glaring back at the thugs. Now that Koga was involved, Leon had no choice. Resolving the issue at hand took precedence over later problems.

"If you plan to escalate this, you will answer to us," Leon warned.

"Dun' worry, I'll go easy on ya," Koga said. He smiled ferociously as he cracked his knuckles.

As if realizing this was a losing battle, the thugs stepped back. Then they noticed the pendants on the men's chests. "A-a snake with wings... Are you guys snakes?!"

Snakes—in other words, members of Wild Tempest.

"Th-that's not good, bro. They're the clan that messed up Edgar."

"Oh, man, these are the guys who crippled him?!"

The thugs talked among themselves in shaky voices for a moment longer, then suddenly spun around and ran off as if they'd been shot at. "W-we'll be back! We won't forget this!" one of them called out from over his shoulder.

Leon and Koga could only laugh at their pitiful escape.

"Thanks to Noel, they think we're monsters," Koga said.

"Good. Let's be grateful we didn't have to resort to violence," Leon said. When he turned around, the priest and nun were bowing deeply.

"Thank you very much. You saved us."

"Don't worry about it. Anyway, I imagine those ruffians will be back. Shall we stop by more often?" Leon couldn't bear to leave them unprotected now that he was involved. However, the priest slowly shook his head.

"I appreciate the offer, but this is our problem. I wouldn't want to bother you either," the priest said firmly, leaving no room to argue. He knew that if the issue wasn't resolved at the root, just shooing the thugs away wouldn't help.

"Understood... Please be careful."

"Thank you, truly. There isn't much I can do, but at the very least, I plan to protect the children who live in this orphanage." His voice was filled with conviction, though he didn't appear capable of fighting anyone.

Leon looked down at the priest's feet to see that a child now crouched there. The nuns ran this orphanage, and there was no full-time priest. But Leon could tell that the children utterly trusted him.

The church bells rang in the new hour, and their exhausting shift at the orphanage was finally at an end.

"Thank you very much for your help today," the nun said. "It's not much, but we've prepared extra meals for you as well. Please join us. I'm sure it will make the children happy too."

Leon and Koga accepted the nun's invitation to join them for dinner. They were exhausted from being tortured by the snot-nosed kids and wanted to go home as soon as possible, but they had become fond of the little ones after all.

"Leon, Koga! Eat with me!"

How could they refuse a child's request? When they sat at the dining table, Leon noticed that the priest had disappeared for a moment, only to return carrying a large table by himself. Leon ran up to help him.

"Oh, thank you."

"Should I just take it to the courtyard?"

"Yes, please. The leg bent, so I was going to fix it."

After they brought the table to the courtyard, the priest laughed merrily. "You've really helped me out. Go ahead and sit down, if you would."

"Aren't you going to eat?"

"I need to fix this. I use the little time that I have efficiently. I still have church work to do as well."

"I see. You're a busy man." Leon admired the priest's work ethic. He always thought priests were arrogant and uptight, but this one seemed different. Perhaps it was in part because they were close in age.

"Umm..." He realized then that he wanted to make a confession to the priest. "Father, can I have a moment?"

"What is it? If there's something I can do for you, I'd be glad to."

With that, Leon poured his heart out. He talked about how he'd left his friends because of his own cowardice, his concerns about whether his new clan would find success, and everything else.

"Hmm, that's quite a lot to deal with. Being a Seeker doesn't sound easy."

"I...don't know if this is right for me," Leon said timidly. It was the path he had chosen. All he could do was continue on it. He knew that, but he didn't know how to feel secure in doing so. At that moment, he was like a ship without a rudder, and it was utterly frightening.

"I understand your anxiety," the priest told Leon, his voice calm. "But you made a decision. You made it, and you can't turn back now."

"Yes..."

"In that case, you should trust in it. Trust your judgment. You don't need to waver; nothing good comes from it. The more people waver, the more they seek to place blame. Life is nothing but a series of choices. You can't ignore the process that led you to make those decisions. The crucial thing is to take your own reins and be sure-footed."

"Take my own reins..."

"You are your own boss. Don't forget that."

The advice was a bit extreme for a priest, but it was clear that that was exactly why he was sympathetic. Leon felt a bit lighter. "Thank you very much, Father," Leon said, bowing his head. The priest nodded kindly.

"I'm happy to have been of service. Now please, eat. I think everyone is waiting for you."

"Agh! I-I almost forgot! I'll go now!" Leon sprang to his feet and ran inside.

It would be a mess if the hungry children started running amok. After seeing Leon off, the priest allowed his gentle smile to twist into a cold grin.

"You can't move forward if there *is* no path. Poor little ants."

With that, he crushed an ant crawling on the table beneath his finger.

"What are we going to do now, bro?"

The two thugs who had run from the orphanage were at a bar, discussing their next move. They'd thought the job would be easy, but they'd gotten nowhere thanks to those snakes.

"If we can't get a hold of that deed, we're in deep trouble... That's it. We'll have to use our last resort."

"Seriously?"

"Yeah. It's the fault of those orphanage assholes anyway for not obeying. They have no right to complain. We'll set the place ablaze..."

Once the building was nothing but ashes, it would be easy to snatch up the land. It was a risky move, and they didn't want to resort to it, but they felt they had no other choice.

The thugs loitered at the bar for some time, then left in the middle of the night. They headed to the orphanage, slipping through back alleys to avoid being spotted.

It was in one such alley that they came across a strange shadow.

"Huh? Who are you?"

A woman in an Asian-style dress appeared, blocking their way. The fox ears poking out of her black hair tipped them off that she was a hybrid beast. Her graceful limbs and voluptuous figure showed through her thin garment, tantalizing the men. However, they didn't attempt to pursue her. It was odd for a woman to be walking alone in the middle of the night, and down a back alley, no less. To make matters worse, her face was covered with a strange skull-shaped mask. Something was definitely weird about her.

She narrowed her eyes as if laughing. "That's interesting. A *very* interesting trick, actually."

"Huh? What are you talking about?" The younger thug cocked his head to the side. Immediately after, blood poured from his lips, and he crumpled to his knees.

"Hrk... Blegh!"

Realizing something was wrong, his cohort panicked. "H-hey! What happened?! Hey, hang in there!" He shook his friend, but there was no response. He was dead.

"I-It can't be... Wh-what did you do?" He looked up at the fox woman, his face ghostly white, but she just shrugged her shoulders.

"Don't look at me. I didn't do anything."

"Then what happened?!"

"Do you know what ikizukuri is? It's a way to prepare a dish on an island nation in the far east, where fish is served live. A skilled chef can keep the fish alive, even after chopping it up."

"Wh-what are you talking about?!"

"I guess you don't know? What a fool. Anyway, I'm saying that you're the fish."

He didn't understand, but he could tell she was making fun of him. The furious thug tried to scream at her—however, instead of his voice, only blood came out.

"Ack! Urgh!" Coughing up all his blood was the last thing that thug ever did. The fox woman grinned and skipped up to the corpses.

"Ah ha ha ha! It's a miracle. They were still walking around hours after being killed!" As she approached the blood-soaked bodies, she checked for the wounds. "Hmph, nothing on the outside. Significant internal injuries though. How strange... I didn't believe a regular, unenhanced blow could do such a thing. So this is the work of the King Slayer... Ha ha ha. It really is wonderful."

As the woman peered gleefully at the corpses, a fly landed on her shoulder and buzzed its wings in a complicated manner, transmitting a message. *Did you see the attack too? No one around noticed it, but there's no doubt they were hit by the King Slayer. It was at the speed of light, without any wind or sound.*

"Yeah, I agree. They're not as good as Edgar, but they'll make fine elements. I'll leave the rest to you."

Then, countless flies appeared in the dark and started gathering around the dead bodies. The fox woman looked on with pleasure.

"I only wish we could have heard them scream. Edgar's crying before the end was so pretty."

4   More Savage than Heaven

NEEDED CLOTHING appropriate for a social event. The symposium was to take place in three weeks, so I decided to order a bespoke formal suit.

In recent years, it had become common practice for men to wear tuxedos for social occasions, but to be honest, I looked terrible in a tuxedo. I was too short, and I had a feminine face. I just wasn't masculine enough to pull it off. Thus, I ordered a tailcoat instead. With tailcoats, the front of the jacket was shorter, drawing the eye upward. It also made my legs look longer—more flattering for my short stature. I would look more dignified when speaking at the podium and would easily catch the attention of the audience.

I wasn't the only one who needed formal attire. The symposium I had planned wasn't just a formal event for experts; there was a strong social aspect to it, so I needed a partner of the opposite sex. If she were to be on my arm, Alma would also need to dress appropriately.

"Hey, pick something less revealing."

"What?! This is way cuter, though!"

Today, I was accompanying Alma to the tailor. Alma had a great body, but she tended to choose clothes that were too revealing. Basically, she was a tease. I didn't trust her to pick out formal attire on her own, so I'd decided to join her. Boy, was I right. Just as I expected, Alma was about to choose an extremely skimpy dress. The neckline was so low that her breasts were about to spill out, and the fabric was nearly translucent. Nothing she chose was appropriate for a public setting.

"Noel, you're too close-minded. Something flashy would stand out more!"

"There's a limit to *how* flashy you can be! What is that in your hand? These aren't clothes you wear; they're just pieces of fabric you stick on each of your body parts. You'll be arrested for public indecency!"

"You're clueless. This is what's hot right now," she insisted.

"With every breath you take, a lie comes back out! I've never seen a woman wear anything like that!"

There were more revealing options for women than there were for men, but there was no reason she couldn't select a tasteful option to show off her beautiful silhouette. And yet, the clothes Alma picked were clearly crossing the line.

"You can't choose. I'll pick for you."

"Ugh! You're like a bossy husband."

"I would rather marry a fly than boss you around," I snapped back.

After that, I took it upon myself to choose something that would look good on her. In the end, I went with a long white dress with a low neckline. It was revealing but not outright erotic, and it was within the realm of good taste. If she wore high heels with it, she would look like a charming, mature adult.

"Wear this. This is fine."

"It's frumpy. You're good-looking, but you have no fashion sense."

I told her to drop dead and handed the dress to the female clerk. "I want to buy this. She has some peculiarities, but can you adjust the size?"

Size adjustments could be done within two weeks. I'd also requested minor adjustments when I ordered my tailcoat. However, with a peculiar body shape like hers—small frame, large bust—her outfit would probably need major design adjustments too.

"I believe the woman with you will need a custom-made gown. Even if we use one of the existing designs, it will have to be reconfigured for her body type. If you order today, the earliest we can get it back to you is one month from now."

"One month... So it has to be custom-made, huh?" The symposium was in three weeks. A month was too long. "I can pay extra. Can't you finish it a bit sooner?"

"I can wear this without any size adjustments!" Alma said, showing off a garment that she could stick to her skin, but I completely ignored her.

"Perhaps if we fitted her with a breast minimizer, a size adjustment would be enough."

"Oh, you can do that? Let's try that, then." I nodded at the clerk's suggestion and looked at Alma. "There you go. Shame about that outfit, but put it back."

"Ergh! You're so boring!" Grumbling the whole way, Alma went into the fitting room with the clerk.

"This garment will minimize your breasts."

"So basically a wrap? No, it looks so uncomfortable."

"Don't worry. A wrap would just push your breasts down, but this minimizer gently covers your chest area, reducing the size. It's quite comfortable, and it won't ruin your figure."

"Wow. Okay, I'll try it... How's this? Is it smaller?"

"Hmmm. You have a rather ample bust, so it's not easy to keep it down. We might have to tie it a bit tighter. Let me help you."

"Uuugh. Ow! Th-this is just a wrap!"

"I-I'm sorry! But we must make it tighter! Hrngh! Uhn!"

"Owww, you're crushing me! My lungs are gonna collapse!"

I couldn't help but snicker at the commotion going on in the fitting room. "Alma deserves it. Make it tighter," I heckled from the other side of the door.

Each utterance of agony relieved some of the stress from my daily life. Just when I was feeling content, I suddenly remembered something my grandfather had told me.

Apparently, before they married, my grandmother had an established career as a skilled tailor. Back then, she probably had struggles with customers too. For some reason, I felt a rush of nostalgia—she was still young when she died, though, so I'd never actually met her. It really did bring back memories.

It seemed like Alma's fitting would take a while yet. Bored, I decided to look out the window. There were busy people and horse carriages passing by. It was the usual daily scene.

"I guess a Valiant announcement doesn't affect them..."

The other day, the Seekers Association had announced at a press conference that a Valiant would manifest in a year's time. At first there'd been a fuss, but now things were back to normal. The market had suffered the biggest impact, and stock fluctuations had been severe since. However, nothing changed as far as everyday life was concerned. There wasn't any more anxiety than normal, and everyone was living their lives.

At least they were calm; widespread panic would be a problem. To me, it just looked like the common folk didn't understand that this concerned them as well. They hadn't come to the realization yet, that's all. In other words, it wouldn't take much to trigger mass hysteria.

"Will I be able to use the public's sentiment to my advantage? Or will it create problems?"

Just as I was muttering to myself, I saw a familiar silhouette pass by the window. When I craned my neck to see, the person backtracked and came right into the shop.

"What are you doing in a place like this?" asked Lycia, an elven member of Lightning Bite.

"I could ask you the same thing. Why would you come in here?"

Puzzled, Lycia took a look around the shop. "Noel...do you like dressing as a woman?"

"I'll cut your ears off, you dumb elf!"

This was a women's boutique, but I was just here for Alma. It wasn't as if I were wearing a dress.

"That's horrifying. When you say something like that, I can't tell if it's a joke or not..." Lycia said, covering her ears and taking a step back.

"You're the one talking crap."

"Sorry. But really, why're you here?"

I nodded my head toward the fitting room. We could hear Alma and the clerk from inside.

"You came to buy Alma clothes? Like for a date?"

"Do you think I would go on a date with Alma?"

"Nope. Definitely not," Lycia answered quickly with a straight face. I wasn't sure I liked that answer either, but I didn't say anything else.

"We needed formal clothes. Both Alma and I."

"Hmph. Is that right?"

"So what about you?" I asked her.

"I'm on my way to meet my party."

"Huh? Then what are you wasting time here for? Hurry up."

"Don't be so cold! Anyway, it's all your fault!" she exclaimed.

"What?! What did I do?"

I had no idea what she was talking about, so she caught me up. Apparently, Lightning Bite was going to merge with King of Dukes and Red Lotus, and then they would form a clan. Veronica, leader of Red Lotus, had come up with the idea—the other parties had both agreed. In order to decide who would take charge of the merged party, the party leaders were going to duel.

"I see. Well, that's good news. The clan application process is strict right now, since the Association's preparing for the Valiant to manifest next year. If your parties merge, I'm sure you'll be approved."

"Th-that's true, but we don't have to rush! Deciding the leader by duel, really?! It's all because you blew everything up!"

"Nah, you do need to rush. That's exactly why I provoked Wolf and Logan," I said. "Whether your clan contributes to the Valiant battle will be the gold standard for assessing our value as Seekers. If you don't seize this opportunity next year, it'll be decades before you get another chance. If not now, when will you finally pick up the pace?"

"Ergh... But only one person can be at the top."

"So what? Everyone involved understands that. If you're really a Seeker, you should respect Wolf's decision. He made his choice: the path toward becoming a true Seeker."

"I do respect it... That's why I didn't object. But sudden change is scary. We've been Lightning Bite for so long. Whether he wins or loses, we'll never be the same again..." Lycia closed her long lashes and let out a sigh. "I wonder if we elves hate change because we're so long-lived. Are other races different?"

"No, it's the same for all races. That's why so few move forward."

"I see. Yeah..."

"Lycia, I understand how you feel. But just remember one thing. There is nothing in this world that doesn't change. Maintaining the status quo is nothing but stagnation; it's just waiting for a soft end. If you really think something is important, don't fear change."

"Are you lecturing me? I'm way older than you are."

"Nah, this is just advice from a friend."

For just a second, Lycia looked taken aback, but she immediately broke into a huge smile. "You're scary, but sometimes you're sweet."

"I'm always sweet," I replied.

"Yeah, right. Even though you destroyed the Winged Knights to get ahead. I don't know the details, but I know your dirty tricks. That's how you always win."

"That's right. I fit them into my plan and used them to climb the ladder," I said honestly. "Speaking of which, Ophelia from the Winged Knights is from your hometown, right? Are you planning to tell me off on her behalf?"

"No, I'm not. I'm a Seeker too. Whatever means you used to win, the losing party should have come up with their own strategy," Lycia said, but she wasn't done. "No matter how close you get to your dream, don't forget the people you climbed over to get there, Noel. Even if Leon did join your team, it doesn't cancel out what went down to make that happen. You don't get strong by crushing people's hopes; you get stronger by bearing them."

"Is that a lecture?"

"Nope, just some friendly advice." She smiled.

"I'll bear that in mind," I said with a shrug. Just then, the fitting room door flew open.

"Woo, my old clothes are the best! Boobs need to be free!" The grin Alma wore as she came out of the fitting room melted the moment she saw Lycia. "Huh? What are you doing here, Lycia?"

Lycia chuckled and explained the situation.

"That sounds interesting. I wanna watch too," Alma said, her eyes shining with excitement. "Since it's a duel, don't you need an official to judge it?"

"Yeah... That may be true." Lycia nodded, then gave me a sidelong glance.

"Ahh, fine," I relented. "I'll judge it."

"Yay! Everyone'll agree if it's you!" Lycia cried out happily, clapping her hands. I was the one who'd instigated all of this after all. I couldn't exactly pretend like I was unaffected by what was going on.

Lycia took us to the arena, a training area in the capital. In order to make it as close to a true battle as possible, there was a variety of replicated environments throughout the spacious facility. The three party leaders who would be dueling were lined up in a desert environment, where the terrain was mostly sand.

"Hey, it's Noel!" Wolf saw me first and waved, smiling and running toward me. "And Lycia and Alma too. What are you doing here?"

"You're going to duel to decide who's going to lead the three merged parties, right? Lycia's asked me to referee it. If none of you object, I'll do it."

Wolf was surprised, but he flashed me a grin. "That's even more than we could have hoped for. Having the master of the major new clan Wild Tempest here makes our duel even more significant."

"Ahh, so you plan to use me in your clan declaration after the merge?"

"Well, if we're going to move forward from here, we'll need that extra boost." Wolf shrugged and looked over to where everyone was gathered. "I'll explain it to them. Please, be our referee."

"I know. That's the entire reason I'm here."

"Thanks. Oh, and—" Wolf suddenly stopped, his smile genuine. "Congratulations on your clan."

"Thank you. But do you really have the confidence to be over here congratulating someone else right before your duel?"

"No, I really don't. But hey, I'm really happy with what you've done. I know more than anyone how hard you've worked over the past year." Wolf looked away, donning his war face. "Now it's my turn."

When Wolf returned and explained that I would be the referee, Logan, the leader of King of Dukes, agreed immediately.

"If we have a referee, then no one can complain if they lose," he said, looking at the other two defiantly.

"I hate to say it...but I agree too. However..." Veronica pointed her finger at me, her brows bristling. "You are only a judge! You don't have the authority to make the rules! Your only job is to declare me the winner after the fighting is done. Understand?"

"I know. I don't have a dog in this fight. I have no intention of interrupting," I assured her.

Once all three had consented and explained the predetermined duel rules, I stood far back so I wouldn't get in the way. The members of the three parties were also watching from a distance.

There were twenty-seven Seekers from Lightning Bite, King of Dukes, and Red Lotus combined. The winner of the duel would command these fighters and establish a clan. Together, they had plenty of capable bodies, fighting power, and recognized achievements. Surely, the Association would approve them. They would also probably be able to join the ranks of major clans representing the capital.

"It's a battle none of them can afford to lose..." I muttered under my breath.

There was no rule that the losers would be banished. However, whoever lost would have to drop down from their position and obey the clan master. Wolf, Logan, and Veronica had wildly different personalities, but they were alike in that they all had pride as leaders. They all stood to lose a lot if they failed.

Alma came up to me from the Lightning Bite camp and asked, "Noel, are you going to watch from here?"

"Yeah, it's a neutral spot. I can't be in any of the three camps."

"I see. Then I'll stand here too."

"Don't you want to watch with Lycia?"

"She's got her own team to support her."

Looking over at the Lightning Bite camp, I could see Lycia with her fellow party members, all holding their breaths. The members of King of Dukes and Red Lotus were doing the same. Each one of them was hoping their own leader would win. There was only one person in the Red Lotus camp looking at me—a wolf-man.

"It's Vaclav. So he joined Red Lotus," I noted.

When I made eye contact with him, Vaclav looked away awkwardly.

"I heard the rules from Lycia," Alma said, sitting on the ground cross-legged and resting her chin in her hands. "They're battling for their lives. No hard feelings if someone dies. It's forbidden to save a friend. No items allowed. The battle is over once two participants are rendered unable to fight. The last one standing is the winner. Right?"

"Yeah, that's what I heard." I nodded and pointed my silver flame at the sky. "I'm not just the referee; they're also letting me give the starting signal."

"That's a big job," she said.

"I'm just an errand boy. But today is special."

I pulled the trigger, firing a blank. At the dry, explosive crack, the battle began.

A few minutes had passed since the start of the duel. At this point, no one had made a move yet.

"None of them are moving... Do you think they're waiting for one to take out another first?" Alma asked, seeming vexed, but I shook my head.

"No way. They wouldn't do that."

"Why? Only one person is going to win, so it would increase your chances if you let the other two fight it out first."

"If their only goal was winning, then you'd be right. But did you forget? They're fighting for the top spot after the parties merge."

"Oh, I see... They can't just win; they want to show that they *deserve* to be on top." I nodded in understanding. "As a strategy, snipping from the sidelines while the other two go all out is no way to show off your capabilities. Even if their former teammates understood, the new clan members definitely wouldn't like it. Seekers must be rational, but leaders have to prove their worth in ways that go beyond the rational. It's what they call charisma."

It was the opposite of what I'd said when I lectured Leon. In order to acquire strength as an organization instead of as an individual, you had to touch the hearts of the people under you. If too many clanmates were estranged, it would defeat the purpose of the merger.

This fight wouldn't last long. They wouldn't be advancing and retreating; they would be coming with all their power and strength in order to show off. As if to punctuate that point, the air between the three contenders was dripping with their resolve to fight to the death.

"What they want is a fight where they can use their physical prowess to force the others into submission. I couldn't possibly fight that way."

"That's because you would gain an advantage with your brains before the fight got physical," Alma told me.

I chuckled, fully in agreement. As she'd said, I had my own way of fighting. Still, I couldn't help but envy the integrity of fighting face-to-face.

"Ergh... They're still not moving. By the way, who do you think will win, Noel?"

"Yeah, see..." I had been assessing them as they prepared. My analysis was that there was no significant difference in any of their abilities. In that regard, they were all on par with each other, hence the standoff. Also, back when I was listening to the rules, I'd confirmed that they had all upgraded to Rank B.

Wolf Lehman, Swordsman Class, Rank B, Gladiator.

Logan Howlett, Fighter Class, Rank B, Monk.

Veronica Redbone, Wizard Class, Rank B, Magician.

Since they were all the same rank, the result wouldn't be influenced solely by power. However, of the three, only Veronica was a rearguard fighter.

A Magician could borrow the powers of spirits to attack with any attribute, and it was proficient in wide-range annihilation. On the other hand, since they were poor at physical combat, they were weak against direct attacks. One-on-one combat was out of the question, and she would be at a huge disadvantage taking on two Seekers with close-quarters combat abilities. Nevertheless...

"I think Veronica will win," I declared.

"Veronica? She looks like the least likely to win to me," Alma said.

She was definitely at a disadvantage in this fight, but I'd heard from Lycia that it was Veronica who had suggested the merge in the first place. She must have had a way to compensate for her lacking combat prowess.

"Veronica is a strong woman. The number of Seeker women is low to start with, and the fact that she has grown into someone tough enough to put together a major force means she's more than a bit like me."

"You mean she has a bad personality?" Alma cracked.

"No! She's good at manipulating situations to her advantage!" I snapped.

Just then, the standoff abruptly came to an end.

"Veronica's making the first move!" someone from the King of Dukes roared.

Veronica had already executed her skill. She made countless birds with an incandescent flame and shot them at Wolf and Logan. A direct hit would dish out far more than burns. Wolf and Logan dodged, but the flaming birds turned and bore down upon them. While they were engaged, Veronica was preparing for a new skill. The flames converged over Veronica's head and melded into a swirling fireball not unlike the sun.

"The heat is incredible..." Alma breathed.

"It's as hot as Leon's *Seraphim's Blade*. It's devastating, but if she misses, she's out of ammo. Veronica is trying to end it now."

Wolf and Logan raised their eyes to the second sun in the sky. For a moment, Logan completely disappeared. Then he reappeared behind Veronica.

Monk skill: *Close Encounter*. This skill closed the distance between a Seeker and a target. Logan simply delivered a chop to the back of Veronica's neck. Defenseless, Veronica collapsed upon the sand. The battle-hardened Seekers on the sidelines knew that she had fallen in an inconceivable manner. Veronica's flame was snuffed out without a sound.

"Veronica!" The Red Lotus members cried out for their fallen leader.

"Heh, this is intense. That's unthinkable. The rear guard really *is* at a disadvantage," I said.

Alma looked at me, sneering. "So you're wrong sometimes too."

"I'm not omniscient." I shrugged with a wry smile. I had seen Veronica collapse—she was out cold, no doubt about it. Still, I had a strange feeling I couldn't put into words.

"Whoa! Amazing!"

The uproar from the crowd was so loud that the entire arena was shaking. While I was busy thinking about Veronica, the battle proceeded at high speed. Wolf and Logan's one-on-one battle sent sparks flying. Logan used *Close Encounter* over and over again to violently assault Wolf. Wolf was engaging with his dual-blade fighting method. He was using his swords to their full potential and perfectly thwarting Logan's unpredictable hits and kicks. This fight was a real crowd-pleaser.

"Go, Wolf!" Alma leaned forward, totally engrossed.

"Logan's doing well. *Close Encounter* is a hard skill to use. Unless he can read his opponent better than they can read him, the opponent will counter him while his guard's down. He clearly trained hard to adjust his positioning so accurately."

Wolf and Logan fought frantically, then both suddenly fell to their knees.

"Agh..."

"Urgh..."

Injury and exhaustion had drained them both. Wolf's sword had torn open Logan's right arm, and Logan had hit Wolf full force in the ribs. Wolf was holding his left side, and Logan was bleeding profusely from his right arm. They were both sweating like crazy and struggled to stand.

"Wolf doesn't just have broken ribs; something hit his internal organs."

"Logan's hemorrhaging. It won't be long now."

Neither of them could fight for much longer. They both managed to stand up and glare at each other.

"Wolf, don't lose!"

"You're the man, Logan!"

Their parties' passionate cheers set the two Seekers' souls aflame. A purple flash surged from Wolf's body. A nimbus of yellow light emerged from Logan's manipura chakra.

Gladiator skill: *Purple Sword*.

Monk skill: *Close Encounter*.

They both simultaneously initiated the strongest skills at their command. This would be the end of the battle—the moment everyone had been waiting for.

"Hey! Look over here!" A voice like thunder echoed through the arena. The two stopped in their tracks at a voice they knew they shouldn't be hearing. It was rough, without a trace of mercy.

Veronica.

"Wha—?!" Wolf and Logan both cried out in surprise. Veronica had supposedly been dispatched, but there she was, standing tall and bathed in flowing tongues of crimson flame. Her normally chestnut brown hair glowed like a fiery corona. Wolf and Logan stared at her as if looking at a sunrise.

"Here I come," she said. She smirked, vanished, and reappeared before Logan.

Magician skill: *Warp Drive*. The skill of instantaneous teleportation.

Logan tried to counter Veronica's attack with a left hook, but—

"Too slow!"

Veronica hit him sharply, right in the liver. Logan fell, unconscious before he hit the ground. Veronica dished out just as much as she could take.

"I can't believe it!" Alma cried, leaping to her feet as if she'd been shot from a cannon. "That punch could've come from a front-liner. I thought Veronica was a Magician?!"

"Yeah, normally that wouldn't be possible. But Veronica isn't normal. She used *Sacrifice*."

Magician skill: *Sacrifice*. This skill forged a deep connection with a spirit when the Magician offered up an important part of her body. For Magicians, whose powers all came from the spirits, being linked to them was very important. The *Sacrifice* skill, learned after upgrading to the Magician subclass, improved the wielder's fighting ability exponentially.

However, it wasn't guaranteed to work, as there was a possibility the spirit would refuse the sacrifice and instead claim the Seeker's very life. Very few Magicians dared gamble with their lives to wield *Sacrifice*.

"Veronica has contracts with all the spirits, but she has a special affinity with fire spirits—the efreet. With that power, she's as strong as a spirit herself."

"Assimilation of a spirit, huh? That makes sense," Alma said.

Spirits were the consciousness of the natural elements that made up this world. By speaking with and borrowing power from spirits, Magicians were capable of changing the laws of physics. In a way, Veronica, who had achieved assimilation of spirit through *Sacrifice*, had already become a spirit. That is to say, she had the power of a raging inferno.

With Logan safely crumpled in a ball at her feet, she turned to Wolf. He raised his sword against her heavy, flaming fist and stumbled backward.

"Sh-she's strong... But why didn't she start with this tactic?"

"Assimilating a spirit requires an extremely elevated mental state. Just the will to win isn't enough. She could only use the skill because life was in danger."

"So if Logan hadn't knocked her out, she wouldn't have gained the power?"

"Probably. It looks like she was healed after the successful *Sacrifice*, but had the skill failed, she would've been doomed. Veronica took a huge gamble."

And boy, had her bet paid off. Wolf was no match for Veronica now that she had harnessed the spiritual power of fire itself.

"Veronica had something up her sleeve, just as you predicted, Noel." Alma looked up at me, smiling.

I nodded. "They were all of similar power level, but Veronica was the most prepared. She took a calculated risk based on how the battle was going. Looks like she sacrificed her right eye to the spirit. She's favoring her right side; she probably isn't used to the artificial eye yet."

As the empire was a magic-engineered civilization, the technology for artificial hands, legs, and eyes—made using beast materials—was advanced. She would never regain the right eye she'd given to the spirit, but she would be able to see just fine with an artificial eye.

"So it's over..."

Veronica's victory was certain. First King of Dukes and now Lightning Bite seemed to accept their defeat. Only Wolf wasn't ready to give up. I subconsciously held on to that hope.

"Win... Take it back," I whispered.

"Hurry up and fall!" Boiling with rage, Veronica stopped hitting Wolf, who was still refusing to give in, and put some distance between them. Then she created a fireball double the size of the last one.

"Concede or die! This is your last chance!"

"Shut up... Throw it if you're gonna." Wolf laughed provocatively, ignoring the wounds all over his body.

Veronica was ready. The flames she wielded were clearly infused with her determination to kill.

"In that case, die! *Inferno*!"

Magician skill: *Inferno*. Of all the fire-attribute skills used by Magicians, this was the most destructive. The ball of hell roared toward Wolf, but he didn't try to dodge. He brandished his sword, and it drew streams of purple lightning in the air around him. He was going to counter with Gladiator skill: *Purple Sword*.

"It won't work! Run!" Alma cried out desperately. The crowd was screaming too.

Only my shouts stood out from the rest. "Go! Don't give up, Wolf!"

I didn't know if he heard me or not.

In a flash, Wolf charged the fireball. His lightning speed was an effect of the *Purple Sword* skill. An electrical current supercharged his muscles, and the magnetic field rail that formed at swordpoint allowed for massive acceleration. It was a top-class Rank B attack skill in terms of both speed and destructive force. But no matter how fast or strong his body was, *Inferno* would reduce him to ash.

But Wolf knew something: electricity beats fire.

"Did he just...cut through the fireball?!" Alma's observation was accurate. According to the latest physics article I'd read to improve my own tactical acumen, even flames are affected by electrical fields. The stronger the electric force, the bigger the effects.

The electric current generated by *Purple Sword* had enough energy to split Veronica's fireball in twain.

I didn't think Wolf kept up with the latest scientific research, but in his will to live, he was able to find a way to survive in a crisis.

After piercing her fireball, Wolf, his hair gone and his flesh broiling red and black, closed in. Veronica slashed at him with a white-hot dagger, slicing through Wolfe's blade as if it were butter. On the counter-swing, she aimed for him.

That was when it happened. Wolf snapped a high kick to Veronica's right temple. He'd seen that she was favoring that side. The blow dropped her instantly, and she didn't wake again.

"Match! The winner is...Wolf Lehman!"

Wolf was the last one standing. I declared him the winner, and the crowd went nuts. It didn't matter if they were Lightning Bite, King of Dukes, or Red Lotus—everyone there accepted Wolf as the winner. It was that good of a fight.

"Amazing. Wolf won..." The dumbstruck Alma looked up at me, smiling.

"I told you, I'm not omniscient."

My job as referee was done, so I turned around to leave.

"Aren't you going to congratulate Wolf?" Alma asked. I shook my head.

"There are winners and losers. They don't need us to get involved."

"Yeah. Gotcha."

"Let's go. We have our own battle waiting for us."

I would never be able to fight like Wolf, but I had my own ways.

†

The day of the symposium had arrived. Most of the invited guests had already arrived at the hotel venue.

Nine clans had agreed to participate in the symposium, including ours. Every one of them was famous, and two especially so. One was Zeke's clan and the official host of the event, Supreme Dragon. The other was also a member of the regalia, Lorelai.

Borrowing Zeke's name to hold the symposium made it possible to get all the major clans there, but I never thought Lorelai would come. Whatever their objective was, it was good for me that they were in attendance, and I planned to use them as much as possible.

There weren't only Seekers in attendance. Various people of note, well-to-do sponsor candidates, and even aristocrats had been invited. Clad in gorgeous, formal attire, they lent the symposium some social cachet as they chatted in a spacious hall lit by crystal chandeliers.

On the table were elaborate hors d'oeuvres and plenty of alcohol. It was befitting of a hotel that catered to royalty and nobility. *Modern Opinion*, which had arranged the venue, had really splurged. If the company had invited all those people and tried to hold it at a cheap hotel, it would have been their last day in business.

I was wearing my tailcoat, and Alma stood beside me in her white dress. As long as she kept her mouth shut, Alma was breathtakingly beautiful. She was wearing high heels, so her short stature wasn't obvious. Just having her next to me caught the attention of everyone in the room. Koga and Leon weren't there. Due to security issues, only one representative per clan—and their plus-one, if any—was allowed to attend. Neither Koga nor Leon liked these sorts of events anyway.

"Oh, so you lead the snakes?" asked a merchant to whom I'd just introduced myself. "I heard that you took down that Garmr with only four Seekers. That's an amazing feat, especially for someone so young."

"I appreciate the compliment. It was thanks to my excellent clanmates," I responded.

"You don't need to be modest. No matter how skilled the

team members are, if the head of the organization is useless, there will be no victory. Even I can tell that you are a Seeker with exceptional talent."

"Even if that's true, it's all thanks to my grandfather. I was blessed to be taught by my hero, Overdeath, and he made me what I am today."

Hearing my grandfather's name, the man perked up with interest. "Ah, yes, Overdeath, hero among heroes. Superior blood lines really do produce results."

The higher the social class, the more they cared about bloodlines. I had no problem riding my grandfather's coattails. "I plan to become a Seeker worthy of my grandfather's name. I'm also looking for supporters to help along the way. If you're interested, let's set up a day to talk. What do you think?"

"Sure, let's set up a date."

I shook the man's hand and we exchanged business cards. How much could I squeeze out of this guy? He was a famous, wealthy merchant in the empire. If he were to sponsor us, we could probably get plenty of funding. There was still time until the symposium officially started, so I proactively chatted with the other guests and made the same promises.

"It's been the same conversation over and over," Alma complained, a somber look on her face. "My cheeks hurt from all the fake smiling..."

"Don't complain. We're doing it for money."

"Ugh. Ambitious little boys are nothing but problems," she grumbled.

"I'll say it again, but I'm not your little brother. Besides, there's something else you need to be thinking about. We only have one chance. If you miss it, it's over."

Alma held up her index finger. "No problem. Trust your big sister."

"Whose big sister?"

I had asked Alma to perform another task in addition to serving as my partner at the event. I was sure she would do fine, but she was so aloof that I was a bit worried. I sighed.

Then, I heard a voice from behind me.

"Hey, Noel. Are you enjoying all this time with the rich and fabulous?" asked Zeke. He was dressed all in black, from his shirt to his tie, and had a smile on his face, but Alma and I weren't looking at him. Our gazes were fixed on his date standing next to him.

She was a glamorous, showy blonde who in no way looked like a respectable person. Most of all, she was underdressed for the event, literally. She was wearing the scraps of cloth that just stuck to various parts of her body—the ones that Alma had wanted— and standing nonchalantly next to Zeke.

"Hey, see! She has the same outfit I picked out! Look!"

All I could do was facepalm.

"Ha ha ha. Maybe it's too exciting for a little boy like Noel," Zeke teased.

"Shut up... I really do hate you," I said. Zeke had probably only brought this trollop to mess with me. It was embarrassing to share a gender with this man.

"And is this beautiful woman the snakes' ace attacker, who I've heard so much about? Alma, was it? My name is Zeke Feinstein. I'm the vice-master of Supreme Dragon," Zeke said, bowing politely. "Nice to meet you."

"Likewise," she responded.

"I've heard that you're the granddaughter of the legendary Assassin, Alcor?"

"That's right."

"Wow. The grandson of a legendary hero and the grand-daughter of a legendary Assassin. It's thrilling to be in your presence at once. I'd love to set up a private sparring match."

"That's enough nonsense. Don't be ridiculous," I said.

Zeke just shrugged. "We'll discuss it another time. I have something to tell you."

"Me?" I cocked my head to the side.

Zeke nodded, then lowered his voice. "You should be careful around Lorelai. There are a lot of unpleasant rumors surrounding that clan. I'm sure they won't attack you in a public place, but you don't want them after you."

"I already know that," I answered without hesitation.

His eyes grew round. "You know them and invited them anyway?"

"Yeah. I didn't care which clans came, so long as I could take advantage of their reputations. It's a great achievement to get the regalia to attend."

"I see..." Zeke gave a little nod, then narrowed his eyes. "Noel, you're underestimating the regalia. They're not as easy to handle as you think. You might know a little bit, but if you don't watch out, all you'll know is your own grave. You guys are still weak."

It was harsh criticism. I looked at Zeke straight in the eyes. "Thank you for the warning, but you're wrong."

"What?"

"Regalia or not, it doesn't matter; I'll crush anyone who stands in my way. You're telling me not to underestimate the regalia? Don't mistake me for one of those jerks who can only fight beasts weaker than themselves."

I couldn't grovel to the regalia if I wanted to be one of them. It was precisely the difficulty that made it worth achieving. We stared each other down, until Zeke finally opened his mouth.

"I can barely contain my desire to burn you to a crisp," he said with a satisfied smile, looking around. He was eyeing the other clan masters. All of them were drunk, despite the fact that the symposium would be starting soon. They weren't belligerent, but I doubted if they were capable of making rational decisions.

"Look around. Even though the Seekers Association announced a Valiant crisis, none of the regalia clans are panicking. The major clan masters are nothing but a bunch of stiffs who count their easy victories," I pointed out.

"I don't like being compared to those guppies," Zeke said.

"Of course not. That's the kind of person you are. And that's why I have high expectations for you."

Zeke took a step back and looked me up and down. "I'm really looking forward to how this character is going to stir things up."

"I'll do what I can to not disappoint you," I replied.

"Naturally. You have an obligation. You better not let me down. I don't look it, but I actually have a very short temper. You don't want to see me angry." Zeke laughed savagely and led his wench away from us.

Right after Zeke left, Thomas from *Modern Opinion* ran up, out of breath. "Oh, there you are! I've been looking for you, Noel! It's almost time. Please go up to the podium," he instructed me.

"Thanks, I'll go now."

The cocktail hour had ended. It was time for the real show to start.

There were nine Seekers seated on the stage including myself. The chairs were lined up starting with Zeke from Supreme Dragon, then Johann Eissfeldt from Lorelai, and ending with me. Thomas, the emcee, was close to me and facing the audience.

"Thank you for waiting, everyone. We will now begin the symposium!" Thomas gestured toward us with his hand. "All the Seekers here today are well-recognized in the capital. No doubt, you're familiar with their work. We have invited them here to discuss the imminent manifestation of a Valiant, as was recently announced. I'm sure everyone is interested in how our famous Seekers plan to respond to the crisis that is upon us. We hope that this symposium will give all of those in the empire fearing for their lives some hope."

That concluded the opening remarks. It was our turn next. "Now, each of the Seekers will introduce themselves. First, we have the brilliant mind behind today's symposium: Zeke Feinstein, vice-master of Supreme Dragon. Welcome, Zeke."

Zeke stood up. "I am Zeke Feinstein, vice-master of Supreme Dragon. Thank you all for taking the time to attend. You must have a lot of free time. Do any of you have jobs? Nah, the only job you have is to lie back and relax. Actually, I've been doing plenty of that myself, as you can see by my stomach. Lack of exercise."

The crowd roared with laughter.

"Unlike everyone else up here, I am not a clan master. I'm a vice-master. However, I'm still the most powerful person on this stage. Thanks to my long list of achievements, I'm the only one up here to have achieved Rank EX. Please understand that I fully plan to act according to my position."

This "joke" killed too. I was the only one who understood he was dead serious. Once he was done introducing himself, Zeke sat in his chair and looked over at me for a moment. His eyes, full of curiosity, said, *"Let's see what you've got."*

"Thank you very much, Zeke. Next, Johann Eissfeldt, master of Lorelai. Please introduce yourself."

Johann, a tall man with silver hair, rose to his feet. He was in his late twenties, handsome and wore an ice-blue tuxedo. Just like Zeke, he had many female fans. "I am Johann Eissfeldt, master of Lorelai. Thank you for coming today. I'm not good at jokes like Zeke, so I hope to have a good discussion sans arrogance just for being part of the regalia," Johann threw keen sarcasm at Zeke, making himself sound commendable. The prideful Zeke frowned, offended.

After Johann's self-introduction was over, each of the Seekers introduced themselves in turn.

Lastly, it was my turn. "I am the clan master of Wild Tempest, Noel Stollen. I'm very honored to have been invited here today. I'm still quite new, so I appreciate the opportunity." I kept it short, and then Thomas took over again.

"Thank you very much, Seekers. Now, I would like to get right into today's topic. Everyone, please tell us what you think of the Valiant crisis. Zeke, we will start with you."

Zeke nodded, but Johann raised his hand.

"Excuse me, can I say something?"

"Yes, Johann."

"I think that question is a bit harsh."

"Wh-what do you mean?" Thomas asked.

Johann laughed awkwardly, "It is the regalia who will actually be fighting the Valiant. Naturally, everyone else will have important jobs as well. The Abyss generated when a Valiant is involved will be much larger than normal, and the rate of corrosion will be astounding. Furthermore, we have past data that the underlings will all have the strength of beast lords. So we're looking at an extremely wide danger zone, and we'll need Seekers in every city ready to fight lords. The last time a Valiant manifested, its Abyss spread over three countries before it was defeated."

The audience collectively gulped. They understood the threat of a Valiant, but there was something visceral about the fact that the Abyss had consumed three whole nations. It was as if the audience had all just been awoken from a drunken stupor.

"Everyone here is an excellent Seeker. All of the clans have achieved great things. At the risk of being misunderstood, I'd say there is a big difference between the regalia and other clans. I'm sure everyone understands that. I wonder if it's not a bit loaded to expect everyone to answer this question from the same perspective?"

"That's true... How would you rephrase the question, then?" Thomas asked.

Johann smiled brightly. "You don't need to change the question itself. I just don't think it's necessary for everyone to give an answer. May we have the right to refuse questions?" He then looked at us. "You guys don't want to be forced to answer every question, do you? If you feel something is over your head, feel free to pass it along to Zeke or myself, so you can relax."

The other clan masters started whispering among themselves. Basically, Johann was telling the non-regalia members to abstain from answering. It would have been easy to disagree with him, but whoever argued would be in hot water. They would be going against the regalia. Providing a half-baked answer would greatly hurt the impression of the clan. Shutting up and obeying Johann was the only sure way to avoid unnecessary shame.

That was when I realized why Lorelai—or Johann, rather— was participating in the symposium. Johann planned to eliminate those he thought were in the way and steal all the questions for himself and Zeke. He probably planned to take control of the event and draw information about Supreme Dragon out of Zeke.

"What do you think, Mister Moderator?" Johann asked. Thomas gave me a sidelong glance. Zeke was listed as the mastermind of the symposium, but only on paper. It was actually me.

Thomas was asking for my decision. I chuckled and raised my hand.

"May I say something as well?"

"Go ahead, Noel."

With his permission, I continued. "What Johann says makes sense. However, doesn't it sound like he's saying that the rest of us aren't qualified to talk, so we should just shut up?"

"That's quite a leap. I almost doubt your intentions. Uhh... Noel, was it? I was only making a suggestion. You are free to do as you like." Johann offered a dramatic shrug. He probably figured he had already planted the seeds, so no matter what I said, he would be the alpha here.

He had no idea. It was me, not Zeke, who'd planned this symposium. It would be easy for me to crush his superiority on a whim.

"Okay, how about this? Johann and Zeke can each be a leader, and we will separate into two groups. Each team will discuss their own opinions about the Valiant. That will reduce the burden of each person to speak, right? With all of these capable Seekers in attendance, it would be such a waste to limit them with the right to reject questions," I proposed.

"In essence, you want to make this a debate? Wouldn't it be troublesome to change the format now? People who want to answer can, and people who'd rather not don't need to. What's wrong with that?"

"We can see through your ostensible kindness," I said, changing my tone and staring directly at Johann. "Your objective is to control this venue. As a fellow participant, I wish to try to stop that."

Johann opened his mouth to protest, but before he could, Zeke raised his hand.

"I am in favor of changing the format. There should be no issues."

Johann's eyes grew wide with surprise. At almost the same time, the audience started voicing their approval as well.

"Zeke and Johann facing off in a debate? That sounds way more interesting!"

"I thought it was going to be boring to just listen to everyone politely ask and answer questions."

"Yeah! Make it more exciting!"

With that, the rest of the audience—who'd been awkwardly watching the argument between Johann and me—finally realized that this was shaping up to be an interesting show. The excitement grew in an instant, and everyone was on board with changing the format.

Johann was taken aback at this unexpected turn of events. He probably couldn't even fathom that I had several plants throughout the audience. There were countless dark rumors about Johann, and once I'd learned he would be attending, I had imagined every possible scenario as well as how to adjust the tracks so that things would still go my way. Hiring actors and instructing them to cheer at whatever I said was the bare minimum of preparations. Once they heard the audience's opinion, the other clan masters started to agree too.

"I'm also in support of a debate."

"Yeah...everyone is excited. I think we should change it too."

"I don't care what format it is; let's just get started."

They were trying to make it sound like this was an intelligent decision, but inside, they were probably just relieved. If the format changed to a debate, they could claim to have participated without saying anything on the record. In other words, they could maintain their positions as clan masters. Every idiot knew it was better to agree with the majority than disagree with the minority.

"Now, since the majority agree, I'd like to switch over to the debate. This topic is not just a yes-or-no issue, so it will be a team event. First, Zeke and Johann will speak on the topic. After that, each of the other Seekers will choose which leader they agree with. Once the seating has been arranged, we will begin the discussion." Thomas smoothly explained the format I'd described through Talker skill: *Link*. This way, Johann wouldn't be able to control me. "This is how we shall proceed, Johann. I hope you understand."

"Fine..." Grimacing, Johann nodded. Considering who was in attendance, he couldn't back out now. He had no choice but to agree. He rested his hostile gaze on me. I was happy to take him on. I would use him to his full potential here, before he figured out my true intentions.

It started with Zeke's speech.

"The Valiant is definitely a threat. Once it manifests, a lot of blood will be shed. On the other hand, by no means is it an enemy we can't beat—a fact that's already been proven." Zeke smiled bravely as he moved on to his main point. "Seekers are constantly evolving. That's because we have a system to inherit knowledge and technology from our forebears. It is the foundation for our progress. It's all thanks to the Seeker training school, the Appraiser Association, and other public organizations. I've run simulations based on the data from the most recently manifested Valiant, Cocytus the Silverfish, and given the current state of the empire, I believe we have an 80 percent chance of victory. At this rate, we won't lose. That's why I want everyone to feel secure in their everyday life."

The crowd broke out in applause. This was the first time I'd heard someone else quantify our chances. My estimate was about 30 percent. I wondered if Supreme Dragon had some sort of secret strategy, or if he was just blowing smoke... Either way, it seemed effective in putting the audience at ease.

After Zeke finished his speech, it was Johann's turn.

"Unlike Zeke, I believe we should have more urgency. We don't need to cower, of course. I plan to win. However, we should be considering ways to fight that limit the damage. No matter how advanced our civilization is, we'll be able to get back that which will surely be lost. It is the role of the regalia to integrate this into our strategy."

Johann's claim was credible, but I didn't believe that was his true opinion. What was his objective?

"Next, I would like to make a proposal. In preparation for the day of battle, I want all clans to entrust authority of their management to me. If you do, I promise to minimize damage and ensure victory."

The venue buzzed at this suggestion.

"Instead of each clan acting alone, if we reorganize and combine into one large group, command will be well integrated, and we can improve coordination. That is the most certain way."

So that was his strategy. He wouldn't be able to achieve it just by saying it here, but the heads of all industries were in attendance. If they agreed with what he said, they would back him up.

Johann Eissfeldt was more intelligent and audacious than I'd imagined.

"You want all the clans to integrate and obey you? Ridiculous. Are you serious?" Zeke spat, gaping at Johann with clear repulsion.

Johann kept his cool. "Actually, it's ridiculous for each organization to fight individually when the survival of the empire is at stake. Everyone should join together to fight."

"And that's why they should obey you? A mere third-tier clan master?"

"So all we have to do is become the top clan, then?" Johann asked.

"Surely you don't *really* think you can?"

"I plan to. Do you have a problem with that?"

Zeke laughed. "Ha ha ha. So you *do* have an even better sense of humor than I do."

The two men were both smiling, but their eyes were cold as ice. I couldn't see things going anywhere but a deathmatch. I looked at Thomas and telepathically sent him instructions for how to resolve the deadlock. Thomas nodded, albeit fearfully.

"J-Johann, does that conclude your remarks?"

"Yes, I'm done."

"Understood. Now then, the Seekers will divide into teams. Seekers, please choose which leader you agree with and sit on either Zeke's or Johann's side."

Following Thomas's directions, I sat on Zeke's side. There were four on Zeke's side and five on Johann's side. He only had one more, but it seemed his speech was pretty convincing.

"Maybe you should learn some rhetorical techniques?" I whispered to Zeke.

"Mind your own business," he said with a scowl.

And thus, the debate began. The content of the discussion boiled down to whether or not all clans should integrate in preparation for the battle with the Valiant. Those on Johann's side claimed to be in favor of it, and those on Zeke's side were against it.

"I'm for it. Considering the threat of the Valiant, I think it is the correct strategy."

"I'm against it. Why do we have to disband our clan?"

"No, wait a second. It's a temporary measure!"

"Who cares if it's only temporary? If we agree to it once, the same thing will just happen again and again, and it'll end up being the same as disbanding."

"All we have to do is arrange that in advance so it doesn't happen. The reality is that if we do not defeat the Valiant, there will be no clans to preserve."

"Where is the guarantee that the arrangement will be fair?!"

"Don't just think about your own rights! What about the danger to the country?!"

With Johann leading the yeas and Zeke leading the nays, the debate was heating up. The exchange was intense, and both those participating and those watching were full of excitement.

However, I purposely refrained from participating, merely observing instead. Everyone was getting whipped up into a frenzy. Eventually, once both camps had said all they had to say, Johann addressed me directly.

"Noel, you've just been sitting there, silent. I think it's about time you spoke up. After objecting to the right to defer questions, you're not going to participate at all?"

"Oh, you want me to talk, Johann?"

"Yes, I'd love it. I can't wait to hear your incredible opinion," he said, an edge to his voice.

Inevitably, all eyes were on me. Since both sides had already shared their thoughts, it was the perfect time for me to talk. "As you can tell by where I'm sitting, I am against the integration of all clans."

"Well, then, let's hear your reasoning."

"Each clan has its own way of fighting. Once the clans are integrated, there's no way to ensure coordination. Actually, there's a high possibility that it'll just make everything more confusing. So I'm against it."

"Don't you think it's rash to just decide that?" Johann crossed his long legs, trying to look undaunted. "I'll admit that each clan has its own way of fighting, but with strict policy and practice, that problem should be easily solved."

"'Should be,' eh? That's quite a passive argument. What makes you think you can control all the clans together with such a wishy-washy way of thinking? Most of all, I can't imagine they would want to join together and fight under someone so undesirable. Just slapping together clans so they look like they're cooperating won't lead to anything good."

"The survival of the country is at stake... Putting your own pathetic pride before the greater good is the epitome of stupidity. I believe that everyone here can make intelligent decisions."

"Heh heh. I'm pretty sure you're the one putting your pathetic pride first."

"What?" Johann's brow furrowed deeply.

I looked at him, my smile growing wider. "If you want to tout the greater good, then why start off by naming yourself commander? It would make more sense to entrust that decision to the Seekers Association, which manages all the Seekers."

"Certainly...it would be necessary to ask the Seekers Association too. But no matter the recommendation, the one who *makes* that recommendation has to show commitment and a sense of responsibility. I named myself as commander in order to show my commitment to my own ideas."

"It's a nice idea, but that doesn't give it merit. There are plenty of others more appropriate for the position of commander. If you want to claim that this is not in your self-interest, then removing yourself as a candidate would convince the other Seekers. I would love to hear your thoughts on that." I promptly turned the tables on him, and Johann was at a loss. However, a fake-looking smile slowly spread across his face and he started clapping.

"Wow, amazing. There is certainly some truth to what Noel says. I will take your opinion into consideration. Thank you *so* much." He was acting high and mighty, even though he couldn't answer my question. Apparently, this guy's MO was to always talk down to others and then avoid inconvenient questions. "Incidentally, what do you think is best, Noel? Can you share with us?"

Johann planned to offer some criticism of his own by switching the subject to me. Ah, but he had no idea. He was intelligent, but no match for me.

"No special measures are necessary. In fact, we shouldn't even take any special measures. If we take out the core beast within the Abyss, it will be purified, and the other beasts will be unable to proceed. All we need to do is quickly defeat the Valiant. That's the best way to prevent unnecessary damage. It is no different than fighting other beasts; if we overestimate the enemy and run around panicking, it will just complicate things."

"Ha ha ha. Pure sophistry. Haven't you forgotten something? We, the regalia, are the ones who will fight the Valiant. It's quite brazen to push something you could never do onto others and call it the optimal strategy. I would love to hear your opinion about that."

Johann smirked as if he had won. So I laughed back. "Ah ha ha, when did I ever say I was pushing it onto others? My clan will fight the Valiant on the day of battle, as part of the regalia, of course."

"Wha?!"

"I swear it on the name of my grandfather, Brandon Stollen, the great hero known as Overdeath: Wild Tempest will become part of the regalia before the Valiant manifests. Have no doubt," I declared.

This set the entire audience into a commotion.

"*He'll* join the regalia?! I thought his clan was only just approved?!"

"They don't have the strength or the track record! There's no way!"

"But that's the grandson of Overdeath!"

"Considering that and how they've advanced since, maybe it's not impossible!"

The audience was creating enough buzz even without my hired actors. All eyes were following my every move.

"That's enough nonsense!" Johann stood up, furious. "Shame on you for making wild claims about the future as a shield. You besmirch the title of Seeker with your lies!"

"Your nostrils are flaring, but I could say the same thing to you. Didn't you say you were going to become top tier? Wild claims about the future, indeed." I repeated his own words.

"Our clan is on a completely different level than yours! The amount of arrogance you must have to compare yourself to us is disgusting!" Johann yelled.

"You're the one who's arrogant. The regalia is not a tenured position; sometimes clans are switched out. So what makes you think you can stay in the regalia forever? Heh, I can see it now, you falling from grace." I chuckled.

Johann was shaking with anger at my provocations.

"Fine, then. If you're so confident, you can prove it. You'll show us evidence that your clan is good enough for the regalia," Johann said, surely confident that I couldn't do it. But that was a huge mistake. I was waiting for those exact words.

This all started with the question of whether or not all clans should be integrated, but thanks to Johann, the symposium was now centered around our clan proving that we were good enough for the regalia.

All according to plan.

"Fine. That's what you want, right?"

"Yeah, that's right..." Johann was recoiling at my confidence, but he couldn't take it back now. All he could do was nod.

"Well, who am I to refuse the request of the clan master of Lorelai, third-tier regalia? Everyone, thank you for your inconclusive debate. I would like a few minutes of your time, if you don't mind."

With that little address, I stood up. Zeke, my accomplice, didn't object, and neither did any of the other clan masters. Obviously. If it weren't for me, they'd have to obey Johann. None of them were dumb enough to go head-to-head with someone who was overwhelmingly better at speaking than they were in such a public place.

"I will construe your silence as approval. Is that okay with you, moderator?"

"O-oh, yes, please," Thomas said with a nod. I went to the center of the stage and faced the audience.

"As you all know, the title of regalia is granted by the emperor. Therefore, any clan worthy of the title must be not only strong, but also have the noble bearing sufficient to be a role model for all clans."

It was benevolence that moved people, not malice. My plot was already in motion.

"In order to prove that my clan is worthy of the regalia title, I promise to root out one of the malignant evils in the capital, right here and now. The name of that evil is fraud. An innocent person was falsely convicted, while a criminal who should be locked up is roaming free. Allowing this is inexcusable for the subjects of His Imperial Majesty," I declared.

The crowd was buzzing again. I smiled and continued.

"Everyone, do you remember the name Hugo Coppélia?"

The crowd broke out in an uproar when they heard the name Hugo Coppélia.

"Did he say Hugo Coppélia?!"

"The Bloody Taxidermist?!"

"Why is he bringing up a death row inmate?!"

It had been two years since the incident with Hugo. In that amount of time, they would have been forgiven for forgetting all about it, but due to the grotesque nature of the incident, most people remembered.

"Two years ago, a wealthy family was murdered. The person convicted for the crime was an extraordinary dollmaker, Hugo Coppélia. They say that Hugo not only murdered the family, but also peeled off their skin and used it to dress his dolls. Used their pelts for show, just like taxidermy. Therefore, as I'm sure you all remember, the media gave him the nickname 'The Bloody Taxidermist.'"

The faces in the audience creased with anxiety, remembering the horrific incident.

"It was a cruel and evil act. One of the victims was even a small child. When I think about their tragedy, it breaks my heart. I can never forgive the criminal who strayed so far off the path of righteousness. The perpetrator should indeed be given the death sentence."

I put my hand to my chest and closed my eyes, as if trying to tolerate the pain. Once I felt that my anger and sadness had been communicated to the audience, I opened my eyes and raised my voice.

"That's why I declare here and now that Hugo Coppélia has been falsely accused! The true criminal is still at large!"

At this allegation, the audience was at a loss for words. Then, after a short silence, they were all roaring again.

"What does he mean, falsely accused?!"

"Does he mean there was a mistake in the investigation?"

"This is an insult to the Department of Justice!"

"But what if it's true?!"

The audience was reaching the point of panic. What scared them was that I'd criticized the Department of Justice for making an error in judgment in a public place. That meant I was criticizing the government. Those present feared they would get in trouble by association, and that freaked them out.

"Quiet, everyone!"

Talker skill: *Peer Support*. When I yelled out with a skill to calm the target, the exclamations quieted to murmurs. It was quite a convenient skill. Versatile and useful even off the battlefield.

"I understand your surprise. However, I do not mean to sound extreme, nor am I trying to confuse you. I can say with absolute certainty that Hugo is innocent."

Now that the crowd was quiet, I puffed out my chest and spoke in a clear voice.

"The reason Hugo was arrested in the first place was because he was the only one alive at the scene of the crime. Considering the circumstances, he was a legitimate suspect. However, when Hugo was captured, he was already unconscious. Someone, or something, had put him to sleep."

According to the investigation, Hugo had been visiting the wealthy home to deliver a doll order. He was invited inside, and as soon as he stepped over the threshold, he lost consciousness. When he finally came to, the wealthy family was already dead. While Hugo was still in a daze, the military police showed up in response to a report and arrested him.

"According to the court records, Hugo was arrested simply because he was there, and alive. It didn't matter that someone else had obviously put Hugo to sleep; he was found guilty based on circumstantial evidence alone. Isn't there something wrong with that?" As I tilted my head to the side, someone from the audience shouted a rejoinder.

"Hugo was crazy! He's just lying about being put to sleep!"

This was one of my performers. Assuming someone in the crowd would voice disagreement, I'd planted these actors in order to control the dialogue. In the end, the other audience members just nodded, and no one else chimed in.

"Hugo was not crazy. The results of his psych evaluation were normal. However, he was *deemed* insane, and all his objections were denied."

"In that case, he's just flat-out lying!"

"That is a possibility. But if that were the case, the police should have investigated. Yet the public prosecutors decided from the start that Hugo was guilty and neglected to investigate, which is clear just by glancing at the court records."

In this empire, the Department of Justice was in charge of both the prosecution and the judiciary. The judge and the prosecutors worked together, so due process was up to the whims of the DOJ. The accused had little recourse when it came to defending themselves.

"The truth is: there was someone besides Hugo in the mansion—the person who reported the crime."

Hearing this fact caught the audience off guard. That tidbit hadn't been included in the court records. It was only in the investigation records that I was able to get my hands on, thanks to my informant, Loki.

"The person who reported it told the military police that they heard a scream coming from inside the mansion, but on the day of the incident, all the doors and windows in the mansion were shut. The mansion was a new construction and equipped with the latest soundproofing. There's also a large yard between the house and the public street. No matter how much someone screamed in the house, it would not have been audible from outside. In that case, how did this person know what had happened?"

The audience was clearly contemplating my question.

"As I'm sure you've all figured out, there is only one answer. The person who called in the report is the true criminal. Apparently, the public prosecutors realized this later, but they had already lost track of the reporting party by that time. Ordinarily, that would mean they should do everything they can to investigate, but in this case, the Department of Justice decided to resolve the case as quickly as possible, declaring Hugo guilty and putting a stop to the investigation."

It was the military police's job to search for suspects, but it was the public prosecutors' responsibility to instruct them to search. Without the Department of Justice's say-so, there would be no investigation.

"The only reason the Department of Justice found Hugo guilty was because they wanted it all over and done with. But why did they want to end the trial so quickly that they were willing to call off the investigation? It has to do with the state of affairs at that time."

I smiled at the audience, who was intently listening.

"Increased unemployment, tax hikes, and inflation. Right now, the economy is improving, but at the time, we were in the middle of a recession. In their dissatisfaction, the people had turned against the government. Amid all that, if it were known that a material witness had run from the scene of a mass murder with nary a shrug from law enforcement, there was a high possibility that the Department of Justice would have been on the chopping block. It most certainly would have been the target of bashing."

After the first perceived failure, the authorities would be condemned until the public found something else to be angry about. In the worst-case scenario, a large-scale riot could've taken place. It wasn't hard to imagine that the Department of Justice was frantic in order to avoid that.

"However, if they could resolve the issue quickly, not only would the Department of Justice maintain its prestige, but they would also be heroes. That's why the Department of Justice gave up on investigating the material witness and propped up Hugo as the perpetrator. That's what really happened."

The crowd created a clamor once more. Everyone looked as though they'd heard something they shouldn't have, but I still had control of the reins.

"That's all just conjecture! Do you have any proof?!"

Another audience plant. I nodded, smile still in place.

"Of course. I'm not a detective in some story, announcing my guesses. I only want you all to hear the confirmed truth."

With that, I gestured toward the entrance of the hall.

"I would like to provide you with proof that Hugo has been wrongly accused. Please welcome former Department of Justice Solicitor General, Count Lester Graham!"

The door opened, and Alma led in an elderly man wearing a judge's robe.

"Lord Graham?!"

"It's really him! I've met him before!"

"Lord Graham is a witness? What does this mean?!"

I understood the audience's surprise. He wasn't just an aristocrat; he was the man who was once the second-most powerful figure in the Department of Justice. He was a household name, and he was acquainted with most of the people in attendance.

"Lord Graham, please come to the stage," I told him.

"Ah, ahhh…" Lester timidly climbed up onto the stage.

He was lagging behind, so I whispered into his ear. "If you don't want me to tell everyone about you-know-what, you'll do the right thing here."

Lester broke out into a cold sweat and gulped, giving me a shaky nod.

He had been Solicitor General at the Department of Justice until six months prior, when differences with the current Minister of Justice forced his resignation. Ever since, he had lived as a hermit, cursing the one who'd kicked him out. He was a typical weakling, an inconsequential person. But that was exactly why he would be easy to use. This man also had a secret that he didn't want anyone to know—he was a pedophile. If that were exposed, he would lose all authority and honor, and his land would be seized. He had no choice but to obey me.

"Wh-what this boy says is…all true," Lester said, mustering the strength to speak. "The Department of Justice decided on Hugo Coppélia as the criminal in order to protect the members of the organization… It's all the Department of Justice's fault…"

"So that means the emperor is unaware?" an actor asked.

"Of course! The emperor had nothing to do with it. It is the result of the Department of Justice's recklessness," Lester insisted.

"I see. Lord Graham, what do you think should be done?"

"The truth should come out...and the boy who was falsely arrested should be released at once while the true culprit is hunted down. I am also responsible, as I was unable to stop the madness while I was Solicitor General."

He was claiming powerlessness, but I knew that this man felt no remorse whatsoever. Surely he'd had no intention of ever trying to help Hugo in the first place. He was certainly good at acting.

This was a great deal for him. Lester wasn't only cooperating due to my threat. Even stronger than that was his desire for revenge on the current Minister of Justice. It was clear he planned to use this incident to drag down the Minister of Justice and then make a comeback in the DOJ. Such a cowardly man would do anything to regain his position and power.

It didn't matter to me as long as he could get Hugo's conviction overturned. For all I cared, he could claim his reason for resigning was that he was the only one in opposition of Hugo's verdict. That would make us look even more justified. I could already see that the audience was mulling it over.

"Everyone, you now know the truth. While the Department of Justice reports to the emperor, it operates like an independent fiefdom for the benefit of its leaders and deceives the people of the capital. This is an unforgivable breach of trust."

The reason I'd instructed the actor to mention the emperor was to emphasize that it was the Department of Justice being denounced, and to clarify that we were not going after the entire government. It was also to make it clear that it was because the Department of Justice was trusted by the emperor—and by extension, the entire country—that this sort of evil could not be allowed to stand. The audience could come to that conclusion on their own.

"Hugo Coppélia was born the third son of a poor shoemaker. He was raised in poverty, never knowing when his next meal would be. However, he was blessed with the talent of a Puppeteer, which gave him the chance to escape that life," I told the audience. "After enjoying great success as a Seeker, he decided to use his savings to become a dollmaker. He was a gentle man who wanted to retire from fighting so he could bring smiles to people's faces with the dolls he made. You all know about his reputation."

Hugo's dolls were loved by all, throughout the entire world. I was sure some in attendance were fans of his work.

"Two years already have been stolen from this wonderful person as he rots away in jail for something he didn't do! Think about the sadness! It tears you apart! I want to save him right now! No, we must save him!"

People silently nodded. I could see some of their faces shining with tears.

"To that end, I ask for your help! First, make a petition and ask for the death penalty to be revoked! We must demand justice for the empire!"

When I was done, there was a round of applause. It started with one of my actors, but more joined in, and thanks to peer pressure, everyone was soon clapping. The venue was filled with thunderous claps and cheers.

Anyone who signed the petition would be publicly committed to their position. News of what occurred there would spread throughout the capital, thanks to Thomas and *Modern Opinion*. There were so many prominent names here that the Department of Justice would be forced to revoke the death penalty. After that, if we could gain even more support throughout the capital, Hugo would definitely be set free. In turn, my reputation would improve, and I would be able to recruit even more sponsors.

"Noel."

While I was busy patting myself on the back, I got a telepathic message from Alma.

"I found him. I'm sure. Just like you said, the mastermind behind the crime is here."

"I see. Good job."

I hadn't been able to find the criminal who framed Hugo even with Loki's help. It was a cold case, after all. All the evidence was long gone. However, with vigorous investigation, we were able to narrow it down to a handful of suspects. Every one of them had been invited to the symposium, and every single one had shown up. They must have been surprised indeed when I started claiming Hugo was wrongly accused. It must have been a bolt from the blue. Their heart had surely skipped a beat.

Because of that, they would react differently than everyone else.

I'd ordered Alma in advance to observe people's reactions. It was hard even for Scouts and Archers, who had superior perception skills, to spot certain behaviors of people in a crowd. But Alma was more than capable.

I could predict what the mastermind would do next. My job now was to use his actions to my advantage. I sensed someone staring intensely at the back of my head and turned around to see Zeke with a satisfactory smile on his face. Johann, next to him, wore an extremely hostile look, having finally understood my true intentions. The other clan masters had seemingly also figured out that the symposium was all my idea. Some looked intrigued, whereas others looked wary.

I faced them and did my best theatrical bow with my hand on my chest and one foot behind me, assuming they would take it as mock courtesy.

"My respected seniors, thank you for listening to my speech."

It didn't matter to me if someone was part of the regalia, an aristocrat, or the emperor of the entire country. I would use everyone, and I would swallow them all whole.

This was how I fought as a Talker.

†

Hugo Coppélia's skills as a Seeker were second to none. However, even with his great abilities, he'd never tried to join a group. Hugo loathed violence. Even though he was blessed with

Seeker abilities, he hated the job, since it was about meting out violence. He'd become a mercenary solely for the money.

From the perspective of those who were working desperately as Seekers, it was an irresponsible and insulting motive. But the Seeker industry, of course, was all about results. Even if one's motives weren't pure, having overwhelming achievements to boast of was enough to shut everyone up.

It was precisely because of the harsh reliance on his abilities that Hugo, who always won no matter whom he faced in battle, became known as the Invincible Mercenary. There were plenty of people who wanted Hugo for their own clan, but he turned them all down. No matter how good the offer, Hugo never even considered belonging to one organization. Most of all, he had no desire to be a Seeker forever.

But some offers were harder to refuse than others.

By the time Hugo was twenty-one years old, he was reaching his peak as a Seeker. Though he was famed throughout the capital, the woman he was dining with that evening was someone he could never offend.

He had been invited to the most prestigious restaurant in the capital. Reservations had to be made three weeks in advance, and just eating there made you the talk of the town. Hugo had grown up on the streets, but a decade after his assessment, he had become a splendid young man who looked like he belonged in a restaurant of this caliber.

When he entered the restaurant and told the host his name,

he was shown to his table. Hugo sat in his seat and smiled at the woman who was waiting for him.

"I'm honored to meet you, Miss Valentine."

"The pleasure is mine. Thank you for coming today."

The woman smiling gently back at him was Sharon Valentine. She was an elf with shiny white-gold hair and graceful features. She was clad in a double-breasted dress jacket that resembled a military uniform. Her goal was to headhunt Hugo, but she was different from the rest. She was vice-master of Supreme Dragon, the strongest clan in the capital and top tier of the regalia.

Hugo had no interest in working as a Seeker, but he couldn't ignore Sharon. As Supreme Dragon's vice-master, she was an excellent strategist; her many martial innovations had had significant influence on Hugo. This was the first time he had met her in person, but he had looked up to her for a long time. Naturally, Hugo was happy to meet her. Considering that, what happened next was regrettable.

"Let's enjoy our meal and save the serious talk for later." Sharon continued to smile cordially and called over the waiter. After their food and drinks came, they ate and talked and laughed.

Once the dishes were cleared, Sharon finally got serious. "Now that we've eaten, let's get down to business." Sharon listed Supreme Dragon's recent achievements and what they were willing to offer Hugo if he would join them. As the strongest clan in the capital, the offer was extremely appealing. "What do you think, Hugo? I think joining Supreme Dragon would be a good deal for you. If the offer isn't sweet enough, I'll consider giving even more. You're worth it."

"I'm very flattered. But..." Hugo cast his eyes down. "I'm very sorry. I have to decline."

"If something wasn't satisfactory—"

Hugo held up his hand. "Miss Valentine, it isn't that I don't appreciate your offer."

"Then...why?"

"The idea is definitely appealing. Belonging to Supreme Dragon would be the greatest honor. It hardly makes sense to refuse. However, I do not plan on continuing as a Seeker."

Sharon's eyes grew wide with surprise. "You don't plan to continue? So you're going to retire?"

"Yes. I plan to retire this year, in fact."

"What will you do with yourself?"

"I am going to make dolls. After a few more gigs, I will have enough funds to live comfortably as a dollmaker for the rest of my life. Please, do not misunderstand. The reason I became a Seeker in the first place was so I could make enough money to become a dollmaker. Once I reach that goal, there is no reason for me to continue as a Seeker."

Sharon nodded, finally understanding. "I see that there's nothing I can say to dissuade you."

"I am very sorry."

"There's no need for you to apologize. I'm the one who asked you for something impossible. But it's really unfortunate. Just imagine the clan Supreme Dragon could be if you joined us."

Looking at Sharon's genuine disappointment, Hugo felt a sense of guilt, but it wasn't enough to change his mind. Hugo had dreamed of becoming a dollmaker for many years, and during that time, he'd never grown to like Seeker work.

"You know, soon..." Sharon said, tracing her wine glass with her finger, "I plan to pass the position of vice-master to my apprentice. That's why I wanted to contribute to the clan as much as possible while I was still vice-master. I suppose I'll have to find another way."

"By apprentice, might you mean Zeke Feinstein?" Hugo asked.

Zeke was a hot topic among Seekers. He was a Swordsman about Hugo's age with extraordinary gifts. Evidently, Sharon was in charge of his education. Hugo had heard that he already surpassed Sharon in his ability on the battlefield.

"Yeah, that dummy," Sharon said with a laugh. "He has a horrible personality and horrible taste in women, and he's not the brightest, but his talent is the real deal. He's even trying to achieve Rank EX, something I could never do."

"Rank EX..." Hugo murmured in wonder.

The class ranks ranged from C to EX, but almost no one ever reached Rank EX. Rank A was generally treated as the highest rank. Were Zeke able to achieve Rank EX, that would make two EX-Ranked members of Supreme Dragon, further securing the clan's top position.

"Supreme Dragon will be even stronger," Sharon said, as if she were reading Hugo's mind. "I'd do anything for that."

"Is it really so important to you?"

"Yes, very. To me, Supreme Dragon is like my child."

Hugo understood that she wasn't at all exaggerating, as was

one of the founding members of Supreme Dragon. He heard that in the beginning, it was just her and Victor Krauser, the master.

Over the next few decades, she had worked to increase their numbers and expand the organization, like a mother raising a child. There was no doubt that Supreme Dragon was the most important thing in the world to her.

"Hugo, you've always been a mercenary, right? Isn't it lonely?"

Hugo gave a wry smile. "No. Not at all." Even before becoming a Seeker—pretty much since birth—Hugo had been alone. He had been able to make it this far on his own, proof that he didn't need anyone else. "I can live without friends."

"My, isn't that a bit extreme?"

"No, I don't think so. I will admit that friends are important, but not necessary. For me, being alone is more comfortable."

"Hmm." Sharon narrowed her eyes and stared at Hugo, observing him.

"What is it?"

"I really hold you in high regard. But..." The gentle beauty flashed a cold, hostile smile. "You don't look so strong."

Hugo felt the blood rushing to his face. He respected Sharon, but where did she get off talking to him like that when they just met? Then he calmed himself down. There was some truth in what Sharon said. At any rate, Hugo should have kept his values to himself instead of sharing them with her. His was definitely an unpopular opinion, but he didn't particularly care if anyone agreed or not. He knew that already and the only reason he'd spoken to Sharon about it was because of the alcohol. Hugo scolded himself, thinking it wasn't like him.

"Please do not torture me too much. I am just a silly kid," Hugo said with a self-deprecating shrug.

"Ah ha ha, sorry, sorry. I have this habit of sounding like I'm lecturing."

"No, I was imprudent. Alcohol does funny things to people."

"Yes. I don't think you're wrong, though. The way I said it came off as insulting, but it's not that I think you're weak. I think you're a strong and amazing person. It just seems like your ideals and the real you don't quite match up."

Just then, Sharon stuck her finger in her own left eye.

"Wh-what are you doing?!" Hugo cried in surprise, but Sharon kept working her finger into her eye socket, pulling her eye out.

"Don't be startled. This is an artificial eye."

He could see that the eyeball in the palm of her hand was fake.

"It's made of extremely expensive beast materials, and I use it like this."

The artificial eye spread its wings and hovered a bit.

"I lost both my eyes in battle long ago. I've been using this artificial eye ever since. It's quite convenient. One flies to wherever I order it, and the other conveys the images it sees back to me. With these, I can spy on anything."

"So...you spied on me with that eye too?"

"Well, of course," she admitted. "Within reason."

Hugo let out a deep sigh. "Miss Sharon...I will trust that you had good intentions."

"Tee hee. Thank you. Your fighting style is as amazing as everyone says. It really is true that Puppeteer is the strongest of all classes. It made me think that it wasn't fulfilling."

"Fulfilling?"

"You're *too* good. Since you're good at everything, you don't need to have passion. Even fame doesn't move you."

He started to understand. "I have no passion for my work. Most of all, like I said before, I am only a Seeker to earn the funds I need. I do not need to be fulfilled," he explained.

"You seem rational, but it sounds like you're holding yourself back."

"Well..." Hugo hesitated, and Sharon put her eyeball back into her eye socket.

"I also looked into your history. Your past has made you too used to compartmentalizing—no, too used to giving up." Hugo stayed silent as Sharon went on. "Friends aren't just there to help each other. They can also serve as rivals that boost each other up and encourage each other to grow."

"Are you trying to get me to rethink my answer?"

"I'm not that persistent. But take this as advice from your elder. You should continue as a Seeker."

"Why is that?"

"You are a treasure in the Seeker world. If you remain a Seeker, you will meet someone who genuinely wants to become your friend. The hole in your heart from your habit of giving up will heal. Maybe it's better to say that your friend will motivate you."

Hugo's lips quirked up once more. He thought it was none of her business, but he lied, "I'll think about it."

After some time had passed, Hugo retired from being a Seeker and became a dollmaker, just as he'd said.

However, the fate of death row for a crime he didn't commit would be waiting for him two years later.

✝

When Hugo awoke from a fitful sleep, the moon was shining through the barred window.

"A dream..."

The expensive restaurant was gone, and he was still in jail. The shock was severe, and he grew instantly depressed.

But his situation had improved from before. First of all, he was in a different part of the prison now. Hugo was being kept in a room for aristocrats. There was a bed and a toilet. It was a far cry from the previous cell, which only had straw and a bucket.

He also had the leisure to work on his appearance. His hair was cut, he was clean-shaven, and though his clothes were simple, they weren't of poor quality. The collar to keep him from using his skills had also been removed. Compared to before, it was downright civilized. The food was better and he received supplements, so he was regaining his strength. He was still skinny, but the malaise that had kept him from standing was gone.

If he asked the prison guards, they would even bring him books or newspapers. It was all thanks to Noel. It was even written in the newspaper on Hugo's bed: "Bloody Taxidermist Framed?! Wild Tempest Clan Master Noel Stollen Exhibits Proof at Symposium!"

The newspaper was from last week. Thanks to Noel, the truth of the incident had been revealed. The true culprit hadn't been apprehended yet, but at least no one thought Hugo was a criminal anymore. Now the world considered Hugo to be a victim, and they were demanding his release.

The Department of Justice held a press conference and explained the situation, but all they did was make excuses, and there was nothing to mitigate the anger of the people. Considering the worsening situation, the current Minister of Justice would surely be removed from office.

Hugo was still officially on death row, but for all intents and purposes, the sentence was as good as revoked. The reason he couldn't leave yet was that he was mid-appeal. No matter how much evidence there was that he was innocent, it had to be presented in court. An acquittal without an official retrial would reduce the justice system to a mere formality.

Once the reexamination began, he was sure to be freed immediately. Despite the long hell he had lived through coming to an end, Hugo let out a deep sigh. "If only I had listened to Sharon, this would have never happened…"

Even after becoming a dollmaker, Hugo hadn't grown close with anyone. He was alone. He had no friends to save him. That was what made him the perfect target to frame for a crime. At the time, he'd never dreamed that he would end up on death row.

Even though it was all hindsight, he was forced to reflect on the error of his ways.

"Friends..."

He wondered if it would even be possible for him to change. Even after everything that had happened, he couldn't imagine living with someone else. Sharon was right; Hugo was too used to giving up.

There was only one thing he knew. "Noel Stollen... I see it now. You are the strongest Seeker."

In his years as a mercenary, he had come to know many Seekers, but he had never seen or heard of anyone who could fight like him. Although Noel was far inferior to other fighters as far as physique, Hugo had already started to consider him to be the strongest.

Part of it was gratitude. Maybe Hugo just saw Noel at his best. But even setting that aside, Noel's talent was exceptional. There was no precedent for a Seeker that led the government by the nose.

"A snake..."

Noel had already established his clan and named it Wild Tempest. Their symbol was a winged snake. The newspapers often referred to the clan as the snakes because of the symbol.

"You're like a snake. You're not just crafty and ruthless; you get close to your prey and then swallow them whole. It's horrifying."

Hugo remembered the words he'd once said to Noel.

"Ha ha ha. You used the name I gave you." Hugo laughed out loud, wiping tears from his eyes. "That's good. Ahh, it really is good..."

Inside Hugo's chest was a tiny, flickering flame that had been set alight.

†

A week had passed since the symposium.

Just as I'd planned, Hugo now had public opinion on his side, and the administration was scrambling to respond. A citizens' group had been formed, and its leader was Count Lester Graham. Naturally, I was secretly the director. I kept in close contact with Lester to make sure that he followed the script I provided him and that he immediately shared any information he got with me.

The current situation was very advantageous to Lester, so he was unlikely to betray me, but he was an idiot. I had zero trust in him whatsoever. Even if he didn't plan on betraying me, acting independently of my directives could lead to him doing it by accident. In order to prevent that, I needed to be aware of everything he did until we managed to free Hugo.

The Department of Justice held a press conference, but it just ended up rubbing the citizens the wrong way. An unjust legal system would inevitably erode the foundation of society. Everyone knew the danger inherent in the guardians of the law actively neglecting the law.

It hadn't been announced yet, but it had already been decided that the incumbent Minister of Justice would be removed from his position and Lester would take his place.

Hugo was still being held on the pretext of an upcoming re-trial. The atrocity of the Department of Justice had been made public, but the true culprit hadn't been apprehended, and Hugo's innocence still hadn't been proven in court. As long as Hugo was still in custody, the matter wouldn't be settled. It went without saying that the administration wanted to resolve this matter as soon as possible. To that end, they were trying to control the situation by negotiating with Lester and promising him the position of Minister of Justice. Their claim was that if Lester became the new Minister of Justice and used his authority to reopen Hugo's case, the new system would be clean. It was a scheme to neutralize the distrust of the citizens.

According to administration estimates, it would take about a month for Lester to become the new Minister of Justice. The current Minister of Justice was a highly ranked aristocrat. No matter what the reason for removal, appropriate preparations were necessary—even more if he was to be treated as a criminal. Until those preparations were in place, the administration couldn't make a move.

Hugo would have to cool his heels behind bars for another month.

"Of course, there's the issue of what I can do in the meantime. Just waiting feels like such a waste. I'll hurry up and get what we need."

All of Wild Tempest had gathered at the newly remodeled clan house. I was sitting in a chair in the office.

Koga cocked his head to the side. "Ya know who was behind

it now, right? So why don'tcha just catch 'im and hand 'im over to the military police? If the true culprit's arrested, there'll be no reason to hold Hugo anymore."

Just as Koga said, apprehending the real culprit would affect his release. Still, that wasn't all there was to it.

"Koga, you really are a dummy," Alma scoffed. She was leaning against the wall as casually as she was speaking. "Noel was able to plant Lester as the new Minister of Justice because we kept the identity of the real killer a secret. If we blabbed and completely resolved the issue instead, we wouldn't have been able to plant Graham, who's under our control, into the Department of Justice."

"Y-yeah, but—"

"You're just incompetent. You should start over from the sperm stage."

"Hey, ya don't gotta insult me!"

I sighed at their never-ending banter. "Our priority is definitely to clear Hugo's name and recruit him into our clan. However, thinking of the future, we need to use everything we can to its full potential."

"If we don't get him released quickly, what if the administration changes their mind and assassinates him?" Leon asked, a note of concern in his voice.

I shook my head. "The administration won't assassinate him. If he were to die in prison, people would pour into the streets and things would get far worse. Also, everyone who's currently guarding Hugo works for me. According to them, the prison wardens are treating him well to get on his good side. Heh heh.

If it were to become public that they were treating an innocent man inhumanely, there's no telling the rage it would cause. Right now, they want to regain trust."

"I hope so..." Leon was convinced, but he still looked worried. "We're going to execute your strategy, then?"

"Yeah. Everything is ready to go."

Leon scrunched up his face. "There's no changing your mind?"

"We're doing it. It's already been decided. Don't worry; it will go perfectly."

"N-no, I'm not worried about it succeeding. It's just that your plan is so—ow! My stomach!" Suddenly suffering from stomach pain, Leon rushed to pull something out of his medical pouch.

"You're so petty."

"Noel, yer just too brave. Yer ideas are..." Koga trailed off, looking exasperated.

Just then, we heard what sounded like a horse neighing outside.

"Noel, a visitor."

Alma looked outside and grinned. "Just as you predicted, Noel. It's Finocchio Barzini."

The other three showed Finocchio, who had come in a carriage, to the office. I entered as well. Per my instructions, my clanmates waited outside the room.

"Long time no see, Noel. I'm glad to see you look well," Finocchio said, flashing a smile. He was wearing his gaudy purple clothes, but his eyes were cold and dark. "You know why I'm here, don't you?"

"Hmm. I guess it's not to be my bestest friend?"

Finocchio snorted, offended. "Don't be coy with me. A snake, right? It suits you perfectly. You really are a wretched person. You already know the mastermind behind Hugo's incident, right? And you know he has an intimate relationship with my family."

My lips crawled up in a grin.

"It's Andreas Hooger, president of Hooger Commerce," he said.

It was the same person Alma had pointed out at the symposium. Hooger Commerce was a major business and prominent in the capital, but it was relatively new. Once Andreas took over, the firm grew rapidly and formed close ties to the Luciano family, which actually controlled the empire behind the scenes.

Once we'd determined Andreas was behind the murders, I'd asked Loki to investigate him again. What he found was that Andreas was smuggling beast materials to other countries. Not only that, but he was also selling inventions and technical information. To countries prospering through magic-engineered civilization, nothing was more valuable than beast materials and the developments that incorporated them. This was a serious crime, but it was the insanely high risk that made it so lucrative.

The head of the wealthy family that Hugo had been framed for killing had been one of Hooger's competitors. Obviously, an expanding business meant more rivals. Besides Andreas, that wealthy merchant had many other competitors. This multimillionaire had caught wind of what Andreas was doing and threatened him, as we'd found out after determining that Andreas was the mastermind behind the murders.

"Andreas killed his burdensome rival and framed Hugo for it.

Now I know the truth that was supposed to have been covered up. I imagine that the Luciano family also wants to settle the issue, given your close relationship with Andreas." I looked straight at Finocchio as I continued. "That's why I knew you would come here. Besides, ever since you were forced to let me go, you've had a major inferiority complex."

Finocchio laughed awkwardly. "Your only redeeming quality is your face. So you have everything in the palm of your hand? Well...it's true that I let you off knowing that you would cause the family trouble again. I'm certainly responsible for that." Finocchio shook his head and recouped. "Andreas is a very important customer. I can't stand by when he has a problem, so you need to decide, Noel. You will need to either forget about the whole thing, or kill me. You can only pick one."

I felt something strange. Magic power that didn't belong to me was flowing through my body. I recalled the time Finocchio had pulled my heart from my body.

Criminal skill: *Judgment*. Criminal was an A-Rank subclass of Scout, and the *Judgment* skill Finocchio possessed could immediately kill the target. If I continued to refuse him, my heart would simply leave my body. Before, I hadn't even felt this awkward sensation, but I could now, thanks to my new rank—though I still wasn't strong enough to resist it.

"Wow, scary. I'm so scared, I think I might wet my pants." I shrugged.

"There's no need for jokes. I'm not in the mood." Finocchio glared at me with eyes like ice.

"What happened to the 'mad clown' character? You look more like a hospital receptionist. Doesn't seem like you're enjoying yourself at all."

"Even if you decide to live as a snot-nosed brat, you *will* play your role... It's called being a man," Finocchio growled.

"I see. How reasonable. Exactly what I would expect of you, Finocchio Barzini. You're not like the petty Albert. You're a real man." I couldn't bring myself to hate this fop. Actually, I kinda liked him. "Finocchio, I'm not like I was then. If you really try to kill me, you're the one who will die. If I say the word, my three clanmates will charge in here."

"I figured. You have a great team. Even at A-Rank, I can't possibly take on all four of you. But I wonder why... Do you really think I would let you live? Huh?!"

"No way! You really are a man. I know that if necessary, you'll throw away your own life without a second thought. But what's the fun in both of us throwing our lives away right here? Is Andreas really worth you putting your life on the line?" I asked.

Finocchio shook his head. "I'm not risking my life for Andreas; I'm doing it for the family. Too bad, little Noel. Your sweet talk is useless on me. Now, I'm ready to hear your decision. Yes or no?"

"Ahh, for the family. That is impressive loyalty. But you're mistaken, Finocchio. If you were really thinking about the family, you would cut Andreas off."

"Is this your gift of gab? I told you—"

I held up my hand to stop Finocchio and pulled out a stack of papers from my desk drawer, then handed it to him.

"What is this? Huh?! A tournament open to all Seekers? Wh-what is this, seriously?" Just the first page had him yelping in surprise.

"It's exactly as you've read. I am going to hold a tournament in the capital. Not one of the underground matches that only the JV fighters show up for. It will be the first official Seeker competition in the empire. You understand the value in that, don't you?"

"I-I do. The main job of a Seeker is to hunt beasts. There have been plans for competitions in the past, but no one wanted to join for fear of injury. If it does happen, this first attempt will be extremely profitable. B-but it's impossible! No one will fight!"

"We just have to set up the right rules. It's all there in the documents, so take some time to read it later. Also, I've already got some big names interested. For example, the vice-master of Supreme Dragon and one of the few EX-Rank Seekers, Zeke Feinstein." I showed him Zeke's signed consent form.

"Zeke Feinstein?! R-really? Are you serious? Er, wow... H-how did you get the strongest man alive to sign? I-I can't believe it..." Finocchio was dumbstruck.

"What do you think?" I asked, smiling. "Sure sounds like it's going to happen, right?"

"Yeah, but...this..."

"If you want, I can fit another page in the plan. Actually, why don't you just run the whole thing? Then you can make it a regular event. How much do you think it will rake in? At the very least, it'll be way more than anything you could get from Andreas. Even more than he would ever bring you in the future."

"W-well..." Finocchio was shaking.

I laid it on thicker. "Finocchio, use that money to become the new Luciano boss. You can control the whole family."

"Huh?! Wh-what did you say?"

"Hey, now, there's no reason to be so surprised. You're second in line, after all. You wouldn't ordinarily become leader of the top family, but you're a candidate for succession. No one would mind if you took over as the new boss."

"Th-that's true, but... We have our own way of doing things..."

"You're hesitant." I stood up and walked toward Finocchio, then looked up at him. We were standing at the same distance as last time. "I am the king of me. No one will hold me back."

"Y-you..."

"Finocchio, you will become the head of the Luciano family and control the empire behind the scenes. I will become top tier of the regalia, and I'll exercise my authority publicly and honorably. If we work together, the empire is all ours."

Finocchio's face grew pale and he took a step back. "Are you... trying to usurp the throne?"

"Don't misunderstand. I have no interest in ruling. What I want is the strongest position, one no one will argue with. Don't you remember? You said, 'After beating me at chicken, you'd better make it to the top, or you will pay.' This is that path to the top."

Hearing me quote what he'd said word for word, Finocchio backed up another step.

"But still, what you're saying doesn't make sense... It's not right..."

"Finocchio, that's two steps."

"Wh-what?"

"Last time, you only took one step back. This time, it's two. How far are you going to go next time? Are you going to just get cold feet and leave? I thought you were a man," I said, explicitly taunting him.

"Y-you dumb brat! I don't care what you say!" Finocchio was furious, emanating bloodlust. I wouldn't have been surprised if he cut off my head right then. But I didn't run away or even avert my eyes.

"Decide, Finocchio Barzini. No, mad clown. Do you want to die for the likes of Andreas, or do you want to climb all the way to the top with me? You can only pick one. Now, decide! If you're a man, then answer me!"

"Ergh..."

Finocchio grimaced, looking frustrated.

But I knew I'd broken him.

Finocchio was angrier than he had ever been in his life on the carriage ride home.

"It's so infuriating!"

His underling sighed as Finocchio stamped his feet. "Boss, please don't throw a tantrum in the carriage. It's bad manners."

"Shut up! I know that! But I'm pissed off, so what do you expect?! Why do I have to be torn down by a dumb brat without a prick?! Where does he get off saying, 'Now, decide! If you're a man then answer me!'? Die, die!"

"And then you agreed to it to show off, right? So you brought it on yourself." His subordinate was unsympathetic.

"Shut up! Dumbass! How can I back down after that?! You're right, I said it! I said I would help! What's wrong with that? I know it's wrong! It's all my fault! Ugh!" Finocchio scratched his head violently and bit down on his handkerchief. "It's so frustrating! Why do I, Finocchio Barzini, have to be treated like a booty call?!"

"Boss, I told you—"

"You! One more word and I'll kill you!" Glaring at his underling, Finocchio really did look like he would kill him, and then he let out a sigh so big, it was like his soul had left him. "How am I going to explain it to the president?"

"Do you have to tell him? Everything today was at your own discretion."

"No, I can't just keep quiet. The president knows that I know Noel, and if I don't tell him, he'll ask me. He'll tell me to do something."

Noel's tournament idea had real appeal, but at this point, it was still just a pipe dream. It wouldn't be enough to convince the president yet.

"In that case, why don't you stay holed up at home for a bit? You can say you don't feel well, so you can't deal with the Noel issue."

"Why would I tell such a transparent lie?"

"Just to buy time. That snake will figure out a scheme to crush Andreas. When that happens, everything will work out, and you won't have to explain a thing. You won't need to tell him about the Seeker tournament, so you can run it all yourself."

"B-but if we don't make a move, then another family might steal Noel from us," Finocchio said, cocking his head to the side.

His underling let out a sinister laugh. "Let's end him ourselves by setting up a revenge killing, using another family's Assassin."

"Oh, my," Finocchio put his hand to his forehead and furrowed his brow. "My, oh, my, that is a dangerous suggestion. To kill our own friend? It's savage. It's scary. What should I do? It's utterly unforgivable." Finocchio was speaking negatively about it, but his words were robotic, as if they had nothing to do with what he truly thought. In fact, his eyes crinkled as if he were imagining something even more pleasurable.

"Just don't get caught, Boss. It's all good if you don't get caught."

"Ugh! You're so bad! I want to see the parents who raised you! I don't know anything! If another family's Assassin dies, I'm sure it will just be an accident! An accident! I've not done a-a-anything wrong!" Finocchio bit his lip to keep from laughing and looked out the window. The scenery flashing by was the same as always, but for some reason, he thought it looked brighter that day.

"If we work together... He can say that now."

There was a saying that if you hadn't seen a boy in three days, to be careful, and Noel really had grown up fast. Much faster than Finocchio had expected. It was as if a new heir to the throne were letting out his first cries.

"It's good for me... Maybe I'll do a little dance on the palm of your hand."

Even though Finocchio had accepted his offer, Noel wasn't done fighting. It wasn't only the Lucianos who were backing Andreas.

Finocchio remembered the advice he'd given as he left.

"Noel, watch out for the Lord of Flies."

Things far more frightening than the mafia skulked around in the dead of night.

"How will you, who walks the path of might, fight against the Lord of Flies...?"

†

The office was large and luxurious, with precious relics on display from all nations and epochs. It looked more like a showroom than an office. A middle-aged man in an expensive-looking business suit walked around within. The watch and rings he wore were all exquisite, and any one of them was worth more than the annual salary of a normal citizen.

Andreas Hooger had gained both fame and universal envy. As head of Hooger Commerce, he was a prominent multimillionaire in the capital. Though he was supposed to be living in the catbird seat, Andreas was pacing nervously like a bear locked in a dark cage.

The truth was that Andreas truly did feel trapped.

"Dammit... Why did this happen..." He kept repeating those words to himself over and over. "Damn you...snake... Noel Stollen..."

It had all started when Andreas was invited to that party. He'd attended thinking it was just a social gathering, but it had turned into something horrible.

Two years prior, Andreas had murdered one of his business rivals. The man had figured out that Andreas was smuggling beast materials into other countries and was planning to blackmail Hooger Commerce with the information. Killing him was the only option.

So too was framing Hugo Coppélia for the murder. The Department of Justice had judged that Hugo was the criminal, and no one even suspected Andreas. That was supposed to be the end of it.

"Dammit!" The furious Andreas slammed his fist on his desk in anger. He hit it over and over until his knuckles started to bleed, and then he dropped his head onto it, sobbing uncontrollably. "It's all over... I'm finished..."

At the end of the party, Wild Tempest master Noel Stollen had claimed that Hugo Coppélia had been falsely convicted. Not only that, but he even revealed the Department of Justice's role in it, calling in the previous Solicitor General, Count Lester Graham.

The truth had been announced in front of many officials and then spread throughout the empire by the media. The people sympathized with the pitiful Hugo and harshly criticized the dirty Department of Justice.

While the true culprit's name hadn't been made public, if there was a new investigation at the behest of the people, Andreas would almost certainly be named as the prime suspect. Even if they didn't hold another investigation, Andreas's crime had already been uncovered.

Noel, who had rallied for Hugo's release, had looked at Andreas at the end of the speech. Andreas hadn't been imagining it; they'd definitely made eye contact. And then that crafty young man had laughed. His eyes had been cold, like a snake sizing up its prey, as he smiled at Andreas.

"That bastard definitely knows I was behind it..."

He probably hadn't exposed Andreas's crime on the spot because he wanted to use the information somehow. Noel hadn't reached out yet, but at this point, Andreas's life was in his hands.

What if he changed his mind and disclosed Andreas's connection to the crime? What if he had already told someone else? Just thinking about it made him numb.

He suddenly heard a voice. It was strange, neither masculine nor feminine. And it said, "Hey, men don't cry."

Andreas turned around, surprised, and saw a figure in a jet-black robe. The door to the room was still locked. No one should have been able to get in. The person's face was hidden by the shadow of the unnaturally dark hood, so he wasn't able to see who it was. Andreas gulped at the sight of this strange-looking intruder. After some time, he realized who it might be.

"A-are you the Lord of Flies?"

The faceless intruder bowed. "That's right, Andreas. I am the Lord of Flies."

"So it *is* you..."

Even after figuring out who it was, Andreas was still nervous.

He was actually even warier now. Andreas knew of the Lord of Flies, but that only meant he knew he could not trust this monster in any way.

He had learned of the figure back when he decided to kill the rich man. Normally, he would have left it to the Luciano family, with whom he had close ties. But they refused, deciding that it was too risky to kill a competitor with so much influence.

For the same reason, the Society of Assassins also refused his request. The old Society of Assassins may have done it, but apparently, the current head always refused risky work.

However, if Andreas didn't kill this competitor, Hooger Commerce wouldn't have a future. Just when he was about to give up, the president of the Luciano family said he might know someone who could help—the Lord of Flies. He was sort of a handyman for the underworld; it was said he would solve any problem for enough cash. In the handyman world, specialists who took dangerous work that normal people refused were called Scavengers. The most famous Scavenger was the Lord of Flies. He was the king of the Scavengers.

The president of the Luciano family introduced Andreas to the Lord of Flies, but he warned that he wasn't to be trusted, although Andreas didn't understand what that meant at the time. Andreas was grasping at straws, so he wasn't thinking clearly.

He finally understood what it meant when he found out days later how the Lord had killed the man. It was true that he'd wanted his competitor dead, but not in such a gruesome way.

Not only that, but a young child was also killed. Andreas truly regretted hiring the Lord of Flies.

Once it was all over, Andreas met him only once. To be more accurate, he met him unintentionally. When he was visiting a museum with his family, someone passed him and whispered in his ear.

"I'm waiting for your next order."

He wasn't able to see the Lord's face then either, but it was the same strange, androgynous voice.

"Lord of Flies... Why are you here?"

"Why? That's cold, Andreas. Why didn't you call me? It seems you're in trouble."

"Do not jest! I'm not asking you to save me!" Andreas cried out. "This is all your fault in the first place! You framed Hugo Coppélia, and now it's all coming back to bite me!"

Andreas hurled blame at him, but the Lord of Flies shook his head.

"That's hindsight. If we hadn't framed someone, the Department of Justice would have pinned it on you. Even if they didn't, they would have found out that you were smuggling beast materials to other countries over the course of the investigation."

"H-how do you know about the smuggling?"

Only the Luciano family was supposed to know about that. Ignoring that question, the Lord of Flies went on.

"The reason the Department of Justice didn't investigate thoroughly and just decided it was Hugo was because they were trying to improve the department's image by solving the case quickly. In that case, a more sensational murder was better for them."

"That's why you killed them in that way?" Andreas asked.

"That's right. I staged a horrendous killing and chose Hugo Coppélia, the up-and-coming dollmaker, to take the fall. You must admit that the plan went extremely well."

It was true that, had the snake never slithered out from under his rock, everything would have gone fine. Blaming the Lord of Flies here was just a criticism of Noel, ultimately.

"Fine... That's over. But what can you do now?"

"It's simple. I can kill Hugo Coppélia in prison."

"Kill Hugo? What will that solve?"

"If Hugo dies in prison, all the blame being cast at the Department of Justice will switch to the administration. The people will be furious, and there may be huge riots that the government can't stop. Actually, we'll make sure there are riots. If that happens, they won't even have time to find the real killer," the cloaked handyman explained.

"They won't be able to investigate during the riots, but what about after?" Andreas pressed.

"We can think of a new plan during the riots. Once the mutiny begins, the raging anger of the people won't be easily snuffed out. You may not be able to stay in the capital, but you can use your connections to flee to another country. Regardless, you need to get away from the snake," the Lord of Flies said, suppressing a laugh. "Evidently, the snake knows that you were behind it, but he doesn't have any concrete evidence. In other words, once Hugo is gone, no one will be able to pursue the case. Surely the snake will give up too. He's not our enemy."

"I-I see... But will it really work?"

"Of course," the Lord of Flies affirmed in a confident voice. Then he added, "If you're not picky about how, anything is possible."

Andreas closed his eyes, thinking. If he asked this monster to kill Hugo, all of his problems would be solved. But as long as he kept relying on the monster, he could sense disaster waiting for him. When he glanced up, the Lord of Flies was standing directly before Andreas. Even standing this close, he couldn't make out the monster's face.

No, that wasn't right. Andreas was shocked by a revelation— the Lord of Flies didn't have a face. Where a face would have been was a swarm of countless flies. This monster was made up of a huge swarm of flies that were just filling the robe.

Andreas felt a chill run down his spine. "Just what are—"

"Choose. Now."

Andreas was petrified with fear. If he said no, he felt that he would be killed right there.

There had always been only one choice.

"F-fine... I'll pay whatever you want. I'll leave it all to you..."

✝

That day, Hugo received a gift from Noel—a leather trunk packed with a suit of clothes. Hugo knew immediately that it was a battle suit made with beast materials, just as he had worn back when he was a Seeker. The suit was woven with thread from an Arachnid, a beast with an abyssal depth of 10. This not only made it resistant to all attack attributes, but it granted the user healing effects. It was the perfect suit for a Puppeteer, a class that expended magic power very quickly. He could see there was other clothing inside the trunk as well.

Hugo looked at the guard who had brought him the case with a wry smile. "I do not believe this is appropriate for a prisoner."

Looking awkward, the guard shook his head. "You are a prisoner, but you're also not."

"In that case, can I keep this?"

The guard nodded, and Hugo chuckled. As the guard said, Hugo both was and wasn't a prisoner. He was still being held under the pretext of a retrial, but at this point, no one thought that Hugo was guilty. He would certainly be released soon, so there was no reason for him to plan an escape. The guards understood this.

After the guard left, Hugo slipped his arm into the suit. It was big on him, since he had lost weight, but once he was back to his normal size, it would fit perfectly.

"Hmph..."

It had been quite a while since he retired, but wearing this suit felt natural and comfortable. He thought he could feel his fighting spirit deep within.

"Even after so much time away, the body remembers..."

Noel truly wanted Hugo to join their team. Hugo was now rather interested in Wild Tempest, but he hadn't decided yet. He didn't want to make a rash decision and then regret it.

"Hmm?"

While he was trying on the suit, he noticed a piece of paper in the breast pocket. It seemed Noel had snuck it in. The message read: *"We'll make a show of it."*

"Hmm." Hugo had no idea what it meant.

That was when it happened.

"Wha—?!"

His body suddenly felt shaky, assailed by dizziness. A strange, sweet scent was tickling his nose. He'd experienced the same thing two years earlier.

"Could he...be here now?"

It was the true culprit, the one who'd framed him for the murders. Experiencing the same hypnotic effect again, Hugo started to sweat profusely.

"D-dammit..." He tried to bite his tongue to stay awake, but he was too weak. He fell to the floor, unable to move a finger. Before he knew it, a black-robed figure was standing next to him. Hugo tried to exert a skill with his last ounce of energy, but it wasn't possible. He was too dazed to control any level of magic power.

So this was it. He had finally prepared himself to die, but then something unbelievable occurred.

An explosion rocked the entire prison. Then a violent wind kicked up, flinging Hugo's door open and slamming the unarmored attacker against the wall.

Although he was facedown on the ground, thanks to the Arachnid silk suit he was wearing, Hugo was miraculously unharmed by the terrible gust. His head was clear once more. The wind must have blown away the narcotic fumes.

Hugo quickly stood up amid a dense cloud of smoke. He put together what had happened, feeling afraid.

"A bomb...?"

Someone had planted a bomb in the prison. The timing of the bomb had coincidentally saved Hugo's life. The attacker looked badly wounded, and although they hadn't collapsed, they were stumbling. They brandished a sword but weakly.

Considering the circumstances, the attacker hadn't set off the bomb. It would have been pointless to stage an attack that put itself at a disadvantage. So there was only one possible culprit.

"Noel Stollen... You even anticipated this... You would go this far?"

Hugo had thought he understood Noel's peculiarities, but he'd still underestimated the boy. Even if he *was* trying to save Hugo, he couldn't go planting bombs in the prison. Just as disasters had no regard for people, that snake was like a storm.

"Heh heh... Ha ha ha!" Hugo cackled aloud. He didn't care who heard him. "Now I get it, Noel. You are definitely the strongest and most notorious," he happily muttered as he initiated his Puppeteer skill.

Puppeteer skill: *Savant Lancer*. The armored doll soldier holding a spear started decomposing and rebuilding the matter around him. Next to the doll, Hugo was glaring at the attacker.

"I hate violence. It is hardly beautiful. However..."

Hugo pulled a magic string from his finger and connected it to the doll soldier.

Puppeteer skill: *Ether Link*. By activating this, he doubled the speed of his labors.

"It isn't so bad to harbor vengeful thoughts once in a lifetime."

I knew that Andreas would try to assassinate Hugo. If Hugo were to die in prison, the political situation would explode, leading to huge riots that no one would be able to control. If that happened, Andreas wouldn't be investigated.

Because we didn't have any physical evidence that Andreas was the mastermind behind the murders in the first place, riots would only muddle the situation and give Andreas some breathing room. Andreas would probably come up with a plan to slip out of my clutches even if Lester became the Minister of Justice. Killing Hugo would just make everything too complicated.

If I used Talker skill: *Confess*, I could get him to admit to it, but there was a big risk in using a psychological skill on someone so high on the societal ladder, so it wasn't practical. If I wasn't careful, they would hang me as a criminal. It wasn't good for me to flip the chessboard, but violence was the most effective plan. Were I in Andreas's position, I would have done the same thing.

Having predicted Andreas's next moves, I was able to turn his plan to my advantage. That was why I'd made Andreas dance on purpose.

He intended to assassinate Hugo, which would be construed as a trick by the administration, and then he would cause riots in order to further control the narrative. There was no mistake.

But if he could not assassinate Hugo, the rest of my plan could be aborted. Catching them in the act would supply irrefutable evidence. There was no point in preventing it before it happened. If they weren't captured at the scene, there would be no proof of the true culprit.

A few days ago, we had rented a house near the prison and stayed there so we could react instantly when Hugo was attacked. When the moon was full at night, we could see the prison, surrounded by a moat, very clearly.

"Noel, they're here," said Alma, who had been standing watch.

Koga, Leon, and I, who had been napping, stood up at the report.

"How many?" I asked her.

"Hmm, maybe about five? They seem strong."

"Okay. It's a good thing we prepared this." I pulled out a small box from my breast pocket. It was a remote control with a red button that would set off the bomb with a flick of my thumb.

"We wouldn't stand a chance against an enemy who could kill an A-Rank like Hugo. So we'll weaken him with the bombs and sneak in."

My role here was to intercept. It was Loki who'd actually planted the bombs. For Loki, who could assume any appearance he wanted, it was a simple task.

Naturally, we would blame the bombs on the attacker. Wild

Tempest, who just happened to be nearby, would apprehend the villain who had tried to assassinate Hugo and had planted bombs in a public facility. If we succeeded, we would be heroes. Even if we were suspected of setting it up, there would be an actual attacker, so it would be easy to talk our way out of that. I was eternally grateful to Andreas, who would serve as our foil. There was a listening device planted in Hugo's room. It was connected to the earring-shaped receiver on my left ear, and I could hear the goings-on in the room perfectly.

"Okay, this is it. Let's go."

"W-wait!" When I was about to push the button, Leon stopped me. "A-are you really going to bomb the prison?"

"Yeah, I'm gonna detonate it right now."

"Please, won't you stop? It's not too late... Bombing is going too far."

I sighed at Leon's fearful plea. "How many times do I have to tell you? It is a bomb, but it's not that powerful. Even a C-Rank close-combat Seeker could handle it. All the guards are melee types. It'll be fine. Even if they're unlucky enough to suffer a wound, they can just be healed. I've also given Hugo an excellent battle suit with protective functions." I explained this for the umpteenth time, but Leon still wasn't convinced.

"B-but the other prisoners will die, won't they?"

"They will. But so what? Hugo's the only innocent locked up in there. How does it hurt us if they die? Or are you still stuck in your Winged Knights way of thinking? You disappoint me, Leon Fredric."

"It's not like that..." Perhaps that provoked him, but Leon's brow furrowed. "I chose you as my master, and I will follow your instructions for the clan. Even if I disagree with the principles. But the fact is, this is too much. Am I wrong?"

"You're not wrong."

I knew Leon was against this. Even if we could get the attacker in one fell swoop, using bombs was a big risk. I wanted to avoid using them if possible.

"Fine, Leon... I'll cancel the bomb plan."

"R-really?!"

"Yeah, really. But if I have this, I'll just press it, so you hold it. Here, the detonator!"

"Wait, what?!"

I tossed the detonator to Leon, and he panicked, trying to catch it. He did catch it, but with too much force—and he ended up squeezing the button, hard.

"Ah...!" Leon let out a dim-witted cry. The ground around the prison shook like thunder, and the night sky lit up. The attacker was trying to kill Hugo just at that moment.

"Aaaugh!" Leon wailed at the top of his lungs, but it was too late. It was all going according to plan.

"W-wow..."

"Noel, you're inhuman..."

Koga and Alma were dumbstruck, but I ignored them and bellowed orders.

"Now we will start battle behavior!"

Initiate Tactics skill: *Battle Voice.*

Koga and Alma prepared to fight at my orders. Even Leon, who was on his knees crying, stood up.

"Order: take out anyone who attacks you!"

Initiate Tactics skill: *Tactician.*

"Defeating evil is just! Swing your sword freely!"

The prison was in pandemonium.

As expected, while the staff suffered some injuries, there had been no deaths. Many had lost consciousness, but they were still breathing. Half of the prisoners had died instantly, while the ones who survived were trying to rise up and escape. The guards intervened, and the halls were filled with violence.

The prisoners were wearing collars that inhibited magic, but their physical augmentations were unsuppressed. Also, they out-numbered the security staff. They were in a complete deadlock.

"Koga, Alma, clear out the riffraff."

"Gotcha."

"Roger."

The two followed my orders with my support and initiated their attack skills.

Samurai skill: *Crazy Cherry Blossoms.*

Assassin skill: *Perfect Throw.*

Countless slashes cut down the prisoners, and innumerable steel needles pierced them. The riot was put down in a bloody instant.

"S-snakes?! Why are you here?!"

I raised my voice to speak to the frightened staff. "We saw

an explosion in the prison! Our clan is here to help subdue the prisoners and catch the perpetrator!"

The staff was confused. Then, the head guard in charge of the site appeared.

"Snakes—I mean, Wild Tempest—thank you for saving us. We couldn't have even hoped for your assistance. But...can we trust you?"

From his perspective, our sudden appearance was too perfect. I understood his suspicion. "Of course. It will take time for the military police to arrive. During that time, we need to prevent any prisoners from escaping. We'll do what we can to protect our beloved empire."

The head guard nodded with a strange look on his face. "Fine. Then, under my command—"

"No, we will move on our own and focus on apprehending the perpetrator. You tend to any injured and secure a perimeter to make sure no one escapes."

"Wh-what did you say?" The man was surprised, to say the least.

I tilted my head to the side. "What's the problem?"

"Stop messing around! This is my responsibility! Follow my orders!"

I moved closer to the angry head guard and smiled gently. "Is there...a problem?"

"Uh, ergh..." The guard scowled, looking frustrated. He lost his spirit with one smile and couldn't say anything else.

That was only natural; I knew his weakness. Thanks to my informant, Loki, I had been collecting information for Hugo's release. I knew the weaknesses of every one of the guards, and especially those of the head guard. No matter how unhappy he was, he was unable to protest.

"I'll ask you one more time. Is there a problem?"

When I repeated it, the head guard hung his head. "No... Do what you want."

Still smiling, I whispered, "You're trash. Just shut up and follow my orders. If you oppose me again, you better be ready for it. I'll make you regret the day you were born."

"Eeek!" The head guard shrieked and jumped a little. Fear was written all over his face.

Fear was the best way to tame a stupid beast. I was sure this man would never try to argue with me again.

I then turned around and gave Leon instructions. "Leon, heal these guards and put up a barrier."

"Understood. Leave it to me."

Knight skill: *Light Veil.*

Knight skill: *Holy Shield.*

Leon's skill surrounded the staff in an aurora of healing light that closed all wounds. The invisible barrier he put up would also protect them from attacks.

Our job was to apprehend the attacker, but we needed the guards to secure a perimeter in order to do so. It would be difficult to apprehend Hugo's assailant if they ran. We weren't going to let a single person escape this prison. The only way out for them was a pine box.

"Let's go."

I moved forward, and the other three obeyed.

On the street, Koga gave me a sidelong glance. "'To protect our beloved empire'? I think about it every time, but lyin' comes so easy to ya. I'm impressed."

"I'm not lying. What we are doing is just. Are we not allies of justice?"

"Hah, or somethin' that *looks* like allies of justice. Dun' be fooled." Koga laughed and threaded his fingers behind his head. "Well, either way, I'm a sinner. I should enjoy my sin."

"Hmm." I stopped and addressed Alma. "How's it looking inside the prison?"

Alma closed her eyes and concentrated. "There are still a lot of guards and prisoners fighting. And there are a lot of wounded people. There are five people with a completely different feel. Of those, four are attackers, and I think the other one is Hugo."

There were supposed to be five attackers, so Hugo probably got one of them.

"Are the attackers all in one location?"

"No. They had to split up due to the prisoner riots. It looks like they've suffered a few injuries from the explosion. If we're going to attack them, now is the time."

"I see. It's a good opportunity."

The explosion strategy had gone well. As I smiled to myself, Alma tilted her head. "But something is strange."

"Oh?"

"The way the attackers *feel* is strange. I sense multiple signals from one attacker. They're really weak, though."

"What did you say?" What did she mean by that? Were they harboring other living beings? When I tried to imagine what their true form might be, I couldn't come up with anything.

"Unknown enemies are dangerous, but we can't retreat. I'm going to tweak the plan a bit. My original plan was to catch at least one alive, but let's kill them all. Do everything you can to wipe them out."

When I gave the new order, Leon looked perplexed again. "Are you sure? I thought you were going to capture them in the act and use *Confess*? If we destroy all of them, we won't be able to connect them to Andreas."

As Leon said, that was my original plan. The possibility that Andreas and the attackers were directly related was low, but if we could trace the relationship, it would be clear, physical evidence. If instead we killed all the attackers, that couldn't happen. However, if we focused only on capturing them alive, there was a good chance we would lose one of our own. That was a risk I wasn't willing to take.

"We need to refocus our strategy on our resources. First, let's go save Hugo. Even if the connection between Andreas and the attackers isn't clear, the fact is that the true culprit ordered an attack. Hugo will be released immediately. After that, we'll use Lester to start the new investigation and Andreas will face catastrophe."

"I wonder if a new investigation could pin it on Andreas."

"Since it happened two years ago, it might be hard. But have you forgotten? He's committed other crimes too."

"Oh, oh right!" Leon clapped his hands, remembering.

Hooger Commerce, headed by Andreas, was smuggling beast materials to other countries. It wasn't carefully hidden, and if there was to be a serious investigation, Andreas would be found out easily, and he wouldn't have a path of retreat. Nobody would need to focus on the murders. Once the Department of Justice acknowledged the injustice of their initial trial, Hugo's name would be cleared. Also, today's attack proved that there was a true culprit at large. The bombs I'd set up had foiled their assassination attempt and turned it into a big incident. Even if we weren't able to prove a relationship, the people would recognize that these attackers were the real killers.

So Hugo wouldn't have to wait an entire month, and whether Andreas lived or died was up to me.

"Naturally, I don't plan to entrust Andreas with the Department of Justice. I plan to squeeze out everything I can."

"Damn."

"You're not human."

"That's tragic."

The three looked at me sternly. I snorted. "What's wrong with it? What do you call this in the far east, Koga? Karma? I'll give him good news in the name of justice."

"According to that logic, something bad will happen to you one day too, Noel. That's why you should do a lot of good deeds now. Specifically, dressing up like a woman and then having se— ow, ouch!"

I pinched Alma's cheek hard, before she could say anymore.

"Wait! Wait a second! Something's changed!" Alma shouted.

"Huh?"

I released my fingers and Alma rubbed her cheek as she continued. "One attacker...and Hugo have started battling. They're moving. It looks like they'll end up on the roof. If we're going to save him, we'd better hurry."

I clicked my tongue. "Tch. What a pain." So the attacker hadn't tried to flee after all. "We have no choice. I'll go save Hugo. You guys search for the other attackers."

If the attackers hadn't given up, there was a good chance the other ones would head to the rooftop too. I didn't want them all together. We had to reach Hugo and find the other attackers at the same time.

"Leon, you're in charge. Once you eliminate the attackers, get out of the building."

"Huh? Ah, sure, okay. But are you two all right on your own?" Leon sounded worried.

I grimaced. "Of course. I have a plan."

Hugo was on the roof, locked in a deathmatch with one of the attackers.

He had been able to kill the first one easily. The attacker had been injured from the explosion and wasn't that strong to begin with. Since the attacker had a skill that could put Hugo to sleep, that attacker had probably been a special type of rearguard fighter.

That was why he'd been able to win. But this one was different.

"So strong..."

The enemy was a Longswordsman. They easily wielded a double-edged sword as long as a human was tall and were trying to cut Hugo in two. Undoubtedly, they were a close-combat class. Hugo was desperately trying to attack with his lancer doll soldier, but he was at a disadvantage. One wrong move, and he would be dead. The Longswordsman had come to kill an A-Rank Puppeteer, so of course they'd be formidable. Hugo knew that. But the attacker was still too strong. Hugo didn't stand a chance.

Hugo's abilities had declined. His actions were awkward. He wasn't able to control his magic well, and he was hardly moving efficiently. He was having trouble controlling the doll soldier. He couldn't even generate more than one doll at a time. Furthermore, he could only use the *Savant Lancer*, which he was most familiar with. In the past, he had been able to create multiple doll soldiers at once even in the middle of battle.

He was frustrated by his own weakness. Even though it had been his choice to stop fighting, Hugo started to consider early retirement a foolish choice. He should have at least continued training. The weak were always trampled upon. Hugo had the strength to fight, but he took it for granted. It was imprudent. Arrogant. He hadn't thought about it enough. It was all so obvious, but he hadn't realized it until right then.

"After this is over, I need to train myself to death!"

Initiate Army skill: *Link Burst*.

This was a skill that could only be used with *Ether Link*; it removed all limitations for the doll soldiers connected to the thread. It actually increased the target's ability by a hundredfold.

It was an extremely strong skill, but the target doll collapsed after only a few seconds.

It was well suited for a last-ditch suicide attack.

"Drill!"

The doll soldier broke the sound barrier with its charge, triggering a thunderclap. The black-cloaked attacker couldn't dodge, blocking the doll's spear with sword and shield. The air itself seemed to rip in two.

"You blocked it?! But..."

Link Burst had greatly amplified the doll's power. It was too fast for the attacker, who'd just barely blocked the weapon. The attacker tried to stomp on the doll, but their foot stomped through the roof instead. The attacker was probably strong enough to absorb a hit from the doll, and then the doll would fall to pieces. But what if the doll could knock the attacker from the roof?

"Push!" Hugo commanded. The doll rushed and pushed the attacker to the very edge of the roof. However...

"Wha—?!"

Hugo saw something he couldn't believe. Just as the attacker began to fall, a number of tentacles sprang from its back and gripped the roof.

"I-it isn't...human?"

Hugo had felt that something wasn't right. The attacker had been moving with incredible, if awkward, speed. Yet it was lacking technique. Even though it had superhuman abilities, the attacker could only swing its weapon at random. That was dangerous enough, but it was just like fighting a wild animal.

It wasn't human; humans lacked tentacles. While Hugo knew what the creature was not, he had no idea what it really was. The first attacker had possessed a hypnotic ability powerful enough to knock Hugo out, but lacked any combat prowess.

These attackers didn't have specialized abilities; it was more like they each had but a single skill. He also felt that they had no malice toward him, like they were being commanded by someone else. So, who had made these attackers? As Hugo stood there, dumbfounded, the doll soldier expired.

"This is bad!" He tried to create a new doll soldier, but his fatigue sapped seconds he didn't have. He couldn't attack the tentacular foe and generate a doll at the same time, and the attacker closed the distance. The longsword came swinging down. Just then, a bright red flame consumed the attacker.

"Grrr!"

The creature, completely covered in flames, flailed about in pain. Speechless, Hugo gaped at the carnage, Feeling a sudden presence behind him, he whipped around.

"The moon sure is pretty tonight."

It was a snake brandishing a gun.

The moon was full, casting a beautiful pale glow upon the roof. I stepped toward the shocked Hugo and pulled a silver pendant from my pocket. It was shaped like a snake with wings.

"Decide."

I didn't say what, but Hugo understood.

"Er, heh heh... So this is the snake," Hugo said, nodding. "You really are a tempest. You do not give a damn about people. But that is why I like you. Fine. Starting today, you will be my master." He looked carefully at the pendant I gave him and said, "I swear allegiance to you, my master."

"I accept your allegiance, Puppeteer Hugo Coppélia."

We swore this oath under the moonlight. My snake had grown another wing.

"Gooo! Sleeep!"

The attacker had survived the flames and was standing up, yelling. There were several tentacles emerging from its cloak. It definitely wasn't normal. It also seemed to have a connection to me.

"Have I met you before?"

The being stayed silent as a gust blew by. The strong breeze lifted the now-tattered robe of the attacker. I was in disbelief when I saw its true form.

"You..."

It was a man. A giant man, his torso covered in black armor. The face was heavily scarred—and had a huge gash where a nose had once been.

"Is that you, Edgar? From War Eagle?"

"Noel..."

It still didn't answer, but it was clearly Edgar. His new form was radically different from the human being he once was. He couldn't focus his eyes and was drooling uncontrollably.

"Do you know him?" Hugo asked me.

I nodded. "We've met."

"You have a wide acquaintanceship if you even know a man with tentacles."

"I'm just as surprised at how I get around as you are."

"Noel!" The tentacles whipped through the air. We evaded, but they were frighteningly fast. They'd tear us apart eventually.

"It looks like he really hates you. What did you do?"

"You see how he's missing a nose?"

"Ah, yes, it *is* gone."

"I did that."

"I-I see... Now I understand."

"Gooo!" Edgar attacked with his tentacles and his good sword arm. We jumped far back and stumbled as we dodged.

"Noel, your friend is too strong! Give me battle orders!"

"I know."

Edgar actually was pretty strong. Just as I suspected, Hugo had grown weak from lack of practice. We had maybe a fifty-fifty chance of beating Edgar, but I didn't panic. It was all in the palm of my hands. It wasn't even close.

"Noel! We're done; everyone is outside!" I heard via *Link*. Perfect timing.

I snapped my fingers. "Okay, Hugo, I'll give you an order. Make sure you land."

"What?! What do you—" Hugo started, then realization dawned on him. "Now surely, you don't mean..."

I smiled and nodded, then pulled out another detonator from my pocket.

We had planted two bombs in the jail. The first had been

located inside; it had torn out the walls and pushed all the air out of the building. The other was underneath the jail, next to the foundation. If I pushed this button, the entire building would collapse.

"Noeeeel!" Edgar moaned, moving closer. Just before his sword reached me, I pushed the big red button.

"Edgar, you're not my enemy."

The jail immediately shook. With its foundation weakened, it imploded. The roof collapsed under my feet.

"Noel!" Edgar didn't have a skill he could use, and he just kept calling my name.

"Shut up! Stop yelling my name!" I aimed my silver flame from midair at the stumbling Edgar. "Just try to dodge this."

The Garmr bullet hit the target, and Edgar exploded like a balloon. The moment the bomb's shockwave subsided, a large hand grabbed me from the side—it belonged to a doll soldier.

"Noel, prepare for impact!" Hugo grabbed the back of my coat. We hit the ground, the soldier doll under us cushioning our fall.

"Ha ha ha. A perfect victory." I laughed through the pain of the impact.

Hugo let out a deep sigh. "What was perfect? I see I am going to be serving someone awful." He acted fed up, but then laughed as if he was enjoying himself. "Well, at least I won't be bored."

"Right?"

"I have high expectations for you," he told me.

We laughed and saw Leon and the others approaching.

"Let's get on with it, then."

THE MOST NOTORIOUS【TALKER】RUNS THE WORLD'S GREATEST CLAN

Epilogue

AFTER THE PRISON BOMBING, Hugo was found innocent, just as I'd planned.

Many newspaper reporters came each day, asking for interviews. Hugo wanted to refuse, but I ordered him to accept. His name had already been cleared, but considering the future, it was better to be thorough.

It wasn't just Hugo; there was plenty of support for me too. After doing everything I could to release Hugo, uncover the fraud in the Department of Justice, and put a stop to the assault on the jail, I was a hero in the capital. Wild Tempest's reputation had skyrocketed—we were getting plenty of sponsorship offers. We hadn't reached 80 billion fil yet, but we had plenty to fund a new plan.

"I told you, Andreas, it's not money we want. All we want is your good faith." I smiled at Andreas, who was standing in front of me.

It was the middle of the night, and Hugo and I were visiting

Andreas's mansion. We didn't have an official appointment; we'd secretly snuck into his study to negotiate. We knew he'd be home, since he was on house arrest.

"Don't worry, we didn't tell anyone we were meeting with you," I added. "That's better for you too, right?"

"I-I..." Andreas was stammering and sweating like a waterfall. The materials I'd prepared were sitting on top of his desk. They contained records of his smuggling.

"If the Department of Justice gets a hold of this, you're finished. But I'm not a monster. I don't want to destroy someone capable like you. Right, Hugo? You feel the same way, don't you?"

"Yes, I agree." Hugo nodded, standing behind Andreas and placing a hand on his shoulder. "The past is the past. We can be friends now, Andreas."

"Uh, er..." Andreas sounded like he was being strangled. Having the person he'd framed for murder standing next to him must've been straight-up horrifying. He was probably scared to death.

"F-fine... I'll prepare the money. How much do you want?"

"Right. We'll start with a billion fil," I said.

"S-start with?"

"Yeah, just to start. We're going to have a long, close friendship. So, one billion fil is fine for now."

"Y-you demon..." Andreas was glaring at me, but Hugo's hand was still clamped on his shoulder. He only had to nudge just a little for Andreas to lose his courage and start shaking.

"So what do you say?"

"I-I'll pay..." Andreas hung his head in defeat. Hugo and I smiled at each other over the success of our negotiations. But then...

"Hrng?! Augh, augh, augh!" Andreas suddenly stood up and started scratching his head furiously. "Ouch?! Ow, ow, ow, ow!"

He ran around the room clutching his head, clearly in agony.

"Noel, could this be...?!"

"Hugo, get away from him! Something's not right!"

As soon as we moved away from Andreas, he gave a horrendous final gasp.

"Ah, aaagh!"

Then, his head exploded, letting loose hundreds of flies. As we looked on, dumbstruck, the flies formed a humanoid shape, which then jumped out of the window and ran away. All that remained was Andreas's dead body, sans head.

"The Lord of Flies..."

I remembered the name Finocchio had warned me about. Loki was still in the middle of researching its true form. However, I had no doubt that that was who was behind this.

"This is bad. This makes it look like we're the killers," Hugo said, looking at the door with bulging eyes. "Let's go, Noel. We cannot let anyone find us."

"Yeah, we'll go." I nodded, and then a smile so wide, I thought my cheeks would tear, spread across my face. "This is getting interesting..."

The Lord of Flies had killed Andreas to get in my way. There could be no other motive. Now that Andreas was dead, we couldn't extract money from him. But why did the Lord of Flies want to thwart me? I could think of a number of reasons, but I didn't know which was most likely. That was all part of the fun, though. It was boring, knowing that I was going to win every time. Having some obstacles would just make it that much sweeter when I reached the top.

I felt a fire burning inside me.

"Lord of Flies, I'm going to swallow you whole."

†

Three shadows lurked in the remains of the slums. One was a monster clad in a black robe—the Lord of Flies. Another was a fox woman with a skull mask. The third was a young man wearing a white coat.

A distorted mirror floated beside them. The mirror didn't reflect the scene around it—instead, it revealed what was happening in a room across town. It was a type of remote viewing. They could see Andreas's headless corpse and the startled faces of Noel and Hugo.

"Is this what you wanted, Malebolge?" the Lord of Flies asked the fox woman.

The hybrid beast called Malebolge nodded happily. "Yeah, thanks. I wanted to make sure the snakes didn't get Andreas in their pocket too. The important thing is to maintain the rivalry and avoid letting things get too one-sided. If you do that, they'll cannibalize each other."

"Malebolge...who do you want the snake to fight with?"

"Lorelai," Malebolge answered, a little smile on her face. "I want the snakes to kill the clan master, Johann Eissfeldt, for me. He's a threat. More so than the other Seekers like Leo, Zeke, or Victor."

"Hmm. He doesn't look like someone you should be worried about..."

"Looks can be deceiving. He needs to be eliminated. You see..."

After hearing Malebolge's reason, the Lord of Flies nodded in understanding. "I see. That is a threat... But can the snake kill Johann?"

"I don't know. But the snake is sharp. Even if he can't kill him, he can probably cripple him. If he does that, I'll be at an advantage."

"Hmph. We just have to pray it goes well. By the way..." The Lord of Flies turned his gaze to the young man in the white coat. "What's he here for?"

"Oh, I forgot to introduce him. He's my new friend."

"Wow, you finally filled the vacancy?"

"Finally. Maybe he'll introduce himself?"

Prompted by Malebolge, the young man slowly opened his mouth.

"I'm Emperro, Soul of the Samurai."